"Fiona, it is true that I took the money," said Frazer. "But Lord Morney did not make it a condition that I should then break the engagement and shame ye. And I would break that challenge and pay back every shilling, if necessary, for I mean to marry ye. I will not let you go."

"I shall not marry you!" Fiona blazed furiously. "You may badger and molest me, but I shall not give in! I shall hate you forever—"

Also by Rebecca Danton:

FIRE OPALS

STAR SAPPHIRE

THE HIGHLAND BROOCH

Rebecca Danton

FAWCETT COVENTRY • NEW YORK

THE HIGHLAND BROOCH

Published by Fawcett Coventry Books, a unit of CBS Publications, the Consumer Publishing Division of CBS Inc.

ISBN: 0-449-50022-5

Printed in the United States of America

First Fawcett Coventry Printing: February 1980

10 9 8 7 6 5 4 3 2 1

To Kay—

> for her friendship,
> her wisdom,
> her many ideas—of which this novel is one

Chapter One

Fiona Cartwright gave a cold, brief smile to her partner, acknowledged his bow with a brief bending of her blue black head, and seated herself, with relief, beside her godmother. She smoothed the violet silk gown with nervous fingers. She had not wanted to come to this ball, she disliked Lord Morney and his cruel wit, she detested society. Why had she ever returned to London?

She glanced down with affection at the snow white head of her godmother, beside her, and knew that was the answer. She loved Mrs. Trent, she had been closer to her than to any other human being.

Mrs. Trent smiled up at her tall goddaughter. Her blue eyes danced with happiness. She looked like a delicate porcelain doll, with her pretty pink complexion, her tiny frame. "Isn't the evening delightful? I declare, I have never seen so many smart persons gathered together! Is it not a colorful company? Only the prince regent is missing!"

Fiona concealed a smile. The company was about

fifty persons, and not all of them the top of the trees of society of London in 1816. But she would not have quenched Mrs. Trent's happiness for the world. "Indeed, it is very smart," she conceded. "The ballroom is most elegant, also."

Even as she spoke, she was glancing about the company. She did not want to admit, even to herself, that she searched for a very tall red-haired man, a stern-faced, enigmatic man, who usually wore a kilt and doublet, and whose blue eyes were as vivid and sparkling as those of her godmother, but larger and widely spaced in his tanned face.

Then she saw him, across the candlelit room, and her breath seemed to halt for a moment. She felt a sort of pain in her chest and felt cross with herself. Men were much alike beneath the smart jackets and ruffled shirts, she had found. Cruel, hard, callous, wanting their own way, brutal if they wanted to be.

Her father had died two years ago, unmourned by her, and few felt his passing with anything but relief. He was bad-tempered, cruel to his daughter, his horses, his servants. They had all felt the lash of his whip. Even now, the scars had not faded on Fiona, and it was necessary for several reasons for her to wear demure gowns. The violet silk she wore tonight was demurely to her thoat, covered her back completely, and she would never be able to wear the deep-cut gowns of her hostess, the spiteful Kate Grenville, Lady Morney. She was bowing and smiling to the red-haired Highlander, with something cruel and curious in her beautiful face, topped with the fluffy blond hair. Her red dress was cut almost to her waist, front and back.

"Now there is a handsome man," murmured Mrs. Trent. Fiona started, thinking she must be referring to Wallace Frazer. But her godmother was looking in another direction.

The young, English Captain Ainsworth was coming up to them. He was pleasant, with brown velvet matching his dark eyes. He bowed and smiled before

Fiona and held out his hand to her as she murmured her greeting.

"I may have this dance? Ah, thank you. It is a week since I have seen you," he reproached her as they took their places in the set forming near her seat.

"Has it been? Oh, yes, in the park, riding," she said indifferently.

"I hoped you would be here tonight," he went on eagerly, ignoring her coolness. "Lord Morney promised his wife had sent you invitations. You are neighbors in Yorkshire, I believe?"

"That is correct," she said colorlessly. She changed partners, moved gracefully through the movements, then returned to him. "I believe you served with him in the Peninsula, then at Waterloo?"

She looked curiously at his handsome young face as she spoke. He seemed so young and untouched by any battles; yet he had fought for more than six years, he had told her once.

His face shadowed. "Yes, ma'am," he said, and looked beyond her shoulder at the distance. "Painful years, they were," he added, under his breath. "Not just the battles, also the fevers, the lack of decent food, the cruel rains with our men lying out there in the mud—wounded—I have nightmares yet. You will laugh at me, ma'am," he added quickly.

"Laugh? Because you have sensibility, Captain? No, I do not laugh," she said, more gently than her wont.

"You are good, Miss Cartwright," he smiled, and escorted her reluctantly back to her chair. He had too good manners to ask her twice in a row, that would stamp her as fast, or cause speculation that they might be engaged.

He bowed, left her after asking if she would care for something cooling. She refused, with a smile.

"A nice young man, but no money," whispered Mrs. Trent, with regret. She knew all the gossip, all the backgrounds of the persons in the room, it seemed. It amused Fiona. "Older brother inherited, has a large family, he has just his regiment."

Fiona nodded, her head turned toward her god-mother. A shadow cut them from the light above, she moved back and stared up at the tall red-haired man. His vivid kilt swung just above his knees, a red-green-blue plaid, with a white line in it. He always wore the same colors, she had noted curiously. His doublet matched, his hose were the same colors. On each of his low dress shoes was a curious silver buckle inset with a yellow brown stone. On his shoulder was a large round silver brooch, centered with a similar stone of a large gleaming golden brown.

He held out his hand silently to her, she rose with unusual shyness to put her hand in his. Without a word they moved to the next set forming.

He was about six feet four, looming over her as few men did. Fiona was tall and slim, about five feet seven. She felt like a child next to him. He was light and graceful on his feet, his arm felt muscular and hard when she put her hand lightly on it.

"I hoped to see you here tonight," he finally said, in his deep musical voice, with the thick accent which burred it.

"Did you, sir?"

"Aye. You are the best dancer in London," and he grinned boyishly, with an unexpected twinkle in his very blue eyes.

She had to smile, in response to his teasing manner. "I thank you, sir. It is good to know I have one talent!"

"I would say," he said, when they met again in the dance, "that you are also very beautiful and most modest. But my tongue trips over compliments."

"I did not note any tripping, Mr. Frazer!"

He grimaced. "Mayhap I am in practice," he said, so ruefully that she had to give a low chuckle. He looked down at her alertly.

"Do you despise the London scene, sir?" she asked.

"Despise?" He took the word, and she could practically see him turning it round and round thoughtfully in his mind. He did not usually speak lightly, he seemed to reflect and consider whatever he did and said. "Oh, aye," he said. "Most seem so frivolous. My life has been a serious one, and I find it difficult to adjust to this. Yet it is most pleasant to dance in a beautiful room, to have a lovely lady on my arm, to note the scents of perfume."

They were separated again, to her regret. He seemed so honest, so straightforward in his speech, she liked to hear what he said and thought. He returned her then to her place, asked, "May I obtain a cooling draft for you, Miss Cartwright?"

Fiona glanced at her godmother, who nodded. "If you will, sir. A lemon drink, without rum in it, if you will."

He bowed and left them, to return a few moments later with the drinks. Only he did not carry them, he came empty-handed, and behind him was a red-haired man, even taller than he, in a kilt like his, with a silver tray of the drinks. The man served them drinks, bowed, and left them, to stand near the door to the garden.

Fiona could not hide her surprise. "That man—is he related to you?" she finally asked as he stood drinking beside them, observing the room with his keen eyes.

"Who? Oh, Jamie Frazer. Yes, a third cousin of mine. He is my piper."

"Piper? What is that?"

"Why—he plays the pipes for me. I am Frazer of Frazer," he said, rather curtly, his attention distracted as Derek Grenville, Lord Morney, came up to them. They bowed to each other formally, warily, Fiona thought.

"Good evening, Frazer," said Lord Morney.

"Lord Morney," said the other man.

Her host turned to Fiona. "May I have the pleasure, Miss Cartwright?" He smiled down at her. His languid air was suited to his peacock colors, of greens and golds, with the ruffled white shirt, the jewels on his hands and at his throat.

She stood and took his hand, though she regretted leaving Wallace Frazer. What curious things he had said! She longed to ask him more. He seated himself beside her godmother, and they were watching as Derek Grenville led her into the next set.

He was chuckling. "So—you have met the Frazer!" he said.

"The Frazer?" she murmured. "What a curious form of address."

"Oh, he is one of those former clan chiefs who keep their old titles. From the Scottish Highlands where those barbarians live. But a splendid fighter for all that. A sergeant in my Highland Regiment, you know," he said, watching her alertly for signs of shock.

"A sergeant? I thought him an officer at least," she said, concealing her surprise as well as she could. "He carries himself well," she added idly.

"Oh, those do." He was chuckling again to himself, his bright green eyes mischievous. "When he came into the regiment, I had my troubles with him, I can tell you. Had to lick him into shape, teach him to obey me! But once I had his loyalty, I had that of the others of Clan Frazer, his cousins, all, I suppose. Odd, that. During a battle, I saw him with French at his front and sides and back. Before I could send to his rescue, his own men were about him, yelling their horrible Scottish cries, swinging their claymores about their heads, and making the Frenchies into mincemeat! He came out with scarce a scratch. Loyalty, that."

"I see," murmured Fiona, not understanding at all. It had been a shock. Most officers bought commissions for themselves, as high as they could get. Did Frazer have no money, then, that he had entered as a common soldier? Surely he was a grand fighter, and she thought probably a good officer. She puzzled about it as Lord Morney danced with her and then took her back to her place. Wallace Frazer had disappeared, she caught sight of his red head at the other side of the room, near the windows, where his even taller cousin

Jamie towered over him, near six feet eight, she decided.

Mrs. Trent was visibly fatigued. She tired quickly now, and Fiona was considerate of her.

"Shall we depart soon, my dear?" murmured Fiona.

Mrs. Trent said, "There's a gentleman coming your way," with resignation.

Fiona would have given a great deal to have gone before the man reached her. Captain Sidney Jenks was a close friend of Lord Morney's. They had fought together in the Peninsula and at Waterloo. He had dark, straggly hair, he drank heavily, and his face was always red. In that dark flushed face, his little piggy, black, mean eyes made her shudder as he looked slowly down over her slim body in the close-fitting violet silk gown.

She could not refuse him. She stood, smiled, in a constrained way, and managed to touch only his fingers in the dance. She retired with relief when it was over. She refused his offer of drinks curtly, and he had lost his smile when he left her.

"I cannot endure him," she muttered to her godmother. "He always smells of wine and cigars, he laughs right in my face, he keeps trying to touch me. Ugh."

"You show it too plainly," said her godmother reprovingly. "Ladies try to conceal their feelings."

"I find it difficult," said Fiona. "Do let us go soon—"

However, another gentleman had appeared, she danced with him, and another. Then Wallace Frazer appeared at her elbow as she moved to be seated.

He held out his hand in silence, she put her hand in his. Somehow they did not need many words. She moved with him into the lively dance.

"I would like to see you in some of the Highland dances," he said presently. "You would be as graceful as the heather on the hill, blowing in the wind."

"I did not know you for a poet, Mr. Frazer," she smiled.

"Nor did I."

He returned her to her place, she and her godmother collected their abigail Mrs. Myrtle Owens, and called for their carriage. Lord Morney was near the door, laughing with someone as they had their cloaks put about their shoulders.

"Do you leave, and so soon, Miss Cartwright?" he said, bowing over her hand.

"I regret it, sir, but it grows late. May I express what a delightful occasion this was, how beautiful your home—"

"So kind of you. I hope to see you at Vauxhall Gardens this next week—"

He saw them to the door, bowed over Mrs. Trent's hand, and saw them into their carriage. Fiona leaned back in the darkness with a sigh of relief.

Mrs. Owens, a Welshwoman of some forty years, and a widow, piped up when they were alone and rolling over the cobblestones. "That's the one what calls you the Snow Maiden, Miss Fiona," she said. "I heard some gents talking tonight."

"Lord Morney—he started that talk?" said Fiona in distaste.

"Yes, and he a married man!"

Fiona grimaced in the darkness. Lord Morney had tried on several occasions to lure her to his greenhouse, into a dark garden, or to Vauxhall Gardens with him. She could not trust him alone, she knew that, nor did she want to. He was a married man, and his wife was keen of eye and spiteful of tongue.

"Him and that Captain Jenks had their heads together, a-laughing and a-drinking, out on the balcony near me," went on Mrs. Owens, who did not miss much, for all her demure appearance at the events. "They was talking about you and that tall red-haired man from Scotland. Seems he served under them, and a handful they must have found him."

"I would not envy him that duty," said Fiona slowly. "They must be—difficult officers."

"He was not an officer himself?" asked Mrs. Trent disapprovingly. "Then he must have no money at all. Such a fine, upstanding young man, and with no money—a pity."

Fiona leaned back in the carriage. All this talk of men and their prospects wearied her. She had quietly resolved years ago not to marry, not to put herself in the rough hands of any man in marriage. She had had enough of being in the power of a bad-tempered, heavy-drinking man, her father.

She knew better than to voice such thoughts. Her godmother looked eagerly for a proper suitor for her Fiona. Even her abigail studied each man at an event, with the view as to whether her Fiona might be happy with him. Marriage was the only proper condition for a lady. And a lady with a fortune such as hers stood little chance of resisting all the proposals that would be hers. Her solicitors handled her money now; when she married, her husband would handle it. She needed a man, that was the view of society.

She was lost in her thoughts, when she heard the coachman cry out hoarsely, "My lady—look to yourself—hey, now—"

There were low scufflings. Fiona sat up in alarm as the carriage door was wrenched open. A leering, masked face peered in, a dirty hand shot out and grabbed her arm, wrenching her forward out of her seat. Mrs. Trent screamed. Mrs. Owens promptly kicked out at him. Another man grabbed at her.

Footpads! The scourge of London. Some men masked and robbed for the fun of it, others for the desperate need for money. They grabbed at her jewels, wrenched at her diamond necklace. Fiona was screaming, not in fear, but in rage.

"Villains! Let me go! Don't touch me!" She kicked out at them, yelled in earnest, hoping some gentlemen might hear. Yet the street was but dimly lit as they had neared her godmother's home. Her town house was in an old and unfashionable part of London.

She smelled the fetid breath of one man as he hauled her from the carriage and dragged her out on the cobblestones. He was saying coarsely, "I got a pretty young one here! Think I'll keep her. Look at them stones!"

He was pulling at her with one hand, and yanking at her diamond necklace with the other. Fiona went to her knees on the cobblestones, felt the hard stones under her legs. She was still fighting desperately, she heard her godmother scream as another footpad grabbed at the tiny woman.

Then—a shrill, outlandish, wild scream! In some language she did not know, men were yelling! Out of the darkness, into the dim light of the lampposts came several very tall men, red-haired, with broad claymores ready. They fell on the footpads with fierce savagery. After the first screams, they fought in silence. One huge man yanked the footpad from Fiona and smashed him to the ground with his broad claymore. Another held a dirk, it shone in the dim light, and it slid smoothly into the side of the man trying to haul Mrs. Trent from the carriage.

It was over in moments. Where three shabby men had been fighting three gowned women, now there was silence. The big Highlanders stood over the men, one went to each in turn and examined them all.

"Dead," he said finally. He straightened and turned to Fiona. "Miss Cartwright, are you badly injured?" He came to her, took her arm with gentle hands, and tried to study her face.

She was shaking with shock. She held to him with trembling hands. "Oh—Mr. Frazer—is it you? Oh, thank God," she said, so faintly he put his strong arm impersonally about her waist.

"You are injured?" he asked more urgently.

"I—don't—know—"

"We must get you home." He lifted her into the carriage, helped Mrs. Trent in beside her. Mrs. Owen lay across one seat, blood on her forehead. He examined her briefly, then straightened. He spoke to the coachman, then to Fiona.

"You'll drive on slowly, we'll walk beside you. Your address, Miss Cartwright?"

She gave it to him faintly, showed him the streets as they turned and twisted in the old section. She was trembling still as the terror of what had happened came to her more fully. She could have been raped, murdered! And her godmother and abigail!

At the house, the coachman pulled up and called. The elderly butler opened the door, two young footmen ran out to help. They carried Mrs. Owens and Mrs. Trent into the house. Wallace Frazer offered his arm to Fiona, and she accepted it, leaning on him as she went inside.

His face was gravely angry as he saw her in the tall lights. Her violet gown was rent from ankle to knees, dirty from the mud of the cobblestones. Her neck had a hard, red line where the diamond necklace had been wrenched on it.

Mrs. Owens had sat up and begun to weep and wail. Fiona was recalled to herself. The housekeeper bustled in, exclaimed in horror, sent maids flying for basins of water and cloths.

Fiona held out her hand to Wallace Frazer. "I cannot thank you enough," she said, in a low tone. "If you had not come—"

He half smiled, holding her hand. "I followed you from the house," he said simply. "I had seen some fellows about, I was concerned. You should not go out all unescorted like that."

"I know," she said. "But godmother—there are so few—" Her eyes explained, apologized for her godmother's ancient house, her few servants. He nodded, understanding at once, it seemed.

"May I call upon you in a day or two, and make sure for myself that you are unharmed?"

"Please come, whenever you wish. You are—most kind."

His hand pressed hers, he bowed, and left them. The

house seemed strangely empty, though everyone was flying about to help. Fiona turned to her godmother, made sure she seemed all right, then went to bathe Mrs. Owens' forehead and send for the doctor.

All the time, she kept thinking of the warm, reassuring clasp of the Highlander's big fingers.

Chapter Two

Wallace Ian Frazer, Frazer of Frazer, stretched out his long legs under the crude wooden table and studied his men in silence. He understood them, he had grown up with them, they had roamed the hills and glens of his beloved Scotland together.

They were all related. When the Clearances had cleared their home in the glen, north of the Great Glen, he had moved his mother and sister to safety in a small house in the nearest village. Jamie Frazer's mother lived with them, so did Ossian's sister and nieces and nephews. Rory's family had died, in the burning of his croft. His invalid mother had died, screaming, as the fire burned the croft to ashes. His father had fought the soldiers and had died of a blow to his white head.

Sholto was the silent one. He had been a shepherd high in the hills, unused to people. Even now he longed for his sheep, his dogs, his silences in the Highlands. Cities were foreign to him, he strode the cobblestones with distaste. But what a fighting man! He fought in silence, striking ferociously with his claymore, studying the lay of the battle with shrewd eyes, going where he was most needed. A demon of a fighter, that one.

Ever since the Rising, the Battle of Culloden, when the forces of Scotland Highlanders under Bonnie Prince Charlie had been defeated and their prince had run away and hid, the Scottish people had lived with uncertainty, fear, starvation. The English had taken their lands, removed the people from one glen and another. Highlanders were unprofitable, sheep were profitable. It was as simple as that to the English landlords, the absentee men who sent factors up to the crude lands to the north to rule in their name.

Wallace Frazer had known no other life but one of changes. His father had died early, from a blow to his body by an English factor when he protested his removal and that of his people. Wallace at sixteen had been head of the clan. Already tall, wise beyond his years, grave always, he had taken over that responsibility. But always he had his dreams, to win back the Frazer lands, to farm them again, to restore his people to dignity, to a life with plenty to eat and something to sing about once more.

They had been forced into the army but had met the duty with dignity. With the Frazer had gone his men, and they would not be parted. Even under the malicious, unpredictable rule of their major, Lord Morney, they had kept their dignity and had earned his reluctant approval by their fighting skills. Toward the end of the Peninsula Wars, he had even asked for medals for his regiment of Highlanders. They had served England well, he had written.

"There be no more wars for the English," murmured Jamie now, thoughtfully, fingering his pipes longingly. The landlady of their aged, crude boardinghouse put up with much, for she had some sympathy for them. But the pipes she could not endure, that loud, sad, sighing, wailing sound drove her out of her mind, she had said frankly, and the neighbors had complained bitterly.

"Aye, but we could turn on them," said Ossian, with a hard practicality. "With the skills we have learned, and with a hundred men at our sides—"

"We have not a hundred men," Wallace reminded him brusquely. "They are in the factories of Glasgow coughing out their lungs, breaking their backs on the docks, or dead under the sod. No, we must be practical. I have been thinking much about what to do. I think I may get an appointment as a factor."

The red-haired men were silent, turning their vivid blue eyes on their clan chief with some incredulity. A factor? Working for the hated English? It showed in their faces, which he could read so well. He nodded his own head slowly, sadly.

"Aye," he said, reverting to the Gaelic. "It may be the only answer. Should I receive such an appointment, I could do us much good. Quietly, we could gather our own people together once more, with the money we earn we could buy some crofts back once more. Our war record will serve us well. Other soldiers receive land in Canada or Australia. We might earn enough to buy some in our own Highlands. I have some hope of this."

"And work for them?" murmured Jamie in distaste. "'Twas bad enough to fight for them!"

"We fought the French," Wallace reminded him mildly. "The Scottish and the French have long been friends. However, Napoleon is no such one as to win our loyalty. Remember the Spanish partisans and how he ordered them hanged. Remember the Portuguese, the Austrians. No, he was a bully and a thief."

"Aye, aye," they murmured with him, nodding their heads. They studied him anxiously. He was their chief, he was smart, he knew the ways of the world, he was educated, his father had seen to that. In him was their hope for the future, and for the future of their families and their clan.

They were loyal to him, as he was loyal to them. They were one, in hope and fear, in happiness and despair. When he led them into battle, they followed, no matter what the major or the captain said to them. It was the Frazer they followed, as their people had always followed the Frazer.

A knock came at the door. Jamie answered, and bowed slightly to the plump landlady. She was breathless from the climb up the steep stairs to the third floor rooms. Wallace Frazer stood up.

"Message—for ye—" she panted, her hand at her stomach. "Lord, those stairs will kill me yet! He waits an answer, below."

Wallace thought at once of Fiona Cartwright. Was she in more trouble? He unfolded the paper, then frowned down at the message.

"Frazer. Come to my club, in the Strand, the Eagle. I have something that may interest you and give you occupation. This morning, elevenish. Lord Morney."

Wallace stared at the note. Did Lord Morney know he hoped for a job as a factor? He might, he was devilish shrewd, and he somehow managed to find out all the news and tidbits of gossip that floated about London.

"Tell the messenger I will come as directed," he said to the landlady.

She nodded, and panted her way down the narrow winding stairs once more. Wallace closed the door after her.

"I am directed to the club of the Eagle in the Strand, by Lord Morney. About eleven. I had planned to visit Miss Cartwright this morning. That must wait. Jamie will come with me, and Rory."

They were curious but asked no questions as he moved to his wardrobe to get his doublet and his long plaid. It was a cold, rainy April morning. He donned the garments, fastened the plaid with his large Cairngorm brooch, made of the beautiful Scottish smoky quartz from the Cairngorm mountains, inherited from his father. He fingered the brooch absently. It was a symbol of his inheritance, like his title, his castle now deserted in the glen, his duties and responsibilities.

They all made ready, and the three of them set out,

Wallace in front, his kilt swinging above his long legs, his *sgian-dubh* stuck in his right stocking. They carried no claymores in the daylight hours, reserving that weapon for the dark night.

About eleven, they arrived at the club. He told his men to remain outdoors. They waited then, patiently in the rain, as he went inside. Lord Morney belonged to the club, he did not, and the grand, imperious marquess of Morney would not admit any but his one guest.

Wallace Fazer gave his name to the supercilious porter at the entry. The man ran his gaze down over Frazer, nodded curtly, and directed him to remain in the hallway while he spoke to Lord Morney. Soon he came back and said, "You may enter!"

He did not say "sir" or show him the way in. Frazer set his teeth and went inside to glance about the shady, pleasant room with the overstuffed chairs, the bay windows overlooking the busy street outside.

His attention was caught by a raised languid hand. He nodded, and went toward the three men in the corner of the room. None of them stood. He had been, after all, a sergeant, not an officer.

He stood beside them. Lord Morney glanced up at him, a secret laugh in his green eyes. What mischief was he up to now? wondered Frazer, impatient with himself that he had answered the summons.

"Frazer," said Lord Morney. "Ah—do sit down," and he gestured to the fourth chair. "You'll have a drink?"

They had all three been drinking and gambling, Frazer saw by the cards and dice spilled about, the glasses and bottles.

"I thank you, no, sir, I planned to make some calls later in the day," he said as pleasantly as he could manage.

"Ah—yes."

Captain Jenks laughed. "Call on the lovely Fiona Cartwright?" he sneered. "Ye'll be wasting your time, I'll warrant! She is an ice woman! A snow maiden!"

Frazer stiffened. No decent man mentioned a woman

like her, a real lady. He kept his face still by an intense effort. They all delighted in ragging him, trying to make him blurt out his fury, so they could reprimand him, call him to order, punish him. He hated Jenks, but he had kept that hate inside himself. He despised Morney but kept that hidden also.

Captain Benedict Ainsworth was not so bad. Led by bad company, Wallace had thought. His only brother had kicked him out, he had no contact with family, no responsibilities. Pleasant enough when not drinking and gambling beyond his means. He exchanged nods with the young man who sat back and looked rather troubled, his glass in an unsteady hand.

Lord Morney leaned back in his chair, his lazy eyes surveyed his former sergeant. "I noted that you danced twice with the lady last night," he said at last. "What d'you think of her, eh?"

Wallace drew a deep breath. "I do not discuss ladies in public, sir," he said very quietly, his burr very pronounced.

Captain Jenks laughed, was silenced by a look from the marquess.

"Come now, I have my reasons, Frazer," said Derek Grenville. He lifted his half-filled glass, tilted it to his mouth. A few drops spilled on his Prussian blue jacket, his modish yellow trousers. He scowled down at his unsteady hand. "Tell me, how close did you get to the lady, eh?"

Wallace began to rise. "I hope you will pardon me," he said very politely. "I will come and see you at some other time, if ye do not mind."

"Sit down, sit down!" snapped the marquess, snarling suddenly. "I told you I have my reasons! I'll make a wager with you."

"I have no money for wagers, sir," said Wallace coldly. "You know the state of my finances, sir."

If he stayed much longer, he would smash his big fist in the grinning mouth, he thought moodily. Why in hell had he come? Hope, eternal hope that the man might have a position for him, that he might somewhere find a decent job where he might help his people.

"Wait," said Lord Morney. He set down the glass deliberately, motioned for it to be filled again. A waiter scurried up to fill it. He waited until the man had left, then continued in a low tone, "You know the name the lady has. Snow Maiden. She has scorned us all, married and unmarried. The word is, she has no wish to marry, she hates men. Yet you seemed to get along well with her, eh?"

"I treated her with courtesy," said Wallace Frazer, with ill-concealed irony. Lord Morney frowned but did not rebuke him.

"I have had an idea. A magnificent idea. She deserves a little set-down, don't you think? Scorning us all. Turning up her nose at gentlemen, she, a maid from the country, presented only this season. None of us good enough for her. You're a handsome chap," he added reluctantly. "You seem to have won her regard to some extent, Lord knows how. What do you say—if you can get her—"

Frazer stood up abruptly. "I'll stay for no more words," he said, and began to walk away.

"Do you know the name of the man who bought your clan lands in the Highlands?" Lord Morney shot after him.

Frazer stood still, his back turned, a shudder went through him. He turned slowly, came back to them, his fists clenched tight. "His name was Smith. There are a million Smiths."

"No, no, after that. Smith acted in his own behalf, then later sold the lands at a profit to another, and he to another. Do you know who owned them from 1803 to 1814?"

Lord Morney motioned to the empty fourth chair. Frazer sank down slowly into it, feeling chills up his spine. He had asked about him, but they knew only the name of the factor, "Phineas Tilden," he said. "That's the factor. Does he own the lands?"

"No. He works for Hugo Horace Cartwright," said

Morney, smiling in enjoyment as he saw the look on Frazer's face.

Cartwright. The same name as Fiona's. Could it be?—the man they hated, the man who had driven out his people, put in sheep, scorned them, harried them from *his* lands, ordered his factor to rope and drag away any man who dared remain—

"The father of Fiona Cartwright," said Lord Morney evenly. He nodded. "The same. I know them well, have for years. Old Cartwright died two years ago, unmourned, I might say. A cruel bastard. His wife died some years before, leaving but one child, a girl. His fortune went to the girl, his country estates, and his property—including the former clan lands of the Frazer in Scotland."

He waited while it sank in. Frazer sat there, his hands clasped tightly together, gazing into space. He did not see the three men watching him curiously, he could not see at all, for the red blaze of blood and hate. The lovely young girl, the smiling pretty girl, the fortune in diamonds about her throat—paid for in the blood of Highlanders!

Jenks was impatient with his silence. Captain Benedict Ainsworth sat in troubled manner, squirming in his chair, his drink forgotten. Morney gazed with bright, malicious green eyes at his victim.

"Well," he said. "It is a surprise to you, yes? He did own the lands, now his daughter owns them. I doubt if she even knows of her property up there, she pays no attention to the land. Her solicitors hold her wealth and manage it. Her factor in the Highlands does as he wishes, so long as the money flows to the girl."

Frazer's stricken look turned to his tormentor, and he saw him more clearly, the malice in his look, the cruel set of his mouth.

"What—had you in mind?" he asked slowly.

"Merely to humiliate the girl," shrugged Lord Morney. "Not to harm her. Just enough to set her back a piece. Now, this is what I thought." He leaned forward. His drink-laden breath offended Wallace, but he controlled his emotions as best he could.

"Come on, out with the plans," urged on Jenks, chuckling drunkenly. "Give the girl a set-down. Lead her on—"

"Shut up. It's my plan," said the marquess curtly. "Frazer, you seem to have caught her fancy. She is cold as ice. I'll set you a task. You court the girl, get her to agree to marry you. Get the engagement in the gazettes in London—and I'll pay you one thousand pounds."

Frazer caught his breath. One thousand pounds! How lightly the man spoke of such money! A fortune to him, how much he could do— But he thought of Fiona Cartwright. A delicate English girl, with direct violet eyes, a shy smile which she showed when she was not in a crowd of society.

Yet—yet she was the daughter of that Cartwright who had helped ruin his people. The men in the docks of Glasgow. The children in the factories, dying early, starved and overworked. The women, depraved and lost.

Morney misread him. "All right, five thousand pounds. What do you say, man?" he urged him impatiently. "You can do it, I saw her soft looks at you last night. Lead her on, show her gallantry, you can court a girl, can't you? She might suspect one of us, she doesn't know you are one of us."

One of them! He could have spit at the thought. One of *them?* Never in a million years. The damned English—

He tried to keep his face impassive. "She would not look to a man without money," he finally said.

"So? She does not need to know you are poor. I will advance you a thousand pounds, dress yourself up, hire a carriage—" Lord Morney tapped the table. He disliked having his plans go awry.

Still Frazer thought. He had never treated a woman so, never had much dealings with ladies. He had danced with them, spoken to them . . . but courting? Seriously, to lead her on?

Jenks watched him shrewdly. "Cartwright made a fortune in the sheep," he said, with a drunken giggle. "He had only a little money when he started, not compared to now. The sheep made him. He said they were better than stinking Highlanders anytime. Worth two million pounds when he kicked off."

Fury blazed up in Frazer. "Ah, God," he groaned, and put his face in his hands. Jenks exchanged a triumphant look with Morney. Ainsworth moved as though to speak, they shook their heads at him.

"Where are your people now?" asked Derek Grenville softly. "Some dead in Spain, they didn't even bring the bodies home. Some gone to Canada, eh? Not many left up there. And it's her land now, and her sheep. She can do what she pleases with it all."

Frazer dropped his hands. "What—would I—have to do?" he asked, in a cold, set tone.

"Court her. Get her to agree to a marriage. Get the story in the gazettes. I want to see the notices," said the marquess of Morney, suavely concealing his triumph. "After that, you can humiliate her how you choose. Leave the country, leave her at the altar, do what you want. Just give the girl the set-down of her life! I hate her cold airs, her nose in the air, the ice treatment she hands out to decent men like me."

Wallace Frazer drew a deep breath. He knew he was not thinking clearly, the red haze before his eyes was like that before a battle, when he contemplated the enemy lines. He could not hold back, however, the rage drove him on.

"I'll do it," he said. "I'll do it!"

"Good man! I'll give you ten thousand for it," said Morney, well pleased and disposed to be generous. "Come to my bank with me, I'll give you one thousand pounds on account. Fix yourself up, smart clothes, some jewels, take the little lady to Vauxhall and the theater. Come along now, we'll go to my bank."

He swept up Frazer, and Jenks tagged along with

them, laughing. At the bank, where the impassive man counted out the one thousand pounds into Frazer's hands, Morney kept chuckling.

In the street he said, "I'll leave you now. Won't be seen together, eh? The little lady might suspect. But do your work, and do it quick! I want you engaged before the end of the season, if you can wangle it. Let me see it in the gazettes before I retire to the country for the summer, eh, Frazer?"

With a condescending nod, he and Jenks went off down the street, leaving Frazer with his hands full of the notes. Jamie and Rory stared at him in dumb shock. He stuffed his pockets full, gave them some to put in theirs.

"What ha' ye done, Frazer?" asked Jamie sternly.

"We'll go back to my quarters. I'll tell you something of the matter," said Wallace slowly, wearily.

They walked back to the quarters, but at the boardinghouse Wallace decided not to tell them. If they knew who Fiona was, they might turn on her in a horrible rage, especially Sholto. No, he must handle this himself.

He finally settled on the story. "It is a wager, something I cannot talk about yet," he told them. "It will not be difficult, or mayhap it will be. We will pay our rent for two months and get some better clothes. And money can be sent to our people, to pay for food and clothing against next winter."

His anger had not died, but it had turned inward, to fester and torment him. He had agreed to this, he would humiliate Fiona, publicly and shamefully, before London society. For ten thousand pounds, and for his honor.

Frazer of Frazer would help avenge his people.

Chapter Three

Two days after the footpads' attack on her, Fiona still felt badly shaken. They had not gone out by day or night. Her godmother had taken to her bed, weeping a little softly. Mrs. Owens had had to have the doctor to stitch her head, and was still feverish.

A footman came to Fiona about mid-morning. He was young and untrained, but willing. Mrs. Trent, her godmother, would not allow Fiona to pay for her luxury. "No, no, my dearest, save your money against your marriage and children. You will want much for them. I can live quietly, I enjoy my old home, shabby though it be. And my servants are comfortable with me."

"Miss Cartwright, there be a strange gentleman to see ye," said the footman dubiously. He had no card on a silver tray. "He had no identity, there be two rough men with him. But I think he be the gent that escorted ye home the other night."

Wallace Frazer! Her feet were suddenly light in their blue slippers, and she sped down the winding stairs to the floor below, to find the Scottish man in his red kilt waiting in the hall.

She held out both hands. "Oh, sir, you are most kind to call. Come upstairs to the sitting room. I will send word to my godmother."

He smiled, a slow movement of his mouth that did not reach his vivid blue eyes. He inclined his head and took her two slim hands cautiously in his big ones.

"I called but to inquire how you did, Miss Cartwright." His tone seemed cold, formal.

She knew she was flushed, she had been too eager. She withdrew her hands, murmured, "Will your—cousins come in?"

"No, ma'am, they will wait here." He gave them a look, and they took up positions in the hallway, feet apart, as though standing guard.

"But that will not be comfortable for them," she said gently. She instructed the butler, "Pray, give them chairs, and tea if they wish in the hallway or in the downstairs drawing room."

The butler nodded impassively.

Fiona turned to go up the stairs, the Frazer followed her, his footsteps heavy on the thin wooden treads. Upstairs, she showed him into the pretty little drawing room, and rang for the maid to inform Mrs. Trent that he was there.

"My abigail is still abed," she said apologetically, for receiving him alone. "Her head had to be stitched."

Wallace Frazer showed his concern, and his face warmed. "I am sorry to hear it, ma'am. It is serious? And your godmother, how does she?"

"Godmother was much shaken, she has been in bed, also. I dread to think what would have happened to us if you had not come, you and your men," she said, with a shaky smile. Her whole body felt chilled as she thought of the masked men, the greedy, dirty hands that had grabbed her and torn her dress, felt her white throat. She could still feel the hands on her, the ruthless horrible hands, and a shudder went through her.

"Pray, be seated, sir. It is a—a lovely day for April, is it not?"

"Aye, ma'am." He seated himself gracefully on the worn davenport, not seeming to see the torn place on the rug near him, the simplicity of the mantelpiece with few ornaments. The little maid returned and curtsyed.

"Mrs. Trent will come as soon as she is dressed, ma'am." And she seated herself on a straight chair near the door, demurely.

"May I offer you tea?" Fiona asked eagerly. She was pleased when he nodded soberly.

"If it be not too much trouble for ye," he said. His burr was very pronounced today. She thought he looked worried about something, but presently, as they spoke, he smiled, and his blue eyes were lighter, more like the sunny blue of a lake.

They talked of the attack; then, when he saw how it distressed her, he changed the conversation. "Do you go to Vauxhall Gardens this week, my lady? There be fireworks, and a concert."

She hesitated. "I do not go out much, sir. I came to London to be with Mrs. Trent."

He inclined his head. "I wish to say, ma'am, that anywhere you wish to go, I and my men will escort you."

He said it so firmly, so solemnly that she stared in wonder and disbelief. "You—escort me, sir? But that would take up much time—no, no, it is not necessary—"

"It is necessary, Miss Cartwright," he said very firmly. His vivid blue eyes gazed straight at her. "There be evil men about, and you and your godmother are ladies, and unprotected. It shall be my duty to escort you."

She was torn between laughter and dismay and a sort of strange pleasure. "But sir—all our gadding about—you cannot wish to escort us to—to the dressmaker's, and to teas—"

"Aye, I will that."

Tea came, she poured out, and handed him the fragile cup. She was pleased with his good manners. He ate and drank sitting upright, did not slurp at the cup, set the cup aside when he had done on a table where it would not upset easily. By this time Mrs. Trent, hastily gowned in gray muslin, had entered the room.

She thanked him over and over for his rescue. "Our savior," she said emotionally, and looked as though tears would spill over. "I cannot be done thanking you, good sir. I shall bless you forever."

He looked embarrassed but bent over her hand gallantly and kissed the fingers. "Nay, ma'am, it was our pleasure to be there at the right time. I have been informing your goddaughter that you and she shall not go out alone again. I and my men will escort you everywhere."

She looked as startled as Fiona had felt. She sank into the pale blue velvet chair opposite the davenport, and he seated himself again. "But sir—you cannot do that—I mean—every day—dear me! How boring it would be for you, dear sir!"

He gazed at her seriously. "Weee-el, ma'am," he drawled out. "I canna say I am too fond of dressmakers and teas and such like, I am not acquainted much with them. However, escort you, I will, and remain outdoors, with your carriage, against the time you are finished with your gossiping and dressmaking."

He spoke so positively that they could not help but exchange glances. Fiona finally spoke up. "You are most kind, sir, and when we do go out evenings, we might call upon you for your kind escort—"

"Ah, nay, ma'am. I mean day and night, ma'am. For those creatures"—it sounded like *craythurs* the way he spoke it—"those creatures do stir themselves both night and day, and desperate they be for a bit of money and jewels to sell. Nay, I'll come round each day, and get my orders."

Then Fiona did giggle. His head turned sharply, that red head of fiery hue, and he frowned at her. She said hastily, "I do but laugh, sir, because you—you speak as though I were an officer, to command you!"

"No, ma'am, you are my lady, to command me," he said softly. "I will take your orders—and I put myself under your wishes."

Mrs. Trent gazed wide-eyed at them both as they stared at each other. Fiona felt a flush from head to foot, and her fingers trembled so that she folded them against each other.

Somehow Fiona did not think he would do this. He remained for luncheon, however, asked them if they meant to go out that day. When they said no, he took himself off.

The next morning, about ten o'clock, he appeared again with two of his stalwart Highlanders, kilts flying, bonnets wide above their tanned, sturdy faces. Fiona thanked him and said she and her godmother wished to pay a call.

He promptly went with them, he and his men, striding along beside the slow-moving carriage. He would not ride inside, it would crowd them. They strode as though they walked their native hills, she thought, Frazer in front, then Jamie, and then Rory or Ossian or Sholto. She was coming to know their names.

He waited for them, though she urged him to come inside with them. He shook his head. "I am not invited, my lady. The Scots are not always welcome. No, I'll wait for ye out here."

He came the next morning, and the next. Whenever they had calls to pay, or errands to do, he would come with them. If they did not go out, he either left, or remained, at Fiona's invitation, to take tea and to entertain them with his slow, burred speech, his serious talk of the Highlands, perhaps briefly of the battles he had seen, though he spoke little of them. "Not fit for ladies' ears," he told them.

Fiona had not wanted to go to Vauxhall, she did not crave the company of the ruffled-sleeved rakes who invited her. However, with the Highlander ready to offer his escort, she decided to go that week. She and her godmother dressed modestly and warmly in velvet, she in blue and her godmother in black, and set out with their largest carriage so the Highlanders would ride with them.

"How splendid, to go to the gardens to a concert once more," exclaimed Mrs. Trent as they neared the Vauxhall Gardens. "I have longed to go, but Fiona would not, without a proper escort. One cannot trust so many gentlemen these days! Not like my day, when a gentleman was a gentleman and took proper care of a lady." She looked with increasing approval on the Frazer.

He bowed silently, in acknowledgement of her praise. Fiona smiled at him shyly. "Yes, I have longed to attend the concerts. Yet it was not safe. However," she hastened to add, blushing, "you must not feel you must escort us all the season, sir! It is too kind of you, taking up so much of your time."

"It gives me great pleasure, ma'am," he said seriously. "And it helps fill my time, if I might be so rude as to say it. Ye see, I do wait to find some suitable employment for me and my men. Each day, I look about, and talk to men about work in the Highlands. But there is little there."

Mrs. Trent looked at him shrewdly. "You would go back up there, though your people were probably driven out?"

Fiona gazed at him wide-eyed. "Driven out?" she echoed. "Why was that?"

"Ah, that is a long story, and not one for a happy evening," he said, his face shadowing, and he half turned from them. "Here we are. Ossian, do find us a fine table not too close to the music, which gets too loud for the ears of the ladies. Somewhere sheltered."

The man answered him in an odd language, and Wallace spoke again in it. Fiona looked at him curiously.

"I have heard you say things that I do not understand," she said, as Ossian strode away. "What is it, French? Or German?"

"Nay, my lady. It is the Gaelic," he answered, and lifted her down easily, with his strong hands holding hers. When she was safely on the ground, he lifted her godmother down by holding her by her little waist. She gurgled with laughter.

"Ah, you lift me like a doll!" she exclaimed with pleasure. "How strong you are!"

He smiled down at her from his great height. "Sure, it is like a little fine doll that ye are, ma'am."

They strolled into the beautifully lit grounds, and back to the table that Ossian was holding for them, feet apart, his belligerent look daring any gentleman to take it from him. They were seated, Wallace summoned a waiter, and their orders for drinks and a meal to be served later were taken. Then he sat down beside Fiona, and presently the concert began.

The music was delightful, some light airs, a singer, followed by a magic act which had them all wonder. Then the orchestra began again, and the food arrived, served by a quick-moving waiter.

They talked under cover of the music. "I do like this music," sighed Fiona. "It reminds me of mother's home in Wales, when the singers would come and all would gather in town to hear them."

Wallace Frazer gave her a quick, surprised look. "Wales? I thought you English," he said.

"Well—Wales is part of England," she smiled. "But Wales is also different. I inherited my mother's eyes and her dark hair, they say, and her voice." Her face shadowed. "She died many a year ago," she sighed. "I wish I remembered her better."

Mrs. Trent's face had shadowed also. "Your dear mother Glynis was the dearest, gentlest soul who ever lived," she said, in a low tone. "How lovely she was, like an angel. Too good for—" She caught her breath and changed the sentence. "Too good for this world," she ended flatly, and patted Fiona's hand.

Frazer looked curiously, thoughtfully, from one to the other; however, he said no more of the matter. Fiona's attention was caught by the sight of three modishly dressed gentlemen strolling near them, staring frankly at them. She averted her look.

Frazer stood and bowed, they bowed back at him and strolled on. He sat down.

Fiona's mouth was compressed. "I cannot like Lord Morney, he is so—so malicious."

"Now, Fiona!" Mrs. Trent said gently. "He has given us many attentions."

Fiona's blue eyes blazed. "I would pity his wife," she said, in a low tone, "but she is just like him. Kate Grenville is the most malicious, the most cruel of tongue of any female I ever met! They are well suited."

"My dear, not in public!" sighed Mrs. Trent. She turned to Wallace Frazer. "Lord Morney was your officer, was he not, sir?"

"Aye, that he was," said Frazer, without expression.

"There, now, we'll have no more of the matter," and she changed the subject with firm determination.

They finished their dinner, to the accompaniment of gentle music. The evening concluded with a great display of fireworks, which amused and delighted them all, even the sober Highlanders. Frazer grinned at the two men with him.

"Now Ossian will write a poem tonight, to the fireworks," he joked.

"Ossian? A poet?" asked Fiona, giving the man a smiling look.

"Oh, aye, he is my poet. He knows all the Highland stories in poems and can recite any that I like. Not much is written down of our history, Miss Cartwright. Were it not for poets like Ossian, all would be lost in a generation or two. They keep our memories green."

She thought privately that sometimes Wallace sounded like a poet himself. She said, "I should like so much to hear him one day. Would he tell me his poems?"

"Mayhap," said the Frazer, frowning a little. "However, most are in the Gaelic. I will have him recite for you one day, if you wish, and I will translate as he speaks."

"I should like that immensely," said Fiona, with such enthusiasm that her godmother stared at her gravely, then looked again at Frazer, with more acute speculation.

Frazer did come another day, one afternoon that rained and was dark and stormy, so that they thought it would not let up. They canceled all their calling, and remained indoors. Mrs. Owens was up and about, though still a bit weepy and frail. The ladies seated themselves in the cozy upstairs sitting room and received Frazer when he came.

"It is just the day for stories and songs," said Fiona. "Would your Ossian tell us poems today, of your history?"

"Aye, that he will, if you wish it," and Frazer called for his two men to come. Jamie, the immensely tall one, had brought his pipes, and Ossian's head was always full of poems.

First Frazer explained the pipes, and how a chief of the clan always had his personal piper to play for him. Then he asked Jamie to play for them, some of the old tunes. And Jamie marched up and down the hallway of the passage just outside the sitting room, and the wail and groan and music of the bagpipes filled the whole house.

Fiona flinched at first at the sound, but as she became accustomed to it, she found the melody, and the sadness of it. She listened intently, noticed that Frazer sat with solemn face and grave demeanor, as though it meant much to him.

When Jamie had finished his tunes, Frazer turned to Ossian.

"And Ossian, here, will ye tell the ladies about the early history of the Scottish kings? Talk ye in the Gaelic and I will translate."

The dreary afternoon was transformed. He spoke so eloquently, and Frazer told them the English in such marvelous words that the dingy room seemed filled with the stately presence of the old, battling, magnificent Scottish kings and queens. Fiona particularly liked the story of Margaret, who was blown ashore in Scotland and became queen to Malcolm, strongly influencing him and his people in the ways of her devout religion. This was the eleventh century, and Fiona was amazed how they spoke of her as though she had lived recently.

Then they spoke the story of Wallace, an ordinary man and not a noble, who had united many men from all over Scotland to fight against the English. He told in a simple way, yet eloquent and moving, how the battles were fought, and Wallace captured, to be tried as a traitor and condemned to death.

Then Fiona said, "And is it this Wallace for whom you are named?"

"Aye," he said, "he is that Wallace. A brave and fine man, who showed the way for the rest of us to fight against oppression and those who would take away our freedoms and our religion."

He went on to speak briefly of Robert the Bruce but then shook his head. "Ah, I go on and on. There is so much history to our land. I fear I will make you yawn."

"No, no, I am most interested!" said Fiona impulsively, her eyes shining. "No wonder you are so proud of your Highlands, and the uniform which symbolizes it. Tell me about the kilt, and the brooch which you wear."

He fingered it. "This was left me by my father. It is of Scottish Cairngorm, a smoky quartz mined in our own Cairngorm mountains, a symbol of our people. The silver is designed with symbols of the Celts, from whom we came."

Mrs. Trent rang for tea. "My, what a delightful afternoon," she said. "You make all those events live for us, sir. We must have more stories and music another afternoon."

This time Mrs. Trent invited Jamie and Ossian to join with them at tea. With a questioning look at the Frazer, they finally sat down with the ladies. Fiona began to realize that Mrs. Trent accepted these men and liked the Frazer immensely. But so did she! So did she! Her heart thumped when he came, she knew his voice, the deep burr and the vitality of the masculine timbre. She knew his step on the stairs, the heavy deliberate step of his boots. She liked to watch the slow smile that came infrequently to his tanned, rugged features. She liked to watch the expressive way his hands moved as he spoke.

They came another day, and another. On nice days, they went out, and Wallace kept his word. He took them to the dressmaker's, and the bonnetmaker's, and waited patiently in the street for them. He took them calling, and Fiona began to insist that he come indoors with them to meet London society. Women were beginning to whisper, and to tease her a little about her "wild Scotsman." Men looked at him dubiously, then began to talk with him, surprised to find him knowledgeable about the politics of England and Europe, the state of agriculture and the economy, and, of course, the battles in which he had taken part. Frazer went reluctantly among them, ever watchful, it seemed to Fiona, of some slight or snub. Some did snub him and turned their backs and spoke sneeringly of the poor Scots people, and how inferior they were to the English. Others accepted him.

Fiona began to realize also that Frazer always wore his kilt, no other dress or day garments. He seemed to have several sets of them, his garments were always clean and well pressed. But he never wore the velvet jackets of gentlemen, the ruffled white shirts, the riding clothes that were popular in the parks, but always his kilt, his doublet, his bonnet with the crest, and on cold or rainy days, the long plaid that was folded about his tall form.

Finally, one afternoon, they were alone for a bit. Mrs. Trent was resting when the Frazer came to call, and Fiona was reluctant to call her. Mrs. Owens sat discreetly in the corner, sewing on bits of lace.

The May afternoon was peaceful, the sun had come out, the lavender sellers had been out yesterday in the Strand, and Frazer had brought her a bunch of lavender and a bunch of heather, brought from Scotland by one of his men.

She fingered the bunch in delight, and drew great breaths of it. He watched her, with a somber expression.

"I would have brought you jewels," he said abruptly. "You should have gems of amethysts, pearls, diamonds, sapphires to set off your beauty, rather than a little bit of flower."

She smiled over the heather at him. "I would rather have the heather, sir," she said demurely. "The gems I could not accept. No lady could, you know. Godmother would be most angry! And I enjoy the scent," she drew another breath of them. "Jewels have no such perfume."

"Miss Fiona," he said abruptly, the first time he had used her name. "I know ye have money. Did ye know I have none?"

She blinked. It had come so fast—she swallowed.

"Yes, I—I surmised that, sir," she managed to answer.

"And must ye marry money?" His accent was so strong that she had to guess at the words.

Instinct told her why he asked. She blushed deeply and buried her face in the little purple heather bells. Then she gathered her nerve and lifted her chin to look at him.

"No, sir, that is not necessary," she said bravely. "My—my father left me—a fortune. I would be happy—to share it—with—whomever I marry—if I should marry," she hastened to add.

"Ah, that is well," he said quietly. "We will speak of it another time. I wished you to know, however, that I have none. Nothing to offer a lass but the strength of my hands and my back, and the loyalty of me and my clan."

She did not know what to answer. Mrs. Trent trailed in, her face brightened at the sight of their visitor. "Well, Mr. Frazer! You have come to cheer us today," she said in a spritely way. By the way she beamed and gave him her hand to kiss, Fiona knew that Wallace Frazer had won her aunt's regard.

But what about hers? Fiona's mind was in confusion. Only a few weeks ago, she had vowed stormily to herself never to marry. And now that man had come along, this odd, stubborn, difficult, serious Highlander, with his outlandish garb, the weight of his history on his back and shoulders, his men devotedly following him, instantly obedient to him. And all her icy defenses were melting!

She felt girlish and shy, yet warm and interested in him. A slight to him at a dinner brought fierce thoughts to her mind. She had crossed several ladies off her list of acquaintances at the way they snubbed her Scotsman, as they dubbed him. Other couples, she felt more warmly toward than in the past because they welcomed the Frazer!

She wanted to learn more about him, she enjoyed his men and admired their devotion. She wanted to hear about his mother and sister, and to meet them. Frazer had said he had sent for them to come to London for a month. He would introduce them, he had said definitely.

Fiona felt an odd thrill going through her. Could the man be serious about her? His questions, his looks, the attentions he paid—they all spelled serious intentions. But how did she feel about it? What could she say?

Chapter Four

The Frazer brought his mother and his sister Margaret to call, one glorious day in May. Fiona had fluttered over what to wear—a grand gown of violet silk, or one of green lace over silk, or a simple white chiffon, or a white muslin.

Remembering his words, that he had no money, she wisely decided to wear something simple. His family would probably not have grand clothes. So Fiona put on the white muslin, and with it she wore a lace scarf about her throat, and only pearl earrings in her small ears.

Her godmother wore her usual gray and looked pretty and delicate with her pink cheeks and sparkling eyes.

When the carriage arrived, and Fiona heard the sounds of their arrival on the ground floor, her heart seemed to flutter and stop, then start again with a great pounding. What if they did not like her? She knew by his face as he spoke of his family that they were close, devoted to each other.

The butler showed them upstairs and announced them solemnly at the door, as Fiona had told him to do. "The Frazer of Frazer. Mrs. Ian Frazer, Miss Margaret Frazer." He bowed and showed them into the small sitting room.

Fiona clasped her hands tightly and then rose to greet them. Mrs. Frazer was a delicately built woman, whose face showed lines of suffering. She was slim, aged, with white hair simply arranged in a chignon behind her neck. She wore black with a red plaid scarf about her thin form.

Fiona went forward to greet her nervously, took her hand in hers, was conscious that the vivid blue eyes were studying her seriously. She smiled down at the woman and received an answering smile so like that of the Frazer that Fiona felt warmer.

She turned to the sister and was surprised. She was about twenty, with brilliant red hair, sparkling blue eyes. She wore a white muslin gown like Fiona's, very simple in make, and over it a swirling red clan plaid fastened to her shoulder and about her waist. She was stunning, thought Fiona, noting the proud tilt of her head, the ribbons that bound back her flaming hair.

They shook hands, Fiona murmured her welcome to the Frazer, and then she introduced them to her godmother.

She was relieved when all that was done, and they could be seated, and talk. Tea was served within a few minutes, it helped bridge the awkwardness.

"You have comfortable lodgings?" asked Mrs. Trent.

"Most comfortable, thank you," said Mrs. Frazer. They talked of London, the gaiety of the season. Wallace had taken them to some gardens, they spoke of the flowers.

There was more than a touch of reserve about the two Frazer women. Margaret spoke little, she seemed to watch all with a grave gaze. But when she spoke, she had such a lilt to her voice, such a poetic turn of expression that Fiona turned often to her and asked her questions for the pleasure of hearing her answer.

"Our seasons are ahead of yours in Scotland, I believe," said Fiona to her.

"Oh, aye. We do not have the roses yet, and the moors are sad with winter yet. The bracken is brown in the hills."

"I should like to see your hills one day," said Fiona, then blushed as the Frazer looked at her. "I mean—I long to travel, I have done little traveling," she added hastily.

"Few come to our Highlands," said Margaret. It sounded like "Hee-lens" the way she spoke. "Some call them horrid and wild. Yet one can find all of God and nature there, the majesty and the upliftin' that one looks for."

Mrs. Trent looked at her with approval, then turned to Mrs. Frazer. "You stood the journey well?" she asked. "It is a long one, I believe."

"We did the journey in three days, thanks to the Frazer," said his mother placidly. "He would not have us travel far in a day, though he hired a fine carriage for us. However, I do find London a wee bit noisy, eh?"

"More than a wee bit," said Mrs. Trent fervently. "A few months, and I am ready to retire to the country. Fiona, you will go to Yorkshire in July, will you not?"

"Yes, and take my noise-hating godmother with me," smiled Fiona. "There in the country, you shall be quiet as you wish."

The Frazer looked grave, he crossed his ankles in the plaid high socks. "When does the London season end, Mrs. Trent? I am not well acquainted with all the social matters."

"June sees the season winding down," she replied. "All retire to the country if they can, against the heat of the summer. Some return in the late autumn, others wait until Christmas or the later winter. The season starts again in February and March."

"Ah, so that is the way of it," said Mrs. Frazer. "How odd to have so many houses to traipse back and forth like that!"

"I have just my country house in Yorkshire," said Fiona hastily. She did not want them to think she lived grandly. "My godmother has this London town house. Between them, we live quite happily. I am her guest, then she is mine." She held her godmother's hand briefly, in affection.

"It is good to have land," said Mrs. Frazer sweetly. Her eyes had a distant look. "Once we had lands, many a year ago. The goodness of the hills and mountains—the beauty of the lochs, and the wheat growing in the green."

Frazer changed the subject swiftly. "That was a long time ago. Now I look for a position in the mountains. I hope to find something soon. We must be going now, mother. We will tire the ladies. May we call again later in the week, Miss Fiona?"

Fiona rose reluctantly as they took their departure. She could not believe two hours had flown so rapidly. "Yes, of course, you must come again soon."

He bowed over her hand, the other ladies murmured their farewells. The house seemed empty after they had left. Fiona brooded at the dusk as she stood at the window, gazing out at the street filling with carriages against the evening pleasures.

Her godmother watched her wisely.

Two days later the Frazers came again. This time they remained longer and spoke more freely. Jamie had come and played the pipes for them. "He canna play in the boardinghouse," sighed Mrs. Frazer. "Too well the English do not like it."

They remained for dinner that evening, at Fiona's urging. It was about ten or later when they departed. She sparkled at her godmother. "I think they enjoyed themselves, don't you think so?"

"Oh, yes, they are fine people. I enjoyed talking with them."

Two mornings later, the Frazer came alone, about

ten. He left his two men in the hallway downstairs and tramped slowly and deliberately up the stairs.

The butler was scarcely ahead of him and had just announced him when Wallace Frazer followed him in. Fiona sprang up, her cheeks blooming with color. She was glad she had worn her yellow gown today, with the amber beads at her throat and ears. She held out her hand to him, he bowed over it.

"How do you do, Miss Fiona?"

"Well, thank you, and you?"

"Well, I thank you. How does Mrs. Trent?"

"She is still laying abed. Her head ached somewhat today. Shall you mind if I do not call her yet?" she asked anxiously. Mrs. Owens sat demurely in the corner with her sewing.

"Oh, aye. That suits me well," he said oddly, and sat down on the davenport, stretching out his long legs. He surveyed her earnestly.

After the first awkward words, she scarcely knew what to say. He spoke so absently, as though his mind were on something else. He put his hands firmly on his knees, then leaned forward and spoke.

"Miss Fiona, I have something to ask you."

"Oh, yes, Mr. Frazer?"

"I ha' it in mind that ye do not find me not to your liking."

She gazed at him as she tried to sort that out. Finally she nodded. "I do—like you, Mr. Frazer," she said demurely.

"Aye, good. I like ye weel meself," he said soberly. "In fact, I ha' not thought to marry for years until I could support a lass. But I had it in mind that a lass needs more than money. She needs a sturdy arm to support her, and protection, as ye do."

Fiona blushed. "That is—very true," she said softly, bending her blue black head. Had that been very daring?

"Ye are of age, twenty," he said; then: "I take it, ye have no guardian? No one closer than your godmother to ask your hand?"

"I—make my own decisions. Only my—solicitors are to be asked for their approval," she said quietly. "And they have little say in this."

He drew a deep breath, stared at her so intently that she felt the blue of his gaze going through her like a shaft of light. "Will ye marry me, then, Miss Fiona?"

"I would like it—very much," she said firmly. He stood up and came over to her. She thought his face had paled. He held out his hand.

He drew her up and kissed her hand slowly, his lips on the fingers, lingering. Then he raised his red head and gazed down at her.

"Then we are engaged," he said. He reached into his jacket and drew out a small silver brooch, with a large smoky quartz gem set in the middle. It looked like his, only it was smaller than his grand brooch. "I ha' not a ring for ye yet, Miss Fiona. I dinna know your size. But I would be honored if ye would wear this brooch on your shoulder. It means much to a Scotsman."

"I should be honored to wear it," she said. His fingers fumbled a little as he clasped it to her yellow gown. She put her fingers on it, felt the gem, and the silver chasing, so delicate and intricate in design. "I shall cherish it always, Mr. Frazer."

"Wallace," he said.

"Wallace. And you will call me—Fiona."

"Fiona," he said solemnly. She was not mistaken, his face had paled under his tan. His hand shook a little. She was touched that he was so moved by this.

Fiona felt very strange herself. She had known him only a few weeks, yet she felt she had known him always. Still—there was so much to know about each other! She wanted to tell him about the misery of her early life, the rough life with her father, how cruel he had been, why she was dubbed the "Snow Maiden," how she had never trusted any man until him.

But all that must wait. The Frazer was formal with her. He sat down now at the small writing desk in the corner, looked for paper and pen.

"I should like to announce our engagement at once

in the gazettes," he said, with an odd timbre in his tone. "You have no objections?"

"Oh—no, of course not!" She thought his haste odd, but perhaps this was the custom. Once engaged, they might even go out alone, with only her abigail. That sent a thrill through her.

She came over to stand at his elbow, answering his questions. Her father's name, her mother's, her birthplace, the name of her home in Yorkshire. He composed it quickly, as though he had thought about the wording, or perhaps he was accustomed to writing more than she was.

Mrs. Trent came in as he was finishing. She congratulated him, wept a little over Fiona. "Sure, he is a grand man," she said, smiling through her tears. "Just such a man as I would wish for you, my dearest Fiona! Someone to guard and protect and cherish you all your days!"

When Wallace left them later, he kissed Fiona's hand again. When she was alone in her bedroom, she touched the Cairngorm brooch wistfully. She would have liked some deeper demonstration of his affection for her. Perhaps he might have said that he loved her. Yet, that might not be the way it was done. She took the brooch to her bedside table so it might be near her in the night as she lay wakeful.

The announcements appeared in the gazettes that week. The discreet wording was followed up greedily in the gossip columns, which Fiona rarely read. She clipped out the little formal announcements and saved them in a little inlaid wood box she cherished, which held her mother's miniature and some letters from her childhood.

When the engaged couple went to a formal dinner that week, Fiona was radiantly happy. Wallace had her on his arm, he had praised her gown of green taffeta and lace, the Cairngorm brooch appeared on it, to match the one on his plaid. They received the best wishes of their friends, and Mrs. Trent beamed on them with joy and scarcely concealed relief. Fiona had

49

been so turned against men that her godmother had been anxious that she might never wed at all! Instead, along had come the Frazer and swept all opposition before him.

Wallace left her that night and dismissed the carriage. The misty rain would not penetrate his warm plaid, and he swept it about himself as he strode off, followed by Jamie and Rory. His feelings were very confused.

He would not be able to sleep, he had slept little that week. He had forced himself through all the motions, the wooing, the proposal, the engagement announcements. Now his revenge was at hand. All he had to do was to say to her that she was the daughter of the man his clan hated more than any man in the world! He could see her face pale, the fear in her eyes. He would smash the self-confidence he himself had been building in her. He would laugh in her face, and all London would laugh with him as he broke off their engagement publicly.

However—could he do it? What did he really want?

The thought of the pain in her face made him flinch. He strode along in the black night, the wind blowing rain in his face, and scarcely noticed the discomfort. He wanted revenge—but he wanted more—to marry her!

The thought of holding her in his arms, making her his wife, seeing the blushes on her beautiful face, the sparkle of happiness in her violet eyes—all made him yearn toward her. His mother liked and approved of her, even though she was English.

His sister had said, "She is half-Welsh. That explains it. She is Celtic like ourselves. No wonder she is sympathetic and kind and beautiful. Her voice is like the chime of bells on Sunday."

Could he hurt her? Could he mock her and discard her? Could he treat her harshly?

It was dawn when he returned to the small boardinghouse and climbed the stairs to his rooms, his steps heavy. Jamie and Rory followed him, not saying a word of reproach, though their cloaks were wet through and their boots muddy.

He undressed and flung himself down to watch gray dawn appear in the skies. He hated himself, he despised himself for his indecision. He was a Frazer, his people had been hurt and killed by her father's men. If he had any clan feelings left, he would strike her such a blow as she would never forget.

But he could not. He groaned and turned over on the bed. She was a delicate, gentle lady. Her eyes glowed trustingly into his. She put her slim hand on his arm and smiled in the dance, her face alight with her happiness. Could he do this to her? Dash the warmth and joy from her young body? She was young, yes, she would recover from this in time. She would marry an Englishman—

"No," he groaned to himself, and turned again on the hard bed. The thought of her marrying another man, of lying in some other man's arms stung him bitterly. He wanted her, he loved her. He wanted to cherish and protect her, as her godmother had innocently said.

If they had but known his intentions—!

"I cannot do it—I cannot hurt her—Oh, God, I must put my people first—yet—she trusts me—"

And the money, he thought. The money she brought to the marriage. Two million pounds! What could that do for his people! She was loving, sympathetic. He had but to play on that, and he would have the money for his clan, though her solicitors might protest and warn her. She would hand it out freely.

The money would smooth all their paths. He thought of his white-haired mother, sleeping in her rooms below. She could have comfort, even luxury, again, with servants to wait on her, good meals, no worries. And his sister, beautiful Margaret. He could afford a good dowry for her. And dresses of the smartest, houses wherever they wished, jewels for their decking.

And Fiona—what of her?

He thought she loved him. She had accepted him at once. Her hand had trembled in his, but lain confidingly when he held it. She trusted him to guard her wherever they went.

She trusted him! The taste in his mouth was bitter.

He slept until noon, then rose again. He went out without seeing his mother. She would ask now about the wedding plans, and he had not gone so far. How could he speak of wedding plans, when he meant to break it off, to humiliate the English girl?

He strode along the Strand, with Ossian and Sholto silently behind him. He had ordered Jamie and Rory to remain in and sleep. He used them hard. He was not a good clan chief. A good chief would be certain and positive in his will.

A footman appeared before him, panting, as though he had run. "Sir? The Frazer? Will ye come into the club, sir? His lordship, Lord Morney, sends me after you."

Wallace stiffened. He was reluctant to see the man yet. But evidently he had been seen from the windows of the club. He turned back, with a curt nod, and followed the footman, his own men behind him marching like soldiers.

He entered the club, ordering his men to remain outside. He followed the footman inside, into the huge room. To his dismay, he found Lord Morney surrounded by a small crowd of men, including Captain Jenks and Captain Ainsworth. He gave them a short nod and ignored the other men crowding about.

They had all been drinking, he smelled it in the air. The room was thick with cigar and pipe smoke, dice lay on the green and mahogany tables. "Ah, Frazer," drawled Lord Morney, lying back in his comfortable chair, and studying him with narrowed green eyes. "I thought you would seek me out at once! Instead I have had to watch for you! You pulled it off, and I will pay like the gentleman I am!" and he laughed aloud.

Everyone was watching curiously. Wallace's mouth tightened. It was an effort not to strike the man. He watched as Lord Morney reached into his pockets, and began to pull out huge pound-notes. He counted it out, slowly, flinging the bills across the table.

He talked as he counted. "I don't begrudge you the sum, not ten thousand pounds, Frazer! You pulled it off. You melted the Snow Maiden. Tell us about it," and he glanced up slyly.

"Naught to tell," said Frazer shortly.

"Come on, man," cried Captain Jenks. "Tell us how you made her give in. Have you had her yet? Have you tasted those ripe lips, kissed those smooth shoulders? By Gad, man, I envy you the task! Cold as she is, she must be Venus herself to the touch!"

"Two thousand, five. Three, four, five, six thousand five hundred, seven, eight—" By slowly counting, Lord Morney was holding all attention, and he knew it. A malicious grin curved his sensuous mouth. "Tell us, Frazer." He held the last bill tantalizingly above the pile. "Tell us a bit, and satisfy us in our curiosity. Is she cold, or did you light a fire in her?"

"Come on, tell us, man! Talk!" urged Jenks, his red face wrinkling up with laughter, his small, mean little eyes almost lost in the thick cheeks. "Come on, does she kiss and snuggle? Or does she save herself for the wedding that will not take place, eh?"

Frazer held himself aloof, he said not a word. He had been long schooled in an impassive stance that drove the tormentors crazy.

Lord Morney flung down the last bill. "Nine thousand pounds. And you have one thousand already, for your courting," he grinned. "Ten thousand pounds to be engaged to that icicle! And well you earned it. The season not yet over, and you engaged already! Never tell me the Scots red-legs are laggards in love!" And he bellowed a laugh.

Frazer longed to throw the money in his face. But he needed it, and his mother and sister, and his men. He bent over, with dignity, and picked it up and folded it, to put in his jacket.

"I thank you, sir, for paying off the wager," he said, and turned to go.

"Not so fast! Stay and have a drink!" said Lord Morney, and held up a languid finger to the footman who darted forward. "What will you have to drink, Frazer?"

"Naught, I thank you, sir. I must be on my way."

"Going to break his engagement, now he has the money!" yelled Captain Jenks, booming with laughter. He said something coarse about Fiona, in an undertone. Captain Ainsworth looked uneasy and disapproving.

Frazer bowed and departed. He seethed with rage, at them and at himself. He had lain Fiona open to their talk. He should never have accepted the challenge.

And worst of all, he did not want to break the engagement. He did not know what to do. He felt so uncertain, it made him angry and upset. A battle he could handle—one only needed to kill the other man before he killed you. Officers he could endure—it took a poker face and a blank mind. But this situation, with Fiona so gentle and trusting in him—how could he bring himself to hurt her?

And how could he endure to let her go? English though she was, he wanted her. He even, he thought reluctantly, loved her. Loved her, wanted to touch and caress her, to hold her, protect her, cherish her. What was he to do?

Chapter Five

Fiona sat in the small, faded living room and nibbled the end of her pen. She had many letters of best wishes to answer, and most of them queried when the wedding would take place. She had few close friends, but some of the London crowd had been friendly and cordial.

She sighed, and set down the pen. She stood, to roam about the room, watched by the wise, dark eyes of Mrs. Owens. Mrs. Trent had gone out calling by herself, accompanied by a lady who lived next door, not needing Fiona today.

The butler came to the door, bowed. "Lord Morney and two gentlemen with him," he said, his face schooled to no expression.

"Show Lord Morney up," she said, after a brief pause. She supposed he wished to offer his best wishes, to sneer a bit, or perhaps he might be pleasant for a change. She had known him much of her life, keeping at a distance from him and his fast crowd, but inevitably seeing him and his wife Kate at local events in Yorkshire.

It was early for calls, but ten o'clock. The Frazer had not yet come, he knew she was not going out today, but he was coming for luncheon, he had said yesterday.

She flinched inwardly when Lord Morney appeared in the doorway and was followed into the room by his two cronies, Captain Sidney Jenks and Captain Benedict Ainsworth. Fiona contrived a smile and gave them all a brief curtsy.

"Gentlemen. You call early. I regret Mrs. Trent is not here to receive you."

Lord Morney held out his hand. She put hers in it reluctantly. She knew his reputation with women. He kissed the hand, which he would not have dared if her godmother had been there. She withdrew it as quickly as he would allow her.

"We came to offer our congratulations, Miss Cartwright," he said, mirth in his face and his sparkling green eyes.

She stiffened. One did not congratulate the bride! "Indeed, sir?" She did not sniff whiskey on them—had they been drinking so early? She eyed them uneasily but could not avoid asking them to be seated. She hoped Wallace would come beforetime, but he was always punctual. "You speak strangely, sir."

Derek laughed, throwing back his blond head in an affected manner. Captain Jenks laughed also, his little black eyes staring at her in an insolent manner. Benedict gave a chuckle and sat down careless in the chair near her. He seemed uneasy, fingering his small brown mustache, watching her alertly.

"Oh, I meant that Frazer is to be congratulated! He pulled it off! We never thought you would marry, you are so cold to men!" He exchanged a mocking look with Sidney Jenks, and the other man winked back at him.

Mrs. Owens sat quietly in the background, doing her

56

eternal sewing. She did not like these men, she had told Fiona before.

Fiona did not quite know how to respond to that. She decided on cool composure. "Indeed, my lord. May I offer you tea?" She stood to go to the bellrope.

"No, no, tea is not my dish! We but came for a short time," said Lord Morney, in his slow drawl.

She seated herself again, in the faded rose chair. "It was good of you to come, on seeing word in the gazettes," she said.

All three men burst out laughing. Now she did eye them in worry. Were they run mad? Or had they been smoking some strange mixture that had turned their minds?

Derek laughed and laughed until his face was red. "*You* have not seen the gazettes, my dear Fiona!" he mocked, in a familiar tone.

"Indeed, I have, thank you. The notice of my engagement—"

He interrupted rudely. "Look at these, then." He pulled the folded papers from his large coat-pocket and tossed them in her lap. "I saved them for you."

She glanced at the pages. "These are the columns of the gossips. I dislike to read such," she said in a cold manner.

"Ah, you do dislike them? But you are in them, my dear! Look," and he leaned over to her in a familiar manner and pointed out the column. "Look, at the place—I know it by heart! 'What little Snow Maiden has melted before a red-leg? And so speedily, also! We can but suppose that the huge sum of money wagered spurred him on to ardent fires.' Do you see the place?"

She smoothed out the paper with trembling hands and stared at it. She read the whole item, puzzling over it. "I do not understand, my lord," she said, in a low tone. "Snow Maiden—is that supposed to be me?"

They all laughed again, Ainsworth flinging himself back in the chair and howling as his other friends did. She gazed at them in growing dismay.

"Yes, yes, of course! You are the Snow Maiden.

Frazer is the red-leg. That is what the Highland soldiers are called, of course," said Morney, suddenly petulant at having to explain all to her in detail. "And I told him, if he could melt you, and get you to agree to an engagement—after you had spurned us all!—I'd pay him a sum of ten—thousand—pounds! So he agreed! And he did it, faster than I had told him! Before the season ended!" He watched her narrowly, savoring his triumph.

She thought she went white. The blood seemed to leave her head. She could not speak. Mrs. Owens made some sound in the background, the men paid no heed, their stares on Fiona.

Her first thought was that he lied. He was malicious and cruel, he would not draw the line at lying. Then she thought of how the Frazer had been dressed last evening, in black velvet doublet along with his kilt, with fine silver and topaz studs at his wrists, with a ruffled silk shirt—all finery he had never worn before in her presence. And he had said he would buy a fine diamond for her engagement ring, he wished for her to go with him today to choose it.

Derek said angrily, "Now do you believe it? Look at that item!" He yanked a page from the pile, held it under her nose, so she had to look at it. "All London knows about the challenge! He told me he could do it, and he did it! So I paid him ten thousand pounds, in my club, this week! Before the gentlemen here, and a dozen others! What did he say to you? How did he convince you of some undying devotion to you?"

The sneer got through to her. "Why—did you—challenge him, my lord?" she said coldly, slowly. "What matter to you, whom I marry or what I do at all?"

"Oh, you have always been Miss Nose-in-the-Air," sneered Derek, more relaxed, leaning back on the sofa where Frazer often sat. "Cold as ice to us all, too good to dance twice in a row with us, Miss Virginity herself! How far has he gone with you, eh? Has he had you yet, in his carriage? Or crawled into your bed?"

"Sir, you'll not speak so to Miss Cartwright?" flamed

Mrs. Owens, standing from her place. "If ye cannot speak decent, you will leave this house!"

Derek looked as surprised as though a hen had flown up in his face and pecked him. Fiona stood, holding to her composure, though she felt like berating him, weeping, storming.

"Mrs. Owens is right," she said, chill in her voice. "You have gone beyond the bounds of gentlemanly behavior. You are no longer welcome in this house. I bid you good day, all of you."

She went to the door and pulled the bellrope. "I say," said Lord Morney, disappointed, "I just wanted to tell you about it. Hasn't Frazer said a word? Has he kept to the engagement yet? Lord, he is playing the fool with you!"

The butler appeared. Fiona said, "Show the gentlemen to their carriage."

"Yes, Miss Fiona." He stood, waiting, and the gentlemen reluctantly arose.

Jenks said, "We ain't going yet. She ain't said how she feels about the Frazer! Are ye going to spite him, Miss Cartwright? What will ye say to him?"

She did not even glance at him. "Goodbye, sirs," she said.

Captain Ainsworth laughed and stumbled for the stairs. "Well, I'll be over next week! After you drop him, you'll want company to Vauxhall and the balls! You may count on me, not that you will lack for gentlemen to come flocking! The Snow Maiden has melted, eh?" And he chuckled to himself, all down the stairs.

Lord Morney was last out, glancing at Fiona as though wishing to say more. She stood frozenly, Mrs. Owens just behind her, outraged by it all.

After they had departed, Mrs. Owens worriedly said to her charge, "Miss Fiona, those gentlemen mean mischief. I would not trust that Lord Morney an inch! Do not believe what they say, I beg of you!"

Fiona drew a deep breath and sat down to look at the gazette pages. "No, but I will certainly ask Mr. Frazer what is afoot," she replied, more calmly than she felt. She was furiously angry, yet hurt, also, and as she read, she felt the sting of the malicious accounts. She scanned them quickly.

"The Snow Maiden—the red-leg—so rapid an engagement—melted the snow, has he?—taking her about to the gardens which she has disdained in the past—"

Her mouth felt dry. Had all he said to her been pretense? There was mention of the sum he won, ten thousand pounds. Would he do that—for money? Why else? Oh, how could she have been such a fool as to believe a man would love her for herself alone!

Men were on the lookout for a wealthy heiress. Indeed, Wallace Frazer had asked her if she had to marry money. How she had blushed as she had said no softly, inviting him to proceed! How he must have laughed at her in secret!

Laughed at her? No, he seemed more somber than usual lately. Was his conscience bothering him? It should, if all the reports were true! She whipped up her anger against him, conscious of a desolation in her, a lost feeling. She had begun to lean on him, to trust him, to need him.

It had all been very hasty, as matters of engagements went. She thought back to meeting him first in March, feeling a reluctant attraction to the grave, courteous man. The first time in April when they had danced. His rescue of her from the footpads. His courtship, strange as it had been, that escorting her all about, in the name of her safety! And she had felt safe with him, so safe.

How quickly he had proposed. She had supposed it was because they were going to remove to the country as soon as the London season was over. Yet—she remembered too well how he had sat down at once at her small table to begin composing the notice to the gazettes! He probably could not collect until the notice was in the gazettes.

She was still staring at the slyly worded notices when the butler came again. "Frazer the Frazer," he intoned.

"Show him in," she said, so coldly that the butler stared.

"Yes, madam."

Frazer came up, his footsteps slow and deliberate. She said to Mrs. Owens, "I wish you would leave us. I must speak frankly to him."

Frazer came in as Mrs. Owens was departing. She swept him a curtsy, giving him a dark look as she went past him.

Fiona closed the door. "I would speak privately with you," she said curtly.

"Oh, aye. Ye have heard about the ten thousand pounds, then," he said, without surprise. He glanced with distaste at the pages of the gazettes scattered about. "Filthy things," he muttered.

"Is it true?" she asked swiftly.

His face was flushed, he could not meet her eyes. Her wrath came up in her fiercely. "Aye," he said slowly. "The fact that I sought you out deliberately. That I courted you. That Lord Morney challenged me to seek your hand, in an engagement, and would pay me the sum to do it, and have it in the gazettes."

She had not expected so sweeping a confession. She felt choked. Her head erect, her violet eyes blazing, she accused him, "And you can stand there and admit it? My God, what gallantry, what chivalry! You would have all London, nay, all England, to mock me! You let them call me——" She pointed at the pages. "Call me the Snow Maiden! You let them write—such—such filth about me—melting my snow! I was asked if I had allowed you into my bed! They will come flocking, those lords and fine captains—ready to take the leavings!"

"Nay, I did not mean——" he began angrily, his blue eyes catching fire.

She swept into his words, her hand slashing him to silence with a gesture. "Well, the engagement did not last long, you have need to fear none of that! I shall send word at once that the betrothal is broken!" she said with heavy irony. "You need not worry that the jest shall go on and encumber you! Let them have their laughs at me! I shall go back to the way I was, trusting no man—by God, I will not trust any man again!" She could scarcely believe her own forceful words. She never swore aloud.

He caught at her wrist as she flailed on. "Listen to me! Nay, I was caught as truly as you were," he said quietly. "I came a-courting you, for the sum promised, and other reasons. I was—curious about you. But I fell deeply in love with you, I swear it. I have been pondering these days what to do. You are an heiress, I have nothing to offer you but my arm and my sword. Yet, you agreed to it. You agreed to marry me—"

She kept wrenching at her arm, trying to free herself. He held her with easy strength, not hurting her, but handling her as carefully as a petulant child.

"I will not marry you now!" she stormed. She blinked back furious tears. "To make my name a mockery! To see their sneers—what have I done to you to deserve that, I do not know!"

He gazed down at her, his blue eyes seemed deep as a mountain lake. "Aye, to deserve that," he said softly. "No, not you, Fiona. I have grown to love and to respect you. I realized that your ice was to cover your vulnerability. Sure, you're as easy hurt as a child, and you were wise to avoid such rakes as them. But ye'll not break the engagement. I have made up my mind, we will go through with it."

"Through with it! Marriage to you, after this? No, indeed! I'll break the engagement. Loose me—I would write to the gazettes, and send the word—they will mock me, but I care not—I will not tie myself to you for the entire world and its wealth! To do this thing to me—it is shameful!"

"Aye," he agreed soberly. "It was shameful. But I would do it again for my reasons. However, ye will not break the engagement. I came today to take you to the jeweler's, to choose a ring for ye. We will go out."

"That we will not!" she cried out at him. "Are you mad? I would not marry you now!"

"Yes, ye will," he said, and his blue eyes began to flash. His hair was flaming about his head, where he had removed his Highland bonnet. She thought they looked like fire, those locks of hair, about his big fine head. "Ye will marry me. Ye shall not break it off! No matter what others say, they cannot part us! Let the world go hang. You love me, you agreed to the marriage, and you are too honest a woman to do so if you did not care for me. And I love you. Let the world go its own pace, and we will go ours."

"I will—not—marry you!" she flashed angrily. She wrenched again at her arm.

In an easy, swift movement, he had her down on the sofa. He was beside her, bending over her, as she stared half-frightened into his flushed face.

"Do not keep saying that," he whispered. "It makes me ver' angry. God knows that I adore you, I will not hurt you—but do not madden me, for the love of God!"

His body was pressed against hers. She felt the heat of him through the thin white muslin of her gown. Her feet dangled over the edge of the sofa, he had her back pressed against the soft cushions. His one hand held her shoulder firmly down. The other hand went softly to her rounded breasts, and she shivered as he touched her with his big fingers.

"Do not—Frazer—do not—"

He bent over her, and his mouth closed savagely on hers. For the first time in her life, she felt the touch of a masculine mouth on her lips, half-opened to protest. His mouth was warm, slightly moist, strange to her, wondrous. Heat flared through her whole body.

His hand caressed her body slowly, from her breasts to where the blue ribbon bound the dress more closely to her, high above her waist. He went slowly downward, until his hand closed about her rounded thigh. She shivered.

"Ah—you will not—" she said, in a muffled tone against his mouth. "Wallace—you will not—"

He shuddered against her, she felt the furious passion in him. His mouth closed again over hers, he kissed her with the pent-up longing of a man long-starved for this. "I want you, I want you, my own," he muttered.

She had been unwise to send Mrs. Owens away, she thought half-coherently. He would not have dared, had her abigail been present. Did Wallace Frazer not respect her? Did he think her loose, as Lord Morney and the other men did? Rage welled in her again.

She pulled back from him, though it meant sinking more deeply into the cushions. His eyes gazed down at her unseeingly, out of focus, glazed with passion.

"I shall not marry you!" she repeated furiously. "You may rape me and molest me, but I shall not give in! I shall hate you forever—"

He drew a deep breath and sat up, still holding her by the shoulder. His other hand went to the top of the sofa, he seemed to be regaining hard control of himself. He gazed down at her as she lay against the cushions, her blue black hair mussed and down about her shoulders, from his fingers through the strands.

"Ah, you are so lovely," he whispered. "I could go mad with joy, taking you. But not today, my lovely. No, we shall be married and then shall know that final joy together."

He stood up. She sat up, pushing back her hair sullenly. She kept her gaze on him suspiciously as he strode back and forth in the small room. Then he came to a stop before her. His breath still came hard, she heard the sound of it, and saw the movement of his chest under the fine shirt as his velvet doublet lay open.

"Fiona, it is true that I took the pounds. But Lord Morney did not make it a condition that I should then break the engagement and shame ye," he said more quietly. "And I would break that challenge and pay back every shilling, if necessary, for I will marry ye," and his brogue had come back stronger and more burred. "I mean to marry ye. I will not let you go."

She lowered her gaze. She pushed back her hair,

then fumbled with it to fasten it again into the neat chignon. He watched her in silence. She noted the fine, strong legs of him under the swinging red kilt. She saw his hands clenched at his sides as he waited her answer.

"How can I believe—" she began. "How can I—believe—that you—marry me—for love? I trusted you before—"

"I know. I know," he said soothingly. "And you hate yourself for the trust. But it was not misplaced, me darling. All those things that brought us together—they will have to be forgot. London will soon forget, in the wake of some fresh news. They have short memories," he added bitterly. "I will not let you back out of the marriage. My mother and sister love you already, and you will fit into our lives—as you fit into my arms. Do ye believe me?"

She was silent, head bent, hands automatically refastening the pins into her hair. Trust him? Could she trust him again? Why had he done this to her? She had thought him honorable and fine, but he had been planning and plotting all this, for ten thousand pounds!

He sat down beside her and took her restlessly busy hand in his. He brought it to his lips. "Shall we go out now and choose the ring, my love?" he asked quietly.

She could not think straight, when his big hand clasped hers, when he sat so close that his warm thigh lay against hers. He stroked her hand soothingly. She finally looked up at him.

"Oh, Wallace, if you—betray me—again—I could not endure it," she blurted out.

He stroked her head with his free hand, tenderly. "Well I know it. I shall not betray you—I have never betrayed you, my dear. I knew soon after we met that I loved you. I canna rest until ye are my bride. We will set the date soon, shall we not? That shall quiet the gossip—and set us all at ease," he added with a faint smile.

She knew she was being weak, but she finally agreed. She called Mrs. Owens, and they went out to choose the ring. It was a splendid diamond, set wih a topaz on either side, and the gold ring on her hand would still the gossips, said Mrs. Owens, in satisfaction.

Yet it could not quite still Fiona's unease with Wallace Frazer. The seeds and the poison of doubt had been implanted in her mind.

Chapter Six

The marriage day was set for the first week of July. Most of smart London would be gone to their country homes, and the notice would attract little attention until the gazettes finally made their languid way to their attention.

Fiona wore a new gown of violet satin with demure white Brussels lace about the throat and wrists. Wallace brought her a fine bouquet to carry, of white roses whose stems were surrounded by sprays of purple red heather.

They were wed in the larger downstairs parlor of her godmother's house. Mrs. Frazer was there, and Margaret, and the four Frazer men who always accompanied the Frazer. Mrs. Trent gave her goddaughter away, and Mrs. Owens wept a little in the corner. An elderly couple, friends of Mrs. Trent, were there, and other than the pastor and his wife, that was all.

A quiet wedding, and a fine one, with the Frazer in his best dress kilt, Cairngorm brooch and buttons shining.

They remained a few nights in London, then undertook the journey to Yorkshire in a leisurely way, making two days of it. Several carriages were used, Fiona had sent for hers. Mrs. Trent, Mrs. Frazer, and Margaret all accompanied them, as well as maids, serving men, footmen, the butler—and a fine procession it was through the July days north to Yorkshire.

Wallace was curious about the countryside of York and leaned from the carriage often to gaze at it, and to ask questions of Fiona. They rode alone in the carriage, the others were in following carriages. Her hand was often in his, or his arm about her slim waist, drawing her to him. Their intimacy was so new and so delightful that both were shy before it. Their eyes would meet, they would smile, then blush, and look away, to look again, longingly.

"And the land is so fertile," he said, marveling at the tall stands of wheat, the thick grasses, the plump cows in the paddocks. "Look ye at the barns, how neat, how nicely kept. And the winding stream yon. How much water is there!"

"Do you not have water in the Highlands?" asked Fiona.

"Aye, water enough, in flood, at times," he said ruefully. "But the farther north ye go, the less the fertile lands. The mountains are covered with rock that a goat can scarce climb. They run sheep there," and his face shadowed. "Aye, sheep," he muttered again. His hand tightened over hers, unconsciously.

"We have about a hundred cows," she said practically. "The man the solicitors hired seems to be good at his job, but I should like you to take over and examine all. You will know more about matters than I."

His face lightened. He seemed eager to get to work. "And how many acres is the land?"

"I do not know," she said ruefully. "I do know it is two miles to the village, which was once part of the land. Many there still work for the Cartwrights. The land became ours about a hundred years ago. I think my ancestor made his money smuggling! No, really I do. He came from Cornwall, with a rich pile of gold. He bought the land, and that is where I was born, and lived much of my life."

He was interested, and questioned her further. She did not know much beyond the one hundred years, the lines of ancestry were blurred. She knew more about her mother's people from Wales.

"I think one of them was a Spaniard from the Armada," she told him. "There is a tale in our family, mother's, that is, that a Spaniard was washed ashore on the coast of Wales and was taken in by an ancestor of mine. He fell in love with the daughter, and because he was a hard-working, good-hearted man, they allowed the marriage. That is where we get our black hair." She smiled at him mischievously. "Do you mind having a Spanish wife, my darling?"

"Better than an English," he blurted out without thought, then quickly reassured her. "No, no, I but jest, Fiona! Do not look so! It is a habit of us Scots, to down the English. We fought against them so many years. Yet—Margaret and mother find it easier to think of you as Welsh!" he added, with a sigh, and a smile at her.

She had reason to ponder his words during the following weeks. She had heard words said scornfully against the Scots people. They were supposed to be more thickheaded, more stupid, uncivilized, a race of men who could fight but do little else. She had accepted all this as gospel, until she had met Frazer and his Highlanders and his family. How long-lasting was prejudice and hate! The remnants still lingered long and caused bitterness.

Frazer took hold eagerly of the work. He had longed for such a job, but to have it like this! He and his wife were now owners of the Yorkshire estates, and he still gasped as he went over the land, realized how vast it was, how many acres were set in pasture land, how much in wheat and rye, how the streams ran through it, how the forestlands were for their own hunting and pleasure.

The house itself was so vast, he felt lost in it, as though it were a castle. It was a huge manor house, built in the seventeenth century on the site of a much earlier building. The central section was of four stories, built of local stone, crowned with turret tops like pepper pots. Out of either side stretched a two-story wing. Servants lived in one wing, and bellpulls were strung and wires set so one could ring for them and they would hear and come running.

The East Wing was the entertaining section. The ground floor held a huge banquet hall, an even larger ballroom with fine parquet floor, a conservatory where their own flowers were grown all the year. Above it were guest rooms, and Mrs. Frazer, Margaret, and Mrs. Trent had their own rooms there, with places for their maids nearby.

Wallace had had it in his mind to dismiss the local man who ran the estate as soon as he himself had the working of it in mind. However, he found Mr. Jacob Proudfoot a kindly man in his forties, a good shrewd Yorkshireman who knew his farming like the inside of his neat little house. His children were grown and had their own little farms some distance away. He ran the estate, his wife was housekeeper for Fiona, and whether she was at home or away, all went smoothly.

Wallace thought about it and decided to keep the man on. There was more than enough for one man to do. He went over the books of the estate with Mr. Proudfoot and Fiona until he could see how it went.

There were many tenants under them, the rents were collected yearly, otherwise they were merely supervised. When Wallace had time, he went about to speak to them, to learn their problems. He found them very contented under Mr. Proudfoot, who was smart, a good farmer, who put up with no nonsense but encouraged them to have their own vegetable gardens and chicken runs.

"Indeed," said Wallace to Fiona, after one such visit, "they live better than a Scotsman in his castle, your tenants! The children go to school, their clothing is fine cotton and even silk for Sunday. They look plump and contented in all."

"It was not always so," said Fiona quietly. "Under my father, there was a man who handled—that is, it did not go well. Father was more interested in gaming in London, and things—went slack."

Wallace waited eagerly to see if she would say more of her father. She spoke readily of her mother, though the woman had died when Fiona was seven. But Fiona's face shadowed, and she would change the subject as soon as her father came into discussion.

There was still much reserve about her, and between them. He had not told her of the Frazer lands above the Great Glen, and how her father had ordered them out. His mother and sister did not know Fiona's father had done this. He was reluctant to bring up the subject, he would have to tell her one day soon, but—how to do it?

For now, the summer was good, he enjoyed riding out on the land that was partly his. He enjoyed seeing his mother's smile of pleasure when they sat on the lawns and enjoyed the evening sunset. He liked seeing the content in his sister's thin young face. Most of all, he adored his new wife.

They had come together physically. He enjoyed sleeping with her, so warm and soft and yielding in his arms. They had a great bed in the master suite, and though he had a bedroom of his own off the master bedroom, he had not used it except to change his clothes. Fiona was yielding, lovable, so very sweet and shy.

Wallace had known few women. His many duties, the war, his own innate fastidiousness had kept him from cheap women. And he had put marriage thoughts from him for years. He had too much to do.

Fiona had been a complete innocent. Wallace was not much more experienced than she. But together they had managed, in their ardent desire and passion for each other. Even when he had hurt her that first night, she had folded him lovingly in her arms and whispered, "It matters not, oh, Wallace, I do love you so much!"

And now after weeks, they were more comfortable with each other. They experimented with their caresses, and he enjoyed seeing her blushes when he left a candle lit beside the bed. He liked to run his lips over her cheeks, down over her chin, over her slim throat, over the white shoulders, down to the taut, high breasts. He could linger for a long time over those tantalizing young breasts, so beautiful in his hands and against his lips.

Then he would rove lower, daringly, and she would squirm, and whisper her protest. Sometimes he needed her, other times the passion in him drove him on, to hold her gently still for his bold caressing.

In the mornings, he would leave to go to the other room, wash in the luxurious bathroom, dress and go out riding, or walk through the gardens. When Fiona came down, they had breakfast together in the sunny dining room overlooking the flower beds. When they were joined by her godmother, or his mother and sister, the talk was general. Other times, he had Jamie to play his pipes for them, stalking around the gardens, while the bagpipes wailed the old Scottish tunes.

It was perfection for a time, and Wallace distrusted that. He was wary, watching for the reactions of the callers who soon began to descend on them.

On Saturdays and Sundays, visitors came from around them, from the village, from the nearest town, even from a city about fifty miles away. And one afternoon, Wallace walked into the drawing room, to find Derek Grenville, marquess of Morney, sitting in the room.

He stopped dead still, eyeing him with the wariness of a wildcat. Derek grinned up at him, rose slowly and condescendingly to his feet, clad in high Hessian boots, and held out his languid hand. "Congratulations, Frazer," he drawled.

"Thank you, sir," he said, and shook the hand as briefly as possible. He turned to find Captain Jenks at his elbow. He was forced to greet him, to welcome him to his new home, and also Lady Morney, a tall blond woman with green eyes like those of her husband. He found out later they were distant cousins, the match had been made by an uncle, to combine the fortunes.

"So here you are, Frazer, safely in a wealthy English home," she shrilled with a laugh. She was tall and lean, she had no children, though they had been married six years.

He bowed stiffly and looked accusingly at Fiona. His wife met his gaze blandly, with little expression in her face. She had that "ice look," he knew, when she was displeased but would not show it in public. That cooled him so he could play host to them.

He looked around again, after he had offered drinks, and Fiona had poured tea for him. He lounged against the mantelpiece, not easy about this. His mother was not here, nor Margaret. Mrs. Trent was trying to make conversation with Kate Grenville, Lady Morney, and finding it uphill work. They had little in common.

Lord Morney lounged in the most comfortable chair, and talked about the land, the hunting, the richness of the land. Almost every word was a jab at Frazer, implying that he had landed well in the lap of wealth.

"So, you have the land you sought," he jeered with a grin. "You were always talking about becoming a factor in the Highlands. This is far from the Highlands, but you have land now, eh?"

"Mrs. Frazer owns the land," said Frazer stiffly. "It has been run well."

"Ah, yes, these past two years, since Fiona took charge. She knows her business, eh? One might think she was a little innocent child, but we know better, eh? She is all business, and understands that the land must be made to pay for itself. That is why you put in cows, eh, Fiona?"

Jab, jab, jab, between commonplace words, the other stings.

Captain Ainsworth put in now, "The hunting was always fine. You'll have hunts this autumn, eh, Frazer? Count on me, if you will. I love the hunt."

Frazer looked at his wife. She replied, with composure, "I doubt if we will have hunts, Captain Ainsworth. I never cared for them, and they ruin the land for the farming. I have known many crops ruined when the huntsmen ride wildly after a silly little fox."

There was a moment of pause as the gentlemen stared incredulously at these bold words. To put down hunting! A female! How dared she! Captain Jenks looked back to Frazer.

"You don't believe that, do you, eh, sergeant?" he asked deliberately. "Surely you will have hunts, great ones, eh?"

"I have not studied the situation," he said slowly. "Fiona is probably right about this. It does ruin cropland."

The gentlemen cried out against this and began eagerly to explain how splendid hunts are. Lord Morney departed with his wife in about an hour, but Jenks and Ainsworth lingered on until dusk, still arguing about hunting, talking about their experiences.

Thinking the guests had departed, Margaret Frazer and her mother came down to the drawing room. They entered, the mother in her usual gray with the red plaid about her shoulders. Margaret wore a green muslin which set off her flaming red hair, arranged simply in loose coils about her shoulders, and tied back in a net with green ribbons.

The two men jumped up. The Frazer women paused, aghast. They did not care to meet the English. Margaret finally set her chin, put her hand under her mother's arm, and led her inside. Fiona had stood to greet them. The Frazer held a chair for his mother.

Both the men were ignoring the mother, staring fascinated at the tall, beautiful Highland girl. Her deep blue eyes were shadowed, she stood near her mother defiantly, her shawl drawn about her shoulders.

"Por Deus, a goddess," murmured Ainsworth, in a daze, his face glowing.

Jenks laughed. "A beautiful lady, indeed! Come on, now, you sly dog, Frazer! Tell us who these ladies are!"

Frazer wanted to kick them. But he must someday introduce his mother and sister to society, he supposed. They did not wish it, but remaining with him and Fiona as they did, they could not avoid it forever.

"Mother," he said quietly, coming to stand at her shoulder and putting his big hand gently on the frail arm. "Permit me to introduce to you two British officers under whom I served. Mrs. Ian Frazer. Captain Jenks, Captain Ainsworth."

The men bowed deeply to her, she nodded slowly but said nothing beyond, "How do you do?" Then they turned eagerly to the girl of twenty nearby. Captain Jenks' eyes roved greedily over her. Ainsworth kept staring at her face, her eyes.

"My sister, Miss Margaret Frazer. Margaret, permit me to introduce Captain Jenks, Captain Ainsworth."

She curtsyed, ignoring their hands, half held out to her. "How do you do, sirs?" she said coldly and swept to seat herself beside Fiona on the large sofa.

She answered in monosyllables, appearing stupid and dumb, and finally Jenks in boredom departed. But Ainsworth lingered, so long that dusk came.

Fiona was finally forced by courtesy to ask him to remain for supper. He seemed in a daze. "Oh, yes, if you will!" he replied eagerly. "If you don't mind—Morney won't, you know. Has a dozen guests, won't miss me."

Supper was served in the dining room overlooking the flowers. Fiona raised her eyebrows and gave Wallace a significant look as Benedict Ainsworth seemed unable to eat, he just stared at Margaret. Finally she took pity on him, thought Frazer, and began to talk to him, for Margaret would not.

"You served in the Peninsula?" she asked.

"Oh, yes, ma'am. Frazer, here, knows it. Fought together. I told you," he said, suddenly wakening from his musing. He looked toward Fiona, his hostess. "I told you that," he said, puzzled.

"I was wondering in what subjects you would be interested," she said bluntly, though with a smile. "Do you care for flowers? Miss Frazer has been assisting me in planning the new flower beds. We thought to put a sundial in the midst of the herb garden."

"How splendid," murmured Ainsworth, gazing back at Margaret.

"Sundials count only the sunny hours," said Margaret unexpectedly. "They ignore the dark and the rain. Only King Sun counts for them, they turn up their stone faces to his light. And the flowers round about are the same, lifting their faces to the warmth of life."

Her voice was so melodious, with the strong burr accenting its charm, that Ainsworth stared at her, so bemused he forgot to glance at the plate the footman offered. He had to be nudged again as the man stood patiently beside him. He finally took some slices of roast beef, added some mustard.

"Ah—you enjoy flowers, Miss Frazer?" he asked.

"Very much. We have but a few in the Highlands. We have our heather, little bells in the wind on the bleak hills. Golden gorse in the summer, purple heather in the autumn, then the winter makes all mist and white snow. Few roses do we have, nor the rare flowers like orchids and lilacs."

"We are experimenting with species in the conservatory," explained Fiona, as Frazer seemed lost in his own dark thoughts. Mrs. Frazer was content to listen, Mrs. Trent was weary from the long hours of entertaining guests. "Some friends of my godmother have kindly given us some starts and seeds and shoots."

"I should like so much to see them," breathed Ainsworth.

They removed presently to the drawing room. Fiona wondered how long Ainsworth would remain, but presently he recollected his manners and stood to make his graceful farewells.

He looked directly at Margaret Frazer as he asked, "You will be coming to the county ball this next Saturday? It is a grand occasion, half the county will come. A crush, but amusing," he added, in languid imitation of Lord Morney.

When Margaret did not reply, Ainsworth looked to the Frazer.

"You will be sure to come?" he cried anxiously. "You have not yet come to any of the county affairs."

"If the ladies wish to come, I shall escort them," he replied.

"Ah, splendid!" he exclaimed, radiant again. "I shall see you there, Miss Frazer!"

"Nay," she said. "I do not come to such."

His face fell, he made his departure very reluctantly. When he appeared again on Monday afternoon for tea, he made his aims very clear. He had come to see Miss Margaret Frazer. But Margaret was cool to him and scarcely spoke at all.

Fiona spoke to her later, saying, "He is not a bad sort, Margaret. It is the company he keeps, I cannot like Lord Morney."

Margaret shrugged. "I do not trust the English," she said bluntly. "It is graved in me at my very heart. I cannot trust them. I have no wish to lead the poor lad on."

Fiona swallowed over an exclamation. "But what about Mrs. Trent—and me?" she finally asked.

"But you are not all English, you are Welsh," said Margaret firmly.

Fiona was silent, pondering. Finally she asked, "Do you not like the young man at all? Is he so disagreeable to you?"

"Oh, weel, he is not so bad," said Margaret surprisingly. "I could like the mon, be he a Scots. But he be English, and I do not trust him an inch. Better not to see aught of him."

And she shrugged in her eloquent way.

Benedict Ainsworth kept coming persistently, but Margaret was cool to him always. He would not get past her guard, she seemed to say. For Captain Jenks and Lord Morney, she had no words at all. They could stare, if she did appear for tea, which was rare. But she did not speak more than a "Yes," or "No, sir," to them, and they gave her up as some rustic incapable of more.

To Ainsworth she did speak at times, in her poetic manner, and he grew more fascinated with her than ever. However, Fiona thought he wasted his time. Margaret was even more stubborn than her brother, and that was much to say.

Chapter Seven

Fiona had never been so happy. She had been an only child, with a hated father. Her mother's memory lay deep in violet mists of time, Fiona had been so young at her death. Mrs. Trent had been closest to her in emotions, her godmother had always been loving, concerned, a refuge to the young girl.

But now she had a real family. Wallace was passionately in love with her, as she with him. They did not understand each other completely as yet, but Fiona thought with contentment that they had all their lives in which to come to know each other.

Mrs. Frazer was a dear. She seemed so quiet, so frail, but her spirit was sturdy, her morals upright and stern. Withall, she was a concerned mother. If all went well with Wallace and with Margaret, she was contented. She never demanded anything, she seemed surprised when anyone was concerned about her. "Aye, I am weel, I thank ye," she would reply. "I need naught."

Fiona had to make sure that her rooms and Margaret's would be kept well aired, dusted, in order, for they would never complain. She consulted with Mrs. Proudfoot, and between them they made quick check on the maids to make sure all went well.

Margaret was like one of those treasure boxes. The further one went, the more was uncovered, of a jewel of a mind and soul. She had suffered much, thought Fiona, when Margaret puzzled her with her reserve on some topics. She seemed much older than Fiona, rather than her same age, twenty. She had been very quiet at first, but now in the comfort of the Yorkshire manor house, she began to unfold her tight reserve.

Margaret could speak so beautifully, it was a keen pleasure to hear her. She was spirited beneath her quiet manner. She could observe with keen blue eyes, and later she would speak and show such perception that Fiona wondered at her. She had not known society, yet she understood human nature.

At first, Margaret would not go with them to any event. She remained at home with her mother. Fiona worried about her.

"She is so young to remain always at home," she said to Wallace. "Can you not persuade her to come to squire's with us? They are a pleasant family."

He looked concerned, yet reserved. "Margaret must make up her own mind," he said, at last. "If she will not, I shall not press her. She has not been much in society, she knows only the Scottish dancing, she has not much light conversation, nor does she play cards."

Fiona made a little face. "My dear Frazer! You make us sound so frivolous!" she protested, and looked up at him hopefully from her dressing table bench.

He bent and kissed her forehead but did not attempt to refute what she said.

Fiona sighed, and resolved to try again to get the girl to come out with them. She would come riding sometimes, she rode sidesaddle gracefully, as Fiona did. And the Cartwright stables were splendid, with more than half a dozen good riding horses, and a dozen carriage horses.

Wallace had become fond of a splendid hunter called Thunder. He was big and sturdy, and he suited Wallace's long legs and heavier weight. They rode out almost every day except in the worst weather of thunder and lightning. Fiona rode one of the gentler mares, and Margaret would ride anything. She had good control of her mount.

They rode about the estate, and Wallace would study the land, and where the needs were most. Then he would go back and consult with Mr. Proudfoot. They agreed cordially, and Fiona was relieved for that. If it came to decisions, she must side with her husband, but they did not usually bother her after the first weeks. They saw she wished them to take hold of the affairs of the land, she would manage the household.

August was a rather quiet month. Everyone was busy about the land, and some had gone away on holiday. Fiona and Wallace attended a dinner at the squire's and enjoyed it.

Squire and Mrs. Arthur Reid, with a boisterous family of five half-grown children, were fair bursting out of their large red-brick home in the village. He had cast a longing eye on Cartwright's manor house, he said with a laugh.

"Sure, that might be large enough for our family!" he said proudly. "Mrs. Reid says we must add on to the house if we do not buy or build something larger."

Indeed, with the company they enjoyed, Fiona thought they must. Several relatives were living with them for the summer and autumn, their children ran wild in the gardens, he kept more horses than his stables could hold. It seemed he had come into some money about two years ago, and in addition to the property and farms he owned here in Yorkshire, there was a spinning mill farther north, and an income from some lands in Kent.

They had a pleasant evening with the Reids. And Fiona had enjoyed talking with the doctor and his wife, Dr. and Mrs. Francis Hopkins. A splendid couple, who had known military service. She was blunt, red-faced, and tanned by the wind, a practical down-to-earth woman who suited her sailor-husband splendidly. He had retired early, after the wars, and taken up a practice in town.

"I think Margaret would have enjoyed them," said Fiona, in the carriage as they went home. "And she would have charmed them, with her intelligence and the beauty of her speech and manner."

"Do not push the girl," advised Wallace thoughtfully. "She has known grief, the man she was engaged to died in the wars. Let her recover as she wishes, Fiona. I think she is more lively of air than she was last year this time."

"Oh—I did not know. I am sorry."

It gave her a pang that Margaret had never even confided this to her. She had told Margaret much, but the girl did not say anything in confidence in return. Yet she listened well and sympathetically.

"Wallace, we must give a ball in return," said Fiona, in a continuation of her thoughts. "We have been entertained much, as newlyweds in the county. Everyone has been very gracious. Do you think—about mid-September, when all return to their homes? We could open the ballroom and have it waxed and shining. And I ought to order new curtains for the room, they are shabby, I noticed the other day."

"A ball," he mused, half frowning. She could just make out the expression on his face in the dim lights as they drew into their own graveled drive, and the torches on the front of the house flared. "Ah—Fiona— do ye think that best?"

She was puzzled by his speech. "Best, Wallace? But we must return hospitality, for we live here, and are part of the county life. Think of how many have entertained us."

"Ah—yes, that is so." He lapsed into silence but seemed troubled.

She wondered what was the matter now. She had to probe delicately, sometimes it was his pride, sometimes some aspect she had not considered.

In their bedroom, after she had dismissed her maid and as she was brushing out her long blue black hair, she tried gently to discover what troubled him.

"About the ball, Wallace. Do you not think we should have one? What other way to return their hospitality?"

He sat down in a chair to tug at his boots, and sigh a little. "Ah, weel, it is so," he said. "We must have them here. I was just thinking, it goes against the grain to invite Lord Morney and his shrew-wife. And that Captain Jenks, as my guest! Oh, aye, I would not like it fine," he said ruefully.

She grimaced also. "We cannot leave them out, they are gentry," she said quietly. "I do not trust them, either, nor do I find them comfortable. Yet we must not snub them, it is not done. I know—we shall ask so many people that they will not bother us much! We shall ask half a hundred, or more, Wallace," and she laughed a little. "They will be lost in the crowd!"

Wallace was silent then, and in the weeks to follow, concerning the subject of the ball. Fiona was excited about entertaining, and he was reluctant to dim her pleasure. However, he thought she was not yet aware of his position—a Scotsman was not welcome by everybody in an English community.

However, he quietly encouraged her to continue with her plans, since they gave her joy. She had new gowns made for herself and his sister Margaret. Mrs. Frazer had declined gently, and Fiona did not press her. The lady was frail of health.

The evening in September was beautiful, a clear sky for a change, with stars sparkling by the time the ball was well under way. The drawing rooms were crowded with the guests in their finery. Lord Morney had come, and Lady Morney, splendid in yellow silk. Captain Jenks followed them about. Captain Benedict Ainsworth took one look at Margaret, in her pale blue chiffon gown with ribbons of her tartan plaid, and began to follow her about as though in a trance. She was lovely tonight, thought her brother proudly, with her red hair dressed high, a black velvet ribbon about her throat, with a locket threaded on it. And her full blue skirts dipped and swayed in the dances, the folk dances she knew. She refused quietly to be drawn into waltzing.

And his wife—the Frazer gazed across the room at his wife. He swelled with pride, she was so beautiful, so splendid a wife, and all his. Her heart belonged to him, he knew that.

How beautiful she was. Her gown was deeper blue than Margaret's, but in the same style, with full chiffon skirts of many layers. Her ribbons were of purple, and another bound her throat. She could have worn diamonds, but instead she had chosen to match Margaret, with a purple velvet ribbon about her slim white throat, and a locket threaded on it. She wore his rings on her hands, and a golden bracelet, with little gold eardrops, and that was all her jewelry tonight.

Music was played constantly by a trio made up of a local piano teacher, violinist, and a flutist. Supper would be served on long trestle tables set up in the wide halls. For now, huge bowls of punch quenched their thirst, and merriment echoed all through the rooms.

Some of the guests were all compliments. Squire and Mrs. Reid had brought their older two sons, who danced without ceasing with one girl and another. Fine young lads, thought Wallace. One day—one day, he might have such a young son. A Frazer, to follow him! Only what heritage of Scotland would he have? the bitter reminder came on the heels of the other thought. He would inherit the Cartwright lands—not the wild Highland glen lands.

Not a Scotsman was permitted to own lands in the Highlands now around the Great Glen. What would happen to those lands? Fiona did not even yet know about those lands. Some day he would have to tell her, but the longer the time went on, the more reluctant he was to bring up the subject.

It lay between them like a sheathed sword, ready to be drawn, to cut—and hurt—

Ainsworth led out Margaret as another set formed. She looked demure, yet there was a deep pink flush in her cheeks. Her brother watched her sharply. He did not care much for Captain Ainsworth. He was English, and a puppy of Jenks and Lord Morney. Until and unless he cut those ties, Frazer would not permit his suit. And Margaret seemed to show no signs of wishing he would pay court to her.

He went into the hallway and out the front door to get a breath of air. The room was close where they danced. He wondered if a storm were brewing.

He strolled around the veranda, past the French windows opened to the night air. He heard the music, heard the laughter, the chatter. Near the end, he paused to draw a deep breath.

Then he heard the voices, his wife and that of Lady Morney. Kate Grenville had a sharp, spiteful voice that was unmistakable.

"It is a great pity, Fiona," said Kate, in a condescending way, "that you had no one to turn to for advice. And to marry him so suddenly—"

"My godmother approves of him," said Fiona steadily. "I wish you would not speak of the matter, my lady—"

Wallace stiffened, he could not have turned away and left for the world. He strained to hear what they said. Murmur—murmur—then Kate's clear voice rose.

"You do not understand, child! The Scots will never be accepted in our society! They are most of them primitive, of a crude culture. Incapable of learning anything, not even the most stupid of tasks!" Her voice was cutting, derisive.

"I will not listen to you! It is a very prejudiced view you have, Lady Morney. I wonder at you! The Highlanders served with distinction under your husband's command—"

"Oh, Morney can get action from a stone!" And Kate laughed lightly. "And fighting—any fool can fight if given a weapon and prodded in his rear! I'm talking about intelligence, culture, the good breeding that one should value when taking a husband! Think of one's children! You could have done much better than to marry a thick-skulled Scots! Even one as handsome as the Frazer!"

"I'll listen no more. You go beyond the bounds—" The voices drifted away, as though Fiona had turned and left and Lady Morney had followed her.

Wallace stood there, seething with fury. His fists clenched, he stared grimly at the night sky. Fiona had defended him, but weakly. Did she think this also?

He could not leave the guests for long. He returned to the drawing room and found his wife much flushed of cheek, glancing about for him. He went to her side at her appealing look.

"Wallace, have you asked Jamie to pipe for us? And Ossian to give us some poems?"

He wished he had not planned this. But his men had been eager to participate, to honor him in this first big dinner at his home. In Scotland, they would have been in a guard of honor.

He could not disappoint them, no matter how he felt now. He bent his head.

"Jamie is ready, he stands in the hall. He will pipe them into the dinner, and later pipe them a farewell," he said quietly.

"Ah, good. I want them to hear how they sound," she told him eagerly, her fingers clinging to his velvet sleeve. "There is so much misunderstanding through ignorance, Wallace!" Her blue eyes pleaded with him.

He softened and nodded again. "Aye, Fiona. That there is. Are ye ready for calling them to the feast?"

"Yes. I'll do that." She smiled as Jamie stood in the doorway, and beckoned him in. The immensely tall red-haired Highlander was in his best kilt and had his bagpipes in his hands. He strode in with a swirl of his kilt. The English country gentry moved back to give him room, eyeing him with wide-eyed amazement, and some amusement, Wallace saw.

"Wallace?" Fiona prompted him softly, her eyes shining.

Margaret was standing near the end of the room. She watched also, her face looking older, rather grim.

The Frazer stepped forward to speak. He glanced about, and something in his look made them fall silent. "Ye are welcome to our home," he said formally. "Were we in the Highlands, I would have welcomed you with our customs. I wish still to give ye a taste of how a Highland chief welcomes his guests. My piper, Jamie Frazer, who has gone with me into battle many a time, will pipe ye in to dinner. The tunes will be those of the old times."

He stood back, nodded to Jamie. The man bowed deeply to his chief, to the guests, then began to play. Women winced, men laughed out at the wild wailing sounds of the pipes, but Jamie turned smartly and strode out to the halls, where the huge dinner was laid in buffet style for them.

"Gad, what an incredible sound. Worse than ever indoors," said Lord Morney, loudly enough to be overheard, as he offered his arm to the squire's wife.

"I would imagine, in battle, it was a welcome sound," she said bravely. Wallace felt a little more kindly to her as she smiled and bent her graying head to him in passing.

The pipes echoed through the halls, all through the dinner. People laughed and talked, calling to each other over the music, as though drowning it out. Wallace endured it, hoping that Jamie would not be horribly insulted. He could brood for weeks over such a slight.

The dinner was finally over, and they returned to the dancing. Wallace hoped the Highlanders would forget about the poetry and more piping. He could not endure for them any more of the rude remarks.

But Ossian did not forget. He hung about, watching the chief eagerly. He wore his finest kilt, also, and he would not forget it if he were ignored.

There came a pause in the music. Fiona stood forward and said into the silence, "The Frazer's own poet, Ossian Frazer, has a poem he will recite for you in the

Gaelic, and the Frazer will translate for us. It is all about Scotland, and the beauty of its hills and glens and lochs." She smiled so beautifully that some of the guests clapped gallantly, though some snickered and whispered behind their hands.

The Frazer and Ossian stepped forward. Wallace was so upset he could scarce keep his mind on the words. They were intoned solemnly, a long, sad poem about the Highlands and the loss of the lands. To the English, it must have been both humorous, and a reminder of the many battles between the English and Scots. Some of the men who had fought had set faces. The women looked confused. Lady Morney got a fit of the giggles and could not seem to control herself.

Finally it was over, Ossian bowed, and some clapped politely. Others were laughing. Fiona gave them a bewildered look, she did not understand at all. Margaret was white with rage, and when Captain Ainsworth came up to ask her to form a set with him, she gave him a curt, "No, thank you."

It was past midnight. The pastor and his wife began to murmur their excuses; Squire Reid said loudly, "Dear me, is that the time? We must be off. Splendid time, splendid!"

They took their departure, with Jamie on his pipes standing near the front door, playing his heart out for his chief. Wallace felt the breaking of his own heart. His piper had played, his poet had spoken—and they had laughed!

The guests departed at last, the carriages rolled away, and the house grew still. Wallace returned slowly to the drawing room. Margaret was standing near the mantel gazing down into the dying fire. Fiona was not there, he could hear her speaking to someone in the hallway.

Margaret looked up at her brother, and her blue eyes had steel in them. "Those English!" she spat. "Laughing! They have no respect for us, for our history. God, they could laugh out of the other sides of their mouths, should we turn on them once more! Even the women would fight, and the bairns! Such people—such scum—"

"We lost all our battles, the ones that counted, Margaret," said the Frazer, with such bitterness that his sister was quieted. "It is the scorn of the victor over the vanquished. No wonder they laugh. We can vaunt our glories, but they know the glories are departed, the glens empty, our people in rags."

They were speaking in the Gaelic. Fiona entered, to hear them talking earnestly, and came up to them shyly. She slipped her hand in Wallace's arm.

"Did it not go well?" she asked shyly, begging for his approval. He gazed down into the violet eyes and could not speak his heart.

"You did beautifully, I was so proud of you," he said gently.

She smiled then and laid her head briefly against his shoulder.

"Aye, you did well, Fiona. Pardon me, while I retire. I will assist you tomorrow, in the letters," said Margaret, and left the room abruptly.

"Will you come up now?" asked Fiona as he continued to stare into the fire.

He could not go into her bed, thinking those harsh, bitter thoughts of the English. He remembered all too well that her own father had driven out his people from their lands.

"Not now. But do you go to sleep, my dearest," he said, and pressed her hand before turning her gently to the door. She looked very puzzled, and a little hurt, but he could not endure going to her tonight.

Fiona too was English.

He waited until the house was darkened, and the yawning footmen had smothered all the flames of the candles and the fireplaces. Then he found his great plaid, wrapped himself in it, and walked out into the night.

He knew his way now fairly well. He walked and walked, out into the hills, and across the moors. The night was silent but for the little scurryings of night creatures, the plaintive hoots of an owl, a few night cries of birds. He wanted the peace to soak into him, nature had not yet failed him.

The fury in his heart raged so high, the hopelessness and gall of it burned his stomach. He could do nothing, nothing for all that laughter and scorn. His people had lost the wars, they were a people enslaved and to be pitied. He walked the moors all the night and did not return until dawn. And still he had found no peace.

Chapter Eight

September came and went, with the golden haze of autumn shining on the blue hills, and across the green and yellow lands. The harvest was gathered in, the cows still grazed but would soon be gathered into the cow barns each night.

Wallace had smothered his rage, but still it burned beneath the surface of his smiling appearance. He knew Fiona felt something lacking in their relationship, he did not come often to her bed. However, it was something he felt so deeply he could not discuss it with her.

One day, he must tell her the full story, of his people and his glen, and how her father had run them out and put in the sheep "which will pay more than those shiftless Highlanders," as many said in England.

He felt truly torn. He adored Fiona—yet, she was English. Not only was she English, but her father had done something so terrible to his people that it was past forgiving. And she had benefited! Her wealth came in large part from their holdings in his land, his Scotland.

His sister Margaret had retreated into herself, to Fiona's puzzlement and concern. She now refused to go out with them, not even to squire's, and she had liked that family. She remained at home and made her mother's health her excuse.

Frazer could not blame her, he hated to go out, to hear the snickers about the piper and the poems, to feel that beneath their courtesy they laughed at him.

How horrible to be laughed at! What poor things they were to endure it, he thought bitterly. But what else could he do? Rather would he be on his beloved hills, wrapped in his worn plaid, striding on his own lands, though in poverty, than here. Here in lush and bountiful Yorkshire, where there seemed to be no poverty at all, in the midst of cultured society, he found no peace.

In October, he was invited to take part in a hunt on the neighboring land of Lord Morney. He was very reluctant to attend. Few ladies hunted, Fiona did not wish to go. Frazer was all set to refuse, when he learned that such a refusal was a deadly slight. The squire told him diffidently, "It is the grand fall hunt, you see, Mr. Frazer. All attend, whether they can ride well or not. It is the going that is important, you see? After the hunt, all go to late breakfast at Lord Morney's and are received in the great hall. He is the lord of this part of the county, and as such must be honored."

The squire had come over especially to see him, to ask for aid for the local school, and in finding a schoolmaster who would replace the present one. The man was aged, and failing in health.

They walked in the gardens. Frazer stared unseeingly at the fine stone sundial his sister had helped to design. "I count only the sunny hours," it read, and about it were planted gay autumn flowers, salvia so red and fine, tall red and orange gladioli, yellow chrysanthemums.

"I canna like the man," Frazer finally said, with a sigh, bluntly.

The squire shrugged and glanced about casually to make sure no one was near. "Nor do I," he murmured, and wiped his forehead. "But none dare say that about, you see. He has much power, he will go to the House of Lords this winter, and make bills. How much power them lords do have, to be sure! If he takes a spite against you, he can do much."

"So that is the way of it. We must smile and smirk at his malice and that of his malicious wife—"

"Aye, Mr. Frazer. That is the way of it," said the squire simply. "Without his word, I could not have bought my house here. His father had taken a disliking to me, and if the present Lord Morney had not put in a good word, I should not have been allowed my place here. Now, I am squire and listened to, and I can protect some of my people."

The Frazer stared down at the plump, earnest man. "Aye, you mean it is like in the Highlands, among the clans. A clan chief must protect his people—"

"It is like that, yes. Only I must answer to those above me, and bow and scrape to them if I wish to keep my position. So you see, it behooves me and my good wife to keep all smooth here so our villagers and the tenants do not feel the wrath which he might visit on their heads. Do you see the way of it?"

"Aye, I see the way, all rect," said the Frazer bitterly. "It is always the way. Those in power must be coddled and cosseted so that others do not suffer. That is why our people gathered in clans. The chief of the clan takes it on himself to protect his people in all. And they in turn promise to come to his aid, and to fight for him, should he need. But the English would destroy us, and our clans, for they do not wish us to have such protection."

"So it is always. The weak must suffer if the strong will not aid them. All of this is a long way about, Mr. Frazer, to saying for the sake of the villagers and your tenants, it would be best for you to attend Lord Morney's hunt, and be gracious to him."

He laughed a little, and Frazer laughed with him, though rather bitterly. He did understand more, however. In every society were the weak and strong. If the strong were of cruel nature, the weak would suffer, unless someone else strong stood up for them. So it always was.

Wallace reluctantly dressed for the hunt, in a fine kilt he used for battles. He fastened his plaid over it all, with the Cairngorm brooch at his shoulder, and touched it caressingly. "I will keep faith," he muttered as he touched the silver and the golden stone that his father had left to him.

"Ah, you look fine, Wallace," said Fiona as he came down early for a quick cup of tea before he departed. She was seated in the morning room, in a violet gown with a purple ribbon threaded through her blue black hair. "You will ride Thunder?"

"Aye, ye are right. He is the best horse in the stables hereabouts," he said more lightly. "What a spendid stallion. I have it in mind to breed him with the mare Daylight. They would make a fine foal."

"I expect they would," she smiled up at him, and he bent and kissed her forehead. "Take care now, the hedges are very high on Lord Morney's land, father used to say." And an anxious frown came to her face.

"I'll take care. I looked over the land last week, with the squire, so as to be prepared." But his face was grim as he went out. He was not accustomed to hunting. He had been warned by the squire that the pace was swift, the methods crude, of lifting the horses over hedge and stream. One place had looked very bad, with a stone fence too close to the hedge, and the hedge not trimmed back.

It was just past daylight when he arrived on horseback at the stables of Lord Morney. Quite a large pack of hounds were there, and about twenty-five men from the county. The squire greeted him cordially, relief on his broad red face.

"Ah, a fine day, Mr. Frazer."

"A fine day, sir. Good day to ye, Lord Morney," said Frazer soberly as his host cantered up to him on a fine gray stallion.

The man looked critically at his horse. "Fine horse there. Would you sell him to me?"

"No, I thank you, Lord Morney. He is the one horse who can carry my weight and height."

The others were laughing and joking, most wore special outfits with hard hats, and he felt out of place with his kilt and bonnet. The morning was drizzling, just right for the hunt, said the squire.

They set out at the clear pealing of the horn. The hounds tore along eagerly, ahead of them, and the hunters spread out along the road, then into the fields. They tore over fields of wheat, not yet cut, and Frazer silently deplored the waste. Fiona was right, the hunts were disastrous to the land. All to get a couple of little foxes!

His hunter was eager to go, and Frazer took pleasure in riding along with the squire, holding back to let the others go ahead. They could talk a bit and exchange smiles at the pleasure of the morning.

A wind rose, blowing rain in his face, he did not mind. Perhaps this would not be bad. The eager hunters raced in the front, tearing across fields, into the small forests, out again, to the cries of the hounds as they sighted a fox.

About mid-morning, as Frazer rode along, having lost sight of the others, he thought about turning back. Surely he had done his social duty, he had shown up, been courteous.

In the mist, he sighted two horses and stiffened as he saw the tall gray of Lord Morney, and the smaller black of Captain Jenks. "Halloo, there," cried Lord Morney cheerfully. "Where did you get to, Frazer? We have killed a couple of foxes already." His eyes glittered, his face shone with sweat, Frazer noted as they came closer.

"Well, congratulations," said Frazer evenly. "I must have lost sight of the pack." He did not say it had been deliberate.

Jenks laughed. "Fine horse you got there, wouldn't mind buying him, eh? But no good at hunting, eh? Can't take a hedge or high fence?"

"He does well enough," said Frazer cautiously.

"Let's see how he goes," suggested Morney. "Come along, the pack is over the hill that way!" He pointed with his short whip across a steep hill, over hedges and into trees. Frazer remembered the stone wall in that direction and was cautious.

"You go ahead, gentlemen," he said, with a tinge of irony. "I would not want to hold you up in my slow pace."

"Nonsense, nonsense, man!" said Lord Morney too heartily. A gleam of a look went between him and Jenks. "Come along, take the hedge there, and we'll follow!"

They crowded about him, one on either side. Thunder snorted, rearing up. Frazer soothed him and backed away from the encounter.

"My stallion is nervous, my lord, do go on," he urged.

He might have known they would not accept that. They laughed, and crowded him again, from behind this time.

"Take the hedge, take the hedge!" cried Jenks. "Say, here comes the pack!" They heard the hounds, the cries of the hunters, another fox must have been sighted.

Frazer hoped to escape when their attention was distracted. He backed away again, soothing the nervous beast. The hunt swept into view, some horses leaped the hedge, one went down, and staggered up again, his rider cursing him and beating him on the thigh.

Frazer's attention was caught by the scene, his mouth had tightened. He hated cruelty to horses. While he was watching the horseman getting up, Jenks hit the crop of Thunder mightily with his whip. "Go on, then, you'll lose them!" he cried.

Caught unaware, the gallant horse tried to respond. He started up at a mad gallop, making for the hedge. Frazer's weight had shifted as he talked to the two other men. He could not recover quite in time. He tried to ease himself in the saddle, to aid the horse over the hedge. The horse faltered in his stride, then he took the hedge.

He was over, but on the other side was a tangle of brush. Frazer went over his head, to land with a thump in the next hedge. His head was dizzy, his bonnet had flown off. He managed to sit up, heard the laughter as Jenks and Lord Morney took the hedge perfectly, and reined up beside him.

"Can't stay the course, eh?" jeered Lord Morney, a gleam in his green eyes. "Get up, Frazer! You're not hurt, man! Dust yourself off and get up again!"

It was just like that harassing in the army on the Peninsula. Tease, taunt, force a man to move too fast, and jeer him when he was overthrown. Frazer tightened his lips, got up, and deliberately dusted himself off as the men laughed. Then he looked about for his horse. His heart seemed to falter, then he began to run. The black beast was down, threshing about.

The men on horseback followed him as he went to Thunder, to bend down and examine him. He was sickened at the sight.

Both the forelegs were broken, twisted under him. The poor animal gazed at him with such agony, he felt thrust through.

Wallace ran his hands softly over the legs. They were broken clean through. The beast was in agony, and with these injuries and the one at his throat, he was finished. The only thing to do was put him out of his misery.

The squire rode up out of the mist. "My boy! What happened! Did the horse balk?"

Frazer looked up at him, at the laughing, jeering

looks of Jenks and Morney. "No, sir," he said, with deadly rage. "These two men forced him into a jump before he was ready. As you can see, they have injured him unto death."

The squire looked shocked, his breath caught. Lord Morney lost his grin. "Are you accusing me of deliberately causing the fall?" he demanded.

Frazer looked at him. "Aye, my lord, deliberately. You and Jenks here, with his ready whip. Did you hope to break my horse's neck—or merely mine?"

The squire swung off his horse and went to lay a hand on Frazer's arm. "Man, man," he urged in a low tone. "Do not belabor it. The gents don't take kindly—watch your tongue!"

Frazer glanced back at the horse. "I'll have to shoot him," he said wearily. He drew out his pistol, loaded it, and fired into the horse's head. The beast lay back with a sigh, dead.

The sound of the gunshot brought others of the hunt. They crowded around, exclaimed, were sympathetic about the loss of the horse. Lord Morney watched with cold impatience.

"About your accusations, Frazer," he said haughtily. The men fell silent. "Do you wish to press charges? Adams, here, is sheriff, do you charge me formally before him? Or was it an accident? That you could not control your horse?"

Frazer was in a deadly rage, but he could do nothing. The squire anxiously hovered at his side. He choked down his wrath.

"Ye know what ye did, and so do I," he said finally. "It will not be forgotten. I bid you good day," and off he walked, on foot.

He heard Jenks' whining laughter behind him. He did not turn back. He heard the muttering, then the horses and the men were lost in the mist as he strode through the bracken and the wheat fields, back toward the road.

He walked about five miles, and his rage grew as he

walked. That poor beast! Dead, for a joke of the two men. No, more than a joke. They had hoped to see Wallace thrown, and had had their pleasure from that. More, they had ruined his fine horse, Thunder. His hopes for the animal were gone, as so many hopes had gone.

He arrived home about one o'clock in the afternoon, having paused many a time to sit on a stile or rest by the roadside, trying to calm his cold rage. He did not notice or mind the fine rain that wet him through.

He walked in as Fiona, Margaret, and his mother were just going to the smaller dining room for luncheon. Fiona paused to see him come in. "Wallace, did you have a fine hunt?— Oh, my dear!" she exclaimed as he came closer, and she saw the state he was in. She looked over him, the grime on his plaid, the mud of his boots, the rain that dripped from his bonnet and cloak. "Wallace—what happened?"

"I ha' lost Thunder. I had to shoot him, he was so bad injured," he said briefly. "Do not stop me—I'll go up and change from this wet stuff." And he went past her, and up the stairs, paying no heed to her gasp of shock.

He sat there, in his dressing gown, his head in his hands. He was weary of it all, he was sick with the happenings of the morning. They laughed at him, jeered at him—and hated him. That had been no accident that morning, they had planned it between the two of them, hoping at least to make him take a tumble. He wished himself a thousand miles away, at least as far as his Highlands. Peace again, in his hills.

He clenched his fists with the rage that swept through him again and again. He hated them, he hated them! But they had power. Morney was the power in the county, whatever he would say would be listened to. A Scotsman was distrusted and had lost many of his rights in court. He did not have a chance that way. If only he might take his dirk and put it to the man's throat!

Fiona came up presently and sat beside him. She put her hand on his one clenched fist.

"Captain Ainsworth kindly came, about two hours ago," she said quietly. "He told us something of what happened. My dear, I am so sorry."

"Aye? What story did you hear? That it was an accident?" said Wallace harshly. "Jenks and Morney planned it between them. They hoped to break my neck, instead of the horse's legs! Aye, they would like to see me dead!"

She gasped, and her fingers clenched over his. "Wallace—do you think? —but they served with you—you fought together—"

He heard the shock in her tone. "Not *with* me," he said, "*over* me. They were my officers, and devils the lot of them! Jeering and taunting, hoping to make me lose my temper to give them a chance to order the lash to me! I made my tongue keep still a hundred times, a thousand times, and my men also. You do not know what it was like, Fiona."

She sat in silence, her head bent. He saw the violet tint of her dress next to his muddy kilt, flung on the chair. He was hurting her, but the hate in him could not be suppressed much longer. He could not endure to be "neighborly" with such men as those.

"Wallace—would you like to leave for a time?" she asked finally. "I have been thinking—all is in order. The harvest will be in soon. Mr. Proudfoot and his wife will continue to take care of matters. Shall we leave?"

"To go where?" he asked wearily. The rage had worn him to the bone, he felt sick and ill with it. "London? For more of their insults when they come? To Brighton? Perhaps the prince regent would like to insult us!"

"No. To Scotland," said Fiona quietly. "I have longed to see your home, Wallace. And I think your mother and sister are homesick for the hills. Could we not go and spend the winter there? You have a home there, do you not?"

He sat thinking, his head down. His home was a castle, he had not seen it for more than ten years. Was anything left of it? His lands—they had been taken from him, but the remains of the castle and the island on which it stood were his, they had not taken that, perhaps because it was so old and in such need of repair no one had thought it worth the taking.

Home—to Scotland. He longed for his homeland with passionate hunger. Home—to peace and quiet, the hills and the blue lochs, and the golden glens in autumn color. The heather and the bracken, the sight of a stag with twelve points suddenly on a hilltop, his own people—

"I would like to go to the home of my people," he said sadly. "I do not know what condition it will be in, we left years ago—"

"Do let us go, Wallace. I know I shall love your home," she urged softly. Her head leaned against his arm, in spite of the stiffness of it. His arm curved about her, he drew her head down to his shoulder, and pressed his cheek on her hair.

"Then we will go, and right soon," he said quietly.

He would have to tell her soon that the land was her land, that the sheep that roamed the hills instead of his Highlanders were her sheep. He would have to tell her the story of how his father's factor had driven them out, burned a croft over the head of Rory's mother, how some had died, how some had gone to the dread mills of Glasgow.

But that for later. He felt strange and withdrawn from her, his own Fiona, whom he loved. She was one of the English who had defeated him, cheated him and his people, tried to kill him.

What would she say when she knew of this? He must find out one day. It might as well be soon.

"Aye, I would like weel to go and see home again," he repeated absently. "And my boys will be glad enough to go. They miss their families."

"Then we will go!" she said eagerly, brushing her cheek against his dressing gown. "I will give orders for the carriages to be made ready, and the packing of trunks. Shall we take sheets and blankets with us, and winter clothing? Yes, we must do that." And she chatted on eagerly, not seeming to note his silence.

Chapter Nine

Fiona tried to persuade her godmother to go with them. Mrs. Elizabeth Trent shook her white head and smiled lovingly at Fiona.

"No, no, my dearest, the cold mountains are not for me," she sighed. "Indeed, in the rains this autumn, how my bones do ache! No, I'll return to my town house in London and wait letters from you. You will write to me, often, will you not?"

Fiona pressed her cheek to the soft pink cheek. "That I will, my dear. If I cannot force you to come with us—"

They both laughed. Mrs. Frazer watched them thoughtfully.

"I fear she is right, Fiona," she said, her gentle voice sad. "The castle may be in disrepair, we have not been there for many a year. The fireplaces will have to be cleaned out, before fires can be set. And there will be no tapestries on the stone walls, I'll warrant. They will be long gone."

Margaret nodded, also, her red hair flaming in the

firelight. "Aye, 'twill be cold. We must make sure to take many blankets and thick cloaks," she said practically. "Perhaps it would be better if mother went first to the village to remain for a time, until we can clean things up—" She looked questioningly at Wallace, but her mother spoke up with firmness.

"Nay, I'll come with ye and will not be put off," said Mrs. Frazer, with a blaze of blue eyes that reminded Fiona of her son's vivid blue eyes. There was a bit of fire left in her after all the years of suffering and hardship. "Do not try to put me off, now! I'll naught have it!"

"Mother, ye shall do as ye wish," said Frazer. "Mrs. Trent, if your heart is set on returning to London, I'll take ye there when you wish. Ye'll not travel alone, too many footpads and desperate men on the highways after the wars."

So it was settled. the Frazer and two of his men accompanied Mrs. Trent, her maid, with two carriages full of belongings and baggage, down to London, to settle her. He stayed two days, to make sure all went well, then returned to Yorkshire.

During the week Wallace was away, Fiona and Margaret set about directing the packing of trunks and cases, filling them with sheets, blankets, thick draperies for several rooms, warm clothes for the winter, and whatever Margaret could suggest. The store in the village provided them with some items, others must be purchased farther away in the nearest town.

By mid-October, and Wallace's return, they were practically ready to depart. Wallace paid a call on the squire and told him their intentions.

"Aye, I heard that you would leave," said the squire, sitting comfortably in his study. They had lit up pipes and put their feet on the fender and talked like friends. Frazer had never thought to like an Englishman so much as he did the squire.

The man was an honest man, forthright when he could be, patient and tactful when he must. His good wife was a fine woman, and he knew the situation here.

"I canna remain here for a time," said Wallace. "Ye know the business of the hunt. Weel, it was like that in the wars, all the time. They taunted my Highlanders and me, all of us, trying to draw us into some quarrel to relieve their boredom. And many a time—" He clamped his lips, thinking of one event."

"Aye?"

"One time," he went on slowly, "I know he did taunt one man into a duel. It was forbidden, but Lord Morney—Major Grenville, as he was then—arranged it that the duel took place on a hill. He took the place above, and it was all over in a minute. The man had his sword through the Scotsman— And the only witnesses were the seconds. There was no doctor."

"So he is a scoundrel as well," muttered the squire, his mouth set. He shook his graying head. "Ah, to have such a one over us. It sets bad."

"I would warn ye. He will not take any offense against him, as he sees it. And he goes out of his way to encourage men to anger against him."

"Then he is as bad as his father," said the squire somberly.

"Worse, to my lights. For his father, as I heard of him, was at least open in his dislikes. This one, bad cess to him, hides the dislike behind smiles and friendship and soft words. Then he turns like a snake on one, and before one knows it—"

"Aye." The squire sucked on his pipe, gazing into the fire. "Well, I shall look to your place for ye, while ye are gone. I need have little fear it shall go well, with your man Proudfoot managing. However, he may need some shelter and wall between himself and Lord Morney."

"I would not have you get into difficulties over it. Send for me, should aught go awry. You have my direction, I have written it out. Once up beyond the Great Glen, any man can direct your groom."

"I'll do it, and gladly. May I say, it's sorry I am that it has to be this way. I was looking forward to many a good talk with you this winter. And your lovely lady graced our occasions, and your sister and mother when they would come."

"It is good of you to say so." They shook hands, and Wallace departed, feeling a little easier in his heart. When he thought of the hunt, he burned so with rage he did not trust himself. He had stayed out of Lord Morney's way and answered no invitations, nor would he permit Fiona to do so. She had agreed, but in a troubled manner.

Squire Reid was a fine man. If he were the only Englishman Wallace met, he might have a better opinion of them. And the good doctor Hopkins, he had been pleasant and forthcoming. The rest of them aped Lord Morney, to the detriment of all of them. They laughed at his malicious jokes, wore his fashions as best they could, sneered down their noses at the Scotsmen.

The group of them left Yorkshire on a gray October morning, and the rain began to fall before they had gone many miles toward the border into Scotland. Fiona shivered in her warm cloak, and Wallace drew up the rug about her.

"Cold already, my love?" he asked in concern. "I fear ye will be miserable when we go into my hills."

"No, no, I shall become accustomed to the cold," she said, with determination. "It is that I have been inside for two weeks, and not much out of doors that I feel chilled. It is only for a short time."

He felt her willpower stronger than her body and watched over her anxiously. They paused to drink tea from bottles, and to eat some cold biscuits and oatcakes, and then went on their way. They had a late lunch in some town north of home and felt they had progressed a good distance by evening. They put up in an inn, with the Tudor style of building, with white stucco and brown timbers making a pleasant pattern of the walls.

The next day they crossed the border into Scotland. They began to see men in uniform guarding the patrol posts, and at the tollgates. They stared suspiciously at the Highlanders in their kilts and cloaks but allowed them to go on with brief questioning. The lady with them was obviously English, with her gentle accent. And the money in their palms helped, thought Wallace bitterly.

They went on and on into Scotland, turning toward the west, and the fourth day they came up into the Highlands. He was out the window half the time, eagerly gazing at his beloved lands. No matter that sheep roamed them, the hills were the same, blue violet in the distance, green and bracken brown close by, with the purple heather covering the lower hills.

Fiona was gazing also, murmuring, "How beautiful! Wallace, I thought they would be stark and bleak. They are so lovely, look at all the rose purple flowers!"

"The heather, our heather," he breathed. "I thought never to see it again!"

She leaned back to gaze at him, puzzled. "Never see it again? Why, Wallace?"

"Ah, I meant in the wars, love. Down there in the brown hills of Spain and Portugal, in the battles. Little did I think I'd live to see my land again."

She held his hand in wordless comfort.

Jamie swung down from his horse and went to pick some of the heather, in great bunches of the flowers. He divided them carefully into three bouquets, tied them with grass stems, and presented them to Fiona, to Margaret Frazer and to Mrs. Frazer. Fiona held hers to her nose.

"Lovely, lovely," she murmured. "I shall never forget my wedding bouquet."

"They sent the heather to me, they had forced it betimes in June," he said gently. "It blooms usually in July and August, but I had to have some for my bride."

She gave him a beautiful smile, shy and sweet and loving. Her violet eyes shone above the purple heather. She was wrapped in a gray cloak. He thought, I must purchase a cloak for her, or have one made, of our tartan. She is my wife, she is a Frazer now.

Then he remembered—she was also Fiona Cartwright, the daughter of the man who had helped ruin them. His face shadowed. He must tell her soon— He must start to tell her today. For by the end of tomorrow, or sometime the next day, they would reach his castle on the island, and she must know the truth.

He did not know how his wife would take it. Margaret knew, he had told her and sworn her to secrecy, he did not want his mother to know. The other Highlanders—they would follow him, and they respected Fiona. But if his people in the glen found out, there might be serious trouble.

He sighed again. How foolish and unthinking he had been! They were all bound to know eventually. He could but hope the knowledge would come slowly. When they saw how gentle and kind Fiona was, and realized she could help them, their anger might not turn against her. After all, she was not her father.

But he must tell her.

Fiona kept looking at him with worry in her eyes. He put his hand on hers, under the cloak, and said, "I must tell you before we arrive, about the glen, and my clan, and what has happened to us."

"Yes, Wallace, I want to hear. Yet I know how sad your heart feels by all that has happened."

"Aye, that it does."

He was silent, searching for words with which to start. He finally began, with telling of the early wars, the hatreds between the English and the Scots.

"There were many border raids, when our men crossed to their land, or theirs to ours," he went on. "Over the years, the hates grew bitter. So many had died, so many houses burned, castles destroyed, prisoners taken and mistreated. I will not go into all that."

Her hand clasped his tightly. "I know a little of it, Wallace," she said quietly. "Do go on. I want to hear about you and your people."

He looked at the little bouquet of heather lying on her lap. With his free hand, he lifted it to his lips. He could scent the faint fragrance. "This is the last of the heather," he said. "August is in full bloom, when the hills are purple with it. Then it gradually dies, and finally there is none left but these last little patches, such as Jamie found. Ah, weel—that is how our people are now.

"You see, after the battle of Culloden in '45, the people were scattered. The English took our lands, harried us who had followed Bonnie Prince Charlie to our doom. Many the land that was taken, even in the scarred hills, where little grew. They made the Highlanders work for them for a time. But the families were large, and the English said there was no profit in the Scots people. Someone began to put in sheep to graze on the sparse green of the hills. They made a profit, more put in sheep.

"And from that, the movement grew. Our clan was deep in the glen, away from towns. We were not touched for a time. A long time. Then the English finally came, even to us. A man named Smith bought the rights from the English crown to take our lands. We had no rights on paper, we had simply lived here for hundreds of years, maybe even a thousand years."

He drew a deep breath. He was coming to the difficult part. The coaches clattered through Inverness, Fiona glanced out at the city, with surprise that it was so large. They went steadily on, through it, and out the other side, crossed bridges, and on into the hills and glens beyond.

Into his wild country beyond the Great Glen. He could not restrain a feeling of joy at homecoming. He leaned from the window, pointed out landmarks.

Fiona looked, exclaimed at the beautiful blue gray lochs, as the clouds drew over, and rain threatened. Eagerly she gazed at the small crofts, with the golden-brown thatched roofs, widely spaced across the hills.

It was growing late in the afternoon. He hoped to go on, and by nightfall reach home. But that was too late.

They stopped at a small inn and stayed the night. He said no more, and Fiona waited for his story. The next day, they went on. "We should reach home by early afternoon," he said encouragingly to his mother and sister.

"Ah, home again, home, to where my heart lies buried," said his mother in the Gaelic. Her blue eyes had a faraway look. Fiona glanced at Wallace for translation, he shook his head. His father lay buried up there in the hills.

He finally picked up the story where he had left it. He told of the efforts of his father to keep the clan together. They withdrew farther into the hills, they retreated to the castle on the lake. Still the English harried them. While his father was gone one week, men came in, and took off half a hundred of the Frazers, carried them off in carts to the cities, where they would find work, they said.

Fiona gasped. "Carried them off—without their wills?" she asked, her violet eyes huge.

"Aye, they did. My father was furious—he fought them, and they—killed him. My mother keened, the men would ha' fought them all and died, but she stopped them." He put his hand over his eyes. "I was but sixteen— I was hiding in the hills, for they would ha' taken me."

"Oh—Wallace—"

He could not touch her hand today. He lay back in the corner of the coach, gazing out into the hills for strength to continue.

"I tried to take my father's place. They would ha' followed me anywhere. But the English finally caught us up. We could enlist, they said, and go to the Peninsula as soldiers. Or we could go to prison or work in a factory, chained to a wheel. I chose for them, we would enlist. We were trained, put in a Highland Regiment and received for our officer one Major Grenville."

"Oh, Wallace!"

"Enough of that part," he said brusquely. "I will tell you another time of Lord Morney and his fellow officers. What happened in the hills is another story. My people were gathered up, some were sent to the factories of Glasgow, some to the docks. Small children were put to work in the mills, where their little fingers could be trained to work with the threads. Many a little one died, the English did not care. Too many Highland brats anyway, they said. The women—ah, some ended up in the—houses along the docks. Prostitutes, until they contracted some disease and died also. A few of my people are still hidden in the hills. I hope to gather them up and protect them."

"But will the English not follow you here, harass you?" Her voice was choked, distressed.

"You see, Fiona," he went on, "the factor is a tough man. But he is not the owner of these lands. Smith sold them to a man from Yorkshire, a friend of his, before he died, leaving no direct heirs. The man's name—was Hugo Horace Cartwright."

Fiona did not make a sound. She was crouched in the corner, the cloak about her. Her eyes gazed straight ahead of her. He did not know what she thought.

"I should ha' told ye long before. I could not do it. I could not say the words, Fiona. Yes, it was your father's man who harried us from the hills, who ordered the putting in of sheep, and made the fortune for him on which you live today. And God help me, the money which puts food in my mouth, and in the mouths of mine."

They had wound round and round the hills, going ever upward. Now the carriages came to the end of a dirt road, and before them lay a blue purple loch, surrounded by hills of brown bracken and low-flung trees hunched against the winds that blew all the winter long. He gazed hungrily out into the loch. There on the brown island lay his castle, his home.

He caught his breath. "Aye—they have burned it," he muttered in Gaelic, in distress. It looked like both wings had burned, and part of the central four-story section and the tower of stone. It shone golden and rust brown from the fires.

The other carriages pulled up. Jamie rode ahead of them on the big horse he favored, and pulled to where the remains of some boats lay on the shore. He and Sholto got down and began to examine them.

Wallace jumped out, eager to see what he could see. He did not look back at Fiona.

Margaret stepped down from the other carriage. Her red hair blew in the wind, above her red cloak, as she hastened down the hill to Wallace's side. "Are any boats still good, Wallace? If not, some must be built before we get to Frazer Castle."

He scarcely heard her. He was gazing across the rippling waters of the loch. The castle, his home. Stark against the purpling gray sky, proudly it had stood for centuries. All about were purple and gray and brown hills, and within them, half-hidden, deep in the Highlands where few English came, was this jewel of a loch. His loch, his hills, his castle. All that remained of it.

Jamie called, "Four boats are still worthy, Frazer!"

"Ah, good," said Wallace easily in the Gaelic. They all spoke the Gaelic now, it came readily to their tongue in their own land. The coachmen and footmen, all English, were staring about with curiosity and fear. In the wilds, they thought themselves, Wallace grinned to himself.

They cleaned the boats, and Wallace and Fiona and Margaret went across first, with Jamie rowing, to set foot first on the Frazer land. Fiona was very pale, she had not said a word for a time. He must speak to her, explain further, Wallace thought, but not now. There was so much to do.

Waves rippled out from the boat, Jamie jumped out and drew it up onto the sand of the beach. He stood back. "I should ha' brought my pipes," he mourned. "To think I forgot that! I'd pipe you back to your castle, Frazer!"

"Tonight, the pipes, Jamie," said Wallace. He lifted Fiona out, and then Margaret. "Welcome to Frazer," he said, with formal courtesy.

They walked slowly ahead, and he strode with them, after sending Jamie back for a load of the household goods. Another boat was coming, with his mother and Mrs. Owens, and two maids.

He entered the castle and found the hallway still stood, and the roof was there, and the tower that was of stone and a fortress and lookout through the centuries. One wing was gone completely, burned out to a shell.

They walked from room to room, saying little. Margaret's lips were thin and her eyes angry, but she did not speak of her fury. "The dining room is whole," she said once. "It needs scrubbing bad."

Fiona said nothing. She gazed from walls to floor, from ceiling to windows as though she did not see much.

"We can use this wing," said Frazer practically. "It has suffered the least damage. Five bedrooms are whole. We will have the front ones, Fiona. Margaret and mother in the rose room. The maids can have the back ones. I'll find rooms for the others— We must get some of the men back from the hills," he mused, with a frown.

It would take much work to make this all habitable again. And he wanted to find his men, to tell them Frazer had returned.

"Tomorrow—" he said. "Tomorrow I shall ride out into the hills with Jamie, and pipe my men home again. I hope to find many of them in the glen. Surely they are still there, they are cunning men, and shrewd."

Chapter Ten

Fiona worked in a daze; she scarcely knew what her hands did. Wallace had slept deeply the night before, with her in the great wide bed. She had lain stiffly, waking again and again, until she had scarcely thought she slept at all.

The shock had been horrible. And Wallace had been so matter-of-fact about it! He had said no more of the matter.

And her father—her father!—had been the one who had driven them from the land, had forced Wallace and his men to enlist. Her father's factor had rounded up Frazers to work in the factories of Glasgow.

And Fiona had grown up in wealth and luxury partly because of the poverty of the Frazers!

The knowledge was too stunning to be taken in all at once. Wallace had gone off early the next morning to ride the hills with two of his men to try to round up the remnants of his clan, find who might be left. They were outlaws, living off stolen sheep, Margaret had told her practically.

Margaret had gazed at Fiona with distance, but some understanding of her pain. "He will come back soon," she said. "You will talk it out. He loves you, dear, and you love him, it will mend."

"You knew? And who else?" asked Fiona painfully.

"I guessed, I had heard the name Cartwright, and it was too much of a coincidence," said Margaret gently. "Mother does not know, she lives much in the past, and takes not much notice of the present. The men do not know."

Fiona worked with them, directing the cleaning of the rooms that still had roofs. They scrubbed the walls and floor and ceilings of the rooms in the one wing that was least touched by fire, and restored some of the former beauty to the great entrance hall. The men worked with a will, both English and Scots, and soon they could see the change they had wrought.

Some of the men slept on the floor. There were a few beds left in some of the rooms. Fiona wandered about from one room to the other, noting mechanically the work yet to be done.

There were places where the tapestries that could not be yanked down had been burned deliberately. Torches had been set to them to destroy the beauty that could not be carried off. Deliberate wanton destruction, she thought, and from orders of her father!

She wondered if Wallace meant for her to leave him. Could they continue this marriage, with such a great wrong between them? What did he think, what did he feel?

Working like this, with her hands, left too much time for thinking. Still numb from the shock, she had worked hard. But now that matters were more straight, and the rooms beginning to look livable, she began also to recover from the first great shock, and to think again.

Should she leave Wallace? Why had he married her? She began to remember the early days of their courtship. How soon had he known who she was?

Not at the first encounters. He had been quiet, withdrawn, yet friendly and courteous. Then—then after the affair of the footpads' attack, he had begun to change. His courtship had become urgent. Why? Had he then learned who she was, who her father was?

And that strange wager. It had seemed so unlike him, it still did, now that she knew him better. She had been stunned to find that he had wagered about her—and ten thousand pounds! At the time, she had put it down to his desperate need for money.

Yet—yet Lord Morney had made sure she knew about the challenge, and its outcome. Did Lord Morney know about her father? Had he told Wallace Frazer? It would be like his malicious nature, he had probably figured that Wallace would jilt her and make a scandal for her, shame her. As he would have, if Wallace had not suddenly decided to marry her, and at once.

By the time Wallace had returned, with about twenty of his men and their families, the only ones he had been able to find, she was more composed. She had a hundred questions to ask him, but not the courage to ask them. Would he fling her out? Would his people accept her, once they learned who she was?

Wallace saw the question in her eyes. They went for a ride on the lake, he rowed them to the far shore, and tied up the boat. He lifted her out onto the sandy beach, and then they walked for a time in the fresh cold air, looking up at the purple hills and the scudding gray clouds.

"Ye have many a question, dear heart," he said gently. "I left ye for a time, it was necessary. It was to gather up my men. And to let ye know your own heart. Do you hate me for keeping all the truth from you?"

"I could not hate you, Wallace," she said simply. "But it was such a shock—are you—do you think—to discard me?"

"Discard you!" he gasped. He studied her worried eyes. "No, no, my heart of me. Never. I love ye. I will to my dying breath." He drew her to him and kissed her lips, and the hard clasp of his arm was good to her.

"And I love you. Is my father to stand between us, even though he died?" she asked. "I know now what he did—will you hold it against me?"

"I fought out that matter a good many months ago, and asked ye to marry me," he said quietly. "No, you are not accountable for your father's deeds. I love ye. My people will come to love ye. You are wife to the Frazer." His head lifted proudly in the wide bonnet. His cloak lay about them both, his tartan cloak.

"But—they do not know—"

"Not yet. One day they will know, and may be angry and hurt. But after they come to know ye, they will accept ye."

She wondered, and doubt lingered. The poison of doubt that had lain between them these many months. But she smiled, and pointed to the beautiful riverlet that flowed down from the hills. "How sweetly it runs," she said. "How it flashes when the sun comes out. I love your land, my dear."

"Our land," he said, with a smile.

She thought, Cartwright land, bought with bloody hands.

The barrier lay between them. It must be ignored, and one day it might melt down. For now, she turned her thoughts to the future. She had always been a practical girl.

"Wallace, what will your people do now?"

"Do?" he asked blankly.

"They must earn a living," she said. "We cannot hire them all for the castle and the island. Can they be employed on the land?"

He frowned, his dark red eyebrows bushy and heavy above his vivid blue eyes, shadowing them like a cloud over the blue loch. "Nay, your factor would not employ them. Phineas Tilden has hired only a few of the men as shepherds, and he brought them in from further south. They are not native here, and they have naught to do with the Frazers, it would be their joys and their lives."

"I could speak to Tilden," she said eagerly.

"He does not know who you are," Wallace told her simply. "Once he finds out, he may not keep the knowledge to himself. Nay, it is better to wait, and let the knowledge out slowly, if possible. Wait a bit, we will bide our time."

She returned to the problem, over her hurt that she must wait to be accepted. She thought of her father, tough and hard, cruel, not hesitating to beat her as he flogged his own horses. Wallace had wondered at the lines on her back, but he rarely saw them, only a few times in bed, when their minds were otherwise occupied. She had never told him they were the scars of her father's beatings. He might have thought they were from a fall from a horse, or some such accident.

"There must be some way to earn livings. I wonder—" she mused as they strolled through the thick brown and golden bracken. The ferns had turned brown, and the fallen leaves made thick, soft paths for them. "Oh—Wallace—" She caught at his hand and held him back as he would have strode forward. "What is that? Over there on the hill?" she gasped.

He stared, and grinned. "Well, I am blessed," he said in Gaelic, and repeated it in English. "It is a stag, a beautiful stag, my heart. A fourteen-point stag! What a rare sight, to be sure! I thought them all driven away by the soldiers—"

They stood quietly, hand in hand, gazing at the magnificent animal as he raised his head and roared across the valley. The whole glen seemed to echo to his cry.

"In rut," Wallace said softly, as though the beast might hear. "He will be calling to the females. This is the time that they mate, before the heavy winter snows."

Something disturbed the animal, he lowered his head, and in a moment he had disappeared in the thick trees. They strolled on, but now her eyes were opened to the wild nature about her. She noted the flight of birds, the lazy flapping of a hawk, its sudden pounce onto some small animal in the brush. She saw the rippling of the waters of the loch below them. She found a last small patch of purple heather and refused to pick it. "No, let it wait against next summer, Wallace," she said. She brushed the little bells tenderly with her hand.

They returned presently to the castle on the loch, and her heart felt more peaceful. Margaret watched them with keen eyes and gave her an approving smile. That was a comfort, her sister-in-law knew the truth, and liked her anyway.

She talked to Margaret, then, from time to time. They discussed various ways that the men might be employed, once the castle was in as much order as possible.

"Nay, the factor will not hire them with the sheep, he would not trust them," said Margaret as the two women sat outdoors on a bench, their cloaks about them, gazing at the lake as they waited for the men to return from their morning of fishing. "There must be some other occupation. What we need is a factory!" she added bitterly.

Fiona's eyes opened wider, she gazed at the loch in thought. "A factory," she echoed at last. "Margaret! Do the men and women know how to spin and weave? Can they make fabrics from the wool?"

"Oh, aye, all know how to do that, even I can," shrugged Margaret. "But they dislike much the factories of Glasgow and other towns. The looms there are—"

Fiona interrupted. "They could do hand loom work, in their homes! Couldn't they? I have seen it done in Wales! The women and the men also make their own looms, and set it to a pattern, and spin and dye their own wools. They make the most beautiful woolens, Margaret! It could be done here!"

"Weel, if it is permitted," said Margaret dubiously. Yet her blue eyes began to glow with more life. "Aye, it would be a marvel! Eh? To make our own woolens! We could call them Frazer wools, belike!"

"Of course!" Fiona was entranced with the thought. She noticed the men fishing, and said, "And there is the fishing, Margaret. Is there enough to take some fish into nearby towns, and sell them? They could be dried here and carried in carts."

"Oh, aye!" said Margaret, looking dazed. "Indeed, Fiona, ye have many an idea!"

Fiona laughed, the first time she had laughed in weeks, she thought. "Oh, I have so many ideas, godmother used to say," she agreed happily. "Let me think. What else could be done?"

Wallace came to sit with them, having sent his fish to the kitchens, and cleaned up. "Well, what do ye scheme and plan, eh, my dears?" he smiled.

They told him their ideas, and he stared. "Well, that would be a marvel!" he said soberly. "I wonder if it could be done?"

"And the sewing," said Fiona, in a continuation of her thoughts. "We could obtain fabrics from the mills, and the women could make little dresses and cloaks for children. Couldn't they? I well recall in London how well such sold in the shops, when I went to purchase a present for a friend. Do not the women sew well?"

"My dear, you will have us all working busily!" cried Margaret gaily, pink rising in her cheeks with excitement. "Of course they can sew! We could make our own fabrics, and design and make garments to sell in London shops. There is the pretty fabric they make in Inverness mills, we could buy some of that. And we could spin and weave our own. What about small cloaks of Scottish plaids, for the little children? Would that not be smart and warm?"

"Would the Londoners buy them?" asked Wallace, more soberly.

"I could write to godmother, and ask her what she thinks. She can be most practical," said Fiona.

They were sitting there in the evening, discussing it yet again, when they heard the sounds of horses on the shore opposite. Wallace stood up, his hand went automatically to his side, where he had carried his sword, only it was not there now.

Jamie came out and stood peering there. "It be the

English," he said somberly. "Shall we break out the weapons?"

Fiona gasped. "But we must find out what they want!" she blurted out. "We are not at war!"

"In the Highlands, we are always at war, in secret," said Margaret, with a sigh.

A voice yelled across the waters. "Is it the Frazers? Phineas Tilden wishes boating to come across!"

Fiona stood up, holding her thick gray cloak about her. She was stiff with alarm. She waited to hear what Wallace would say. He cupped his hands about his mouth and called, "I will send my men with four boats! Come to dinner, will ye?"

A pause. Then the call, "Coming, and thank you!"

Fiona relaxed, so did Margaret. But Wallace stood tense as the Highlanders took out the boats and began to row them across the dusk of the lake. Presently the boats returned, and in the first one was a short, dark-haired man of about forty.

He was wrapped in a black cloak and had a black peaked hat on his head. He gazed up at them as he came up the shore.

He turned to Wallace and greeted him but did not hold out his hand. Wallace bowed stiffly. "Frazer of Frazer, having served my time in the Highland Regiment" he said, his voice stinging with some bitterness.

"Aye, I well recall you as a lad," said the factor. He then turned to Fiona, standing back in the shadows. "And you will be—"

"My wife, Mrs. Frazer," said Wallace curtly. The Highlanders stood in the background. Phineas Tilden grinned at her, and Fiona realized with a shock—he knew!

They went inside and to dinner. The men were courteous and wary with each other. After dinner, Tilden sat with Wallace and Fiona alone in the great drawing room, bare but for a couch tattered with age, and several chairs they had rescued from unburnt rooms.

"I came to pay my respects," he said, then, glancing

about with a grin. "These are not the comforts you are accustomed to—Mrs. Frazer!"

"They do us very well," she said curtly. "In time I hope to add to the furniture. My sister-in-law and I will hang curtains and draperies—"

"You plan to live here, then?" he asked curiously.

"Yes, we do," said Wallace. "May I ask—how did you hear that we had come? The word through the hills?"

"Nay. Not that," said Tilden, and grinned again. "I had a fine letter from an old friend, son of an older friend. Lord Morney was kind enough to write and tell me you had come to—take over your possessions as heiress of Mr. Hugo Cartwright, Mrs. Frazer!"

It was out but not a shock, thought Fiona. "How kind of Lord Morney," she said dispassionately, thinking she would like to run the man through! Lord Morney had interfered too much in her life so far!

"Yes, it was. I might not have known who you were, but for his letter. The Scots do not know, do they?" he asked.

"Not yet. We have not had time to be social," said Fiona, as brightly calm as though in her own drawing room in Yorkshire. "We plan to fix up the castle first, before inviting guests."

Tilden grinned, showing mottled pointed teeth—like those of a rat, she thought. "Ah, so wise. I came but to receive orders, should you wish to give them, Mrs. Frazer. After all, you own all the lands hereabouts! Do you wish to change any arrangements? Do you wish to see the accounts?"

"I believe you send them annually to my solicitors in London," she said quietly. "They will continue to take care of financial matters. They are—most trustworthy."

She remembered now, they had sent a man up here last year because of a low figure in the profits, and had had trouble with the factor, one solicitor had complained to her. They had managed to sort out the matter, and he had paid for the remainder due.

"Well, well, whatever you wish done, shall be done," he said.

Fiona said, to test him, "I had thought to find employment for the Scots who have none," she said, as though casually. "I find some do not wish to go into the cities. And who could blame them, with such beautiful scenes as the hills offer? I may wish to begin a small mill to make fabrics of the wool. Can you supply us with some good wool at this time?"

He lost his good-natured pretense. He asked sharply, "What will you do with a mill? There are enough mills here! The men will not work at them! They are bone-lazy and would rather poach game!"

"We shall see, shall we not?" Fiona's hand closed over Wallace's, for he would have protested sharply. She kept her tone even. "I think it is time they had work to do, if they wish to do it. The wars are over long ago. We can try a mill and also employ some women to make garments for sale in England. It might go well and take them off the dole. That would be good, would it not?"

"The damned rebels do not deserve such treatment!" he told her angrily, his dark face reddening in his fury. "Over the years, the English have had trouble enough suppressing them. Now you will coddle them."

"By giving them work to do?" Fiona asked steadily, surprised at her own calm as she argued with them. "That is not logical, Mr. Tilden. Every man should be given the opportunity to earn his living, do you not agree?" and she smiled.

He cooled so quickly, she was suspicious. "Oh, as you will, as you will! It is your land, after all. Well, well, you have made some splendid changes in the castle. You may make quite a few changes in the glen, as well. Have you seen the village, formerly that of the Frazers', and now a Cartwright village? All who live there work for you, you know, Mrs. Frazer!" And he grinned again, glancing slyly at Wallace Frazer.

"No, not yet, I thank you for reminding me of it. I think we will have much to do yet in the castle, but I

123

hope to visit the village in some months from now," said Fiona, with quiet calm.

After he had left, refusing to remain the night, Wallace said, "I canna like the mon. He means mischief."

"Probably," said Margaret. "It is his nature. He loves mischief and trouble. When it gets too big, he calls out the guards and puts it down, as though he had not created the trouble in the first place! Oh, he is a very devil! I do not trust the English, and he is one of the worst!"

Fiona flinched. Every word she said seemed to stab into her own heart. Margaret sighed, and went inside to see to her mother, who fortunately had not come down to dinner. Margaret had seen that a tray was taken up to her.

Wallace put his arm about her and drew her away. "The breeze off the lake grows cool, love. Come inside."

She went inside but did not feel warm again for a time. An ominous chill was in her heart.

Chapter Eleven

With something practical to do, Fiona felt much more cheerful. She set to work with a will, and soon after Christmas (which was a gray, gloomy one for them all), she had the men build a small wooden structure on the land opposite the island.

Wallace oversaw the work. He had thrown off his doubts, at least in her hearing, and directed the making of several fine looms of various sizes. Tilden, to their surprise, sent several wagonloads of good white wool to them for them to experiment with the dyes, spin the yarn, and set the looms.

By March, all was set up. Five men and two women were employed at the dying, the spinning and the weaving, and with time they could employ more. The first project, Wallace said, was to make a fine Frazer cloak for his wife. This was done, and with much ceremony and merriment, it was presented to her.

Fiona accepted it, joy in her heart. They did not all know who she was, she thought the word was going around the glen, for some eyed her with suspicion. But that might be because she was English, they knew it by her accent. She put on the cloak, and all cheered, and they celebrated with homemade Scotch from some still in the hills. It was a fiery brew, and Fiona gasped as it hit her stomach. Margaret tactfully and quietly watered it down for her.

The months had gone swiftly. It would soon be spring. The winter had been cold, there in the castle, and Fiona had sent for more blankets from her godmother. Mrs. Trent sent all she requested from the London shops, and letters of encouragement to her, along with the gossip.

"Captain Ainsworth has called several times," she wrote at one time. "He is most pleasant and amiable away from his evil companions. I told him so, and he looked grave. I think he would break away from them if he had other good friends. He is a bit too easily led, I told him that also."

Fiona's relations with her husband had grown warmer, after the first chill weeks. Wallace slept with her in the massive bedroom on the first floor which had been that of the Frazer of Frazer for many hundreds of years. They had warmed it with fires in the fireplace, it was easy enough to cut wood from the hills, and it kept some of the Highlanders busy. They had fires in the big drawing room, and some of the men slept on the rugs there, with their cloaks drawn about them.

She loved being with Wallace, she adored him so, and wanted to please him. Perhaps when she had had a child for him, especially a son to be his heir, he would be even happier with her. She had hopes of it, anyway.

On the cold nights, when the chill winds swept through the pines on the shore, and the water churned against the island as though it would tug at it and pull it down the loch, she loved to lie close to Wallace, and listen to the many night sounds. She recognized the calls of the birds, the thrilling call of the stags.

"How do the little animals survive the winter?" she asked sleepily, one night.

He drew her into his arms and caressed her back

through the thick woolen nightdress. "As we do," he said, mischief in his tone. "They lie close and tight in their burrows, and enjoy the coziness of each other. Like this." And he kissed her mouth, then let his lips roam over her soft skin down to her throat.

"Oh—Wallace," she said. "You tease me."

"Oh, aye," he said, with a little laugh, "It is enjoyable to do so. Ye do not mind, do ye?" He sounded satisfied with himself and with her, and she smiled in the darkness.

She curled closer to him. "I do not mind," she told him softly. She dared to put her hand inside his nightshirt, and move her fingers slowly over the hard chest, twining them in the dark red hairs there, to his waist. He was very masculine, she thought, with a thrill. He felt all hard muscle and sinew, yet his skin on his shoulders and chest was almost as soft as hers. Silky, and smelling of the soap he used.

She dared to ask, still caressing him, "When did you first know you loved me?"

He was silent, and she felt a little pang of doubt. Oh, that poison that lingered!

"I think," he said slowly, "it was when I first saw you. The ball at Lady Anne Freemantle's, ye will recall. You wore a violet gown the color of your eyes. Ye turned your head and looked at me in the set, and I could not look away. I had never seen such eyes, like the loch at sunrise before the reddish color touches the waters. And your hair was the color of the shadows in early autumn, back in the hills, blue black like the blackbird's wing. And your voice was like the wind in the pines, so sad and so merry, all at once."

She was still, listening, caught in the poetry of his words. He did not often speak so, though his sister used the words so naturally.

"I thought you could not be real, more like a fairy queen," he went on, in her ear, nibbling at the lobe in a sensuous manner that sent thrills down her spine. "I thought, I'll close my eyes and open them, and flick, she will be gone, leaving only an image shining after.

So I closed my eyes and missed a step, and my partner scolded me with a tap of her fan!"

"Oh, Wallace," she gurgled with soft laughter at the smile in his tone. "You did not!"

"Aye, that I did. Then I apologized, and after the set I looked about for ye. I watched ye for a time, from the corners of me eyes, to see if you would flit away. Then ye stood alone near the windows and looked weary, and I dared to approach ye and asked if I could get for ye a little wee drap of refreshment."

"I remember," she breathed. "I looked up—and saw you—and you were so tall and red-haired and so sober— You seemed to look right through me with your piercing eyes. I said yes, I should like a drink of something cool. And you brought me some lemon drink, and it was refreshing, and did not go to my head—" She had remembered because the gentlemen usually managed to put something strong in her drinks if she trusted them to bring one sometimes. Wallace had been different.

"Aye. And you smiled so sweetly and thanked me. And I heard later you were called the Snow Maiden, and I thought it was because they did not see the lady under the snow. A gentle, shy, fey lady."

"Fey? What is that?"

"Like a fairy queen, something not like mortals." His mouth was going around her ear, down under it to the sensitive flesh beneath, and down further. He gently unfastened the laces of the nightdress that tied it down the front, and put his big warm hand on her full breasts. Then he bent and kissed her all down over the breasts, holding the pink nipples in his lips, touching her with sureness and sweetness, and fire.

"Darling," she breathed, and turned a little to hold him in her arms, her hands going over his broad shoulders. She reached inside his nightshirt again, and her fingers explored down the wide back, to his narrow waist, and up again over the hard spine.

She felt him shudder in her arms, and his kisses quickened, became full of desire and passion. He moved over her and drew up her nightdress to her waist. Their legs strove together in the embracing, and he came to her, and it was so hot and wild that she lost her breath. He was so slow in his deliberate movements then, and he went on and on, she gasped and kissed his throat, and moaned, "Oh, my darling, come to me—oh—come—I cannot wait—"

Instead he lingered, and became more slow. She squirmed under him, thrusting up her hips to him until finally he quickened again, and moved faster and faster, and the passion flared up wildly between them, like a fire in the dry underbrush, blazing and taking hold of everything in its path.

She felt everything seem to break loose inside herself, floating and quivering and deliciously ecstatic. Time seemed to have stopped, she heard nothing, saw nothing, for very dizziness. She could only feel, feel—the hardness of his body on hers, her fingers gripping desperately at him for purchase, as they swept up and up and up—

Then down and down, gently, to lie together in the thick featherbed with the quilts over them, holding close and wet and tight. He groaned with satisfied desire.

"Oh, me love, me lovely darling. How delightful are thy breasts, how lovesome are thy thighs," he murmured.

He could whisper poetry to her by the hour, and she adored it, in the Gaelic which she did not understand, or the English which she blushed to know. Her fingers threaded through his thick red hair, down to his neck, and tugged gently to draw his face to hers once more, their lips met timelessly.

Finally they slept, and she did not know when she slid from loving to sleeping. It was all one, held tightly to him.

And so the nights went by, and the days were full of work, and all seemed to be going well. The winter snows fell, and cut them off from the world around for two more weeks. There was a late March snow, and it covered the hills with feathers, then melted into the blue loch, which glistened in the spring sunshine. The fragile wildflowers began to show, blue and pink-striped, and sunny yellows.

The looms were busy humming. They decided to make two more, for others were eager to be employed at the looms. Mrs. Trent had written she had found a clever man to merchandise any woolen lengths or garments they chose to send. He would give them a fair return, she said.

Children came with their parents to play around in the crisp April air as time went on. Fiona began going over to the mainland every day to watch the work and admire it, to try her hand at spinning, to play with the smaller children. They were so bonny, so quick and bright, with their sparkling blue eyes, many with bright red hair like Wallace's. She dreamed, also, sitting on the riverbank, near the tiny tumbling stream that flowed into the loch, of Wallace's children and hers.

One afternoon, soon after, she heard the heavy sound of horses coming. She looked about in surprise, for few horses came to their quiet glen, and none of the carriages of the gentry made their way here from the town, the nearest one some thirty miles away.

She stood to gaze curiously toward the rough paths and the hills from which the sound came. She saw then that the people were leaving the looms, dropping all, grabbing their children's hands, and running into the thick bushes and up the glen into the hills.

Wallace was rowing across the loch, and two of his Highlanders, glancing toward her in worried fashion. She waited for them, walking down to meet them as they pulled in. And then the horsemen came, with Phineas Tilden leading some half a dozen English soldiers in red uniforms!

Wallace stood beside her, with their Highlanders behind him on the sandy shore as the horsemen rode down in neat file to the loch. Phineas Tilden had a curiously satisfied look on his thin, mean face.

Fiona had a premonition then, and Wallace must

have done. For her husband folded his arms on his chest and waited their coming with a strange droop to his shoulders, though his head was high, the bonnet defiant in the thin April sunlight.

"Good day, Frazer, Mrs. Frazer," greeted Tilden. He slid down from his horse, one of the English soldiers took the reins. The men stayed on their horses, staring curiously at the Scotsmen in the kilts, at the lady in the red tartan cloak of the Frazers.

"Good day to you," said Fiona. Wallace did not speak, glaring at the man from under bushy red eyebrows.

Tilden reached into his capacious pocket and drew out a thick sheaf of papers, which he handed to Fiona. She took them curiously, not attempting to look at them. "What is this?" she asked.

"You will see in the papers, Mrs. Frazer. The lands your father bought are confiscate to the Crown."

He grinned, his teeth sharp and pointed in that curious ratlike look. She could not take in his words.

"Confiscate?" she echoed. "What does that mean?"

"It means, madam, that for consorting with rebels against the English Crown, for comforting the enemy and consorting with them," he glanced contemptuously at Wallace, "and for various reasons listed in them papers, you have lost the Frazer lands. The lands of the glen are closed to you. They are forfeited and will be taken over by the Crown for management, until they sell the lands to someone—who will manage them *properly*."

She could not understand. In England, no one could take their lands from them. She stared at him blankly. "But they cannot take our lands from us," she gasped. "That is against the law! My solicitors will inform you—"

"They are in London and don't know the situation here in Scotland," said Tilden complacently. "I took it on myself to inform the Crown, and certain of the lords in London, of what was going on here. A bill was passed in the House of Lords, and you will have to give up the lands. Those will go," and he pointed to the wooden sheds with the looms. "They are on forfeit lands."

"No!" she cried. "We built the buildings ourselves, we built the looms—"

"Tear them down, lads," said Tilden gleefully to the English soldiers. Fiona turned to Wallace desperately.

"Tell him he cannot do this! It is not his property, it is—it is mine!" she said violently. Wallace did not move.

His Highlanders did not move, even when two British soldiers slid down from their horses, put ropes to the buildings, and pulled them down. They stood, arms folded, watching grimly as torches were set alight and put to the buildings. The smoke that went up smelled of wool—for all the looms went, and the wool, and the cloths partly made, and all the hard work of months.

Fiona turned on Tilden in a rage. "You will be made to pay for all this!" she flared. "I hereby discharge you as factor! You have acted against my interests all along! You will quit your post at once, do you hear me?"

"You are not my employer, madam!" he smirked. "The lords in London done appointed me to act in the Crown's best interests while settlement is made. The new man who buys the lands from the Crown will hire me, no doubt. I serve their interests well!"

"You serve the devil well!" she cried. Then Wallace took her arm and drew her back from the anger in Tilden's face.

"Say no more, Fiona," he said quietly. "He will not be moved. Let them go in peace. We will speak later."

"Aye, your good husband knows what is what!" Tilden sneered. "He knows it does no good to fight against the English! He will always lose! It would suit us better for him to reenlist, if we had some war now! For he fights not badly—when directed by the English!"

Fiona felt the arm about her tense, the muscles

strain against her back. A murderous look was in the Frazer's blue eyes, turning them darkly purple.

It warned her. The English soldiers were armed and ready, and on horseback. "You will go now," she said more quietly. "You will hear from my solicitors in due time! And you will be made to pay for this!"

"No, Mrs. Frazer. It is you who will pay!" Tilden swung up into the saddle. "You will pay in the lost lands and the lost revenues. England does not take kindly to those who coddle the enemy, as you have done! The Scots have to be taught a lesson that no one defies us! You have sympathized with the enemy, you will find no help in London!"

He wheeled the soldiers, and they rode smartly away, leaving the small pathetic remains of the mills in charred ruins.

Fiona kept her head up and her back straight long as they were in sight. Then she sagged. "Oh—Wallace—" she whispered. "How can they do this? How can they?"

"They won the battles," he said, in a deadly quiet rage. "Aye, they won the battles. But there is one more battle to fight! I'll gather the clan, and we will fight them, by God! They will know a Scotsman can fight and can die, if necessary, for his home and his land!"

Then Fiona awoke to the realization that this was not a horrible dream, not a play enacted before her eyes. They had meant all this. Tilden had brought the soldiers because he had thought, he had even hoped, that the Highlanders would protest and fight! He had hoped—to kill them all!

"Wallace, that will do no good, it will only kill your men—and you," she said desperately. "Come—let us talk it over quietly in our home, and come to some solution. I will write to London, to friends there, someone in the House of Lords, to the prince regent himself. Surely he will not endure this! It is against English law to take property from a person in such an arbitrary manner."

"This is not England, it is Scotland," said her husband, his teeth grinding out the words. "And Scotland has lost her wars, God pity her! We must endure and starve, we must go hungry and cold and work ourselves to the bone in the grime of the cities—even then our lords of London will not be happy! They will not be satisfied, the emnity has gone on too many centuries. No, Fiona, there is no help for it. I shall gather the clan for one more last fight, and have an end of it."

"An end of you!" she whispered, appalled. "Wallace, I beg of you, dear heart—"

He did not seem to hear her. They took boats back to the island, to the castle. She told Margaret what had been done, and his mother, and they joined her in the efforts to dissuade Wallace from gathering the clan. Highlanders were willing, he said ominously. It would not take much effort to gather half a hundred men, and wipe out the soldiers.

"And be wiped out in turn," said Margaret, tears in her eyes, but her voice severely practical. "It has been happening for these many years, my brother. What good does it achieve?"

"We will have our revenge!" Wallace growled, pacing up and down the great hall before the immense crackling fire. "By God, they have gone too far this time! They would take all the little we have left! Better to die in glory, than to live in whining poverty!"

Fiona exchanged a despairing look with his mother, who shook her white head sadly.

"I will raise my people," he said, red head held high, blue eyes glittering like frost in a winter morning. "I will raise them, and lead them—one more time! The Frazer name will be remembered in many a poem and song, after our time!"

"Aye," said his mother, "with many a greeting woman to sing it, and many a grizzling child to mourn her da. The men will be dead, and the lads, so many bonny lads. And for what good? You will kill, and be killed, but your women will be a-working in the mills, their fingers worn to the bone. Your children will be put to work there, too, or on the docks, young girls

134

sold into the houses that line the docks. And for what good? That someone should sing a poem of it? Nay, my son."

Wallace flung up his long arms, in a wide gesture of futile longing. "But what can we do? They will not let us live in peace, they will not let us live! Where can we go that they will not follow to harass and dispossess us? Where can we live in God's peace, and work in quiet? Where can a man roam the hills and call them his own? What is there left but to fight and die?"

"There must be something," muttered Fiona, huddled in cold chill against the fire's warmth, her tartan plaid about her. "There had to be some way—" Her sharp mind, inherited from her father, was turning over the possibilities. Land in Yorkshire, could she take the Highlanders there and begin again?

She remembered how the neighbors had laughed over the pipers and the poet. She flinched for them.

Somewhere else? Cornwall? Or Wales, her mother's land? Would they be welcome? Was their land she could buy?

Where could they go, to be in peace? The Scots people knew they would not be left alone in their glens to live, to hunt, to spin and weave. They would be hunted like wild animals themselves.

"What to do," she muttered aloud, nibbling a finger. "What to do? Where to go?"

Chapter Twelve

Wallace went about the glen, striding on foot up through the pathless hills to find his people. He would come on a small croft, greet the people gravely, and sit down to talk to the men.

They were sullenly angry. The English had ruined again what the Scots had tried to do. "Honest work!" said one man, his white head erect, his blue eyes blazing. "They begrudge us honest work. They would drive us to thieving to give them an excuse to hang us!"

"I know all this," said Wallace, for the hot angry words went on too long, and the women were muttering in the background as they stirred some meat broth for the luncheon. They would take a sheep now and then, and dry the meat. Added to the meat in the water, they would have vegetables they could grow in small patches, up there in the cold hills, well hidden from General Wade's roads where the English soldiers roamed. "The question to be considered now is, What to do? Where to go?" he added, thoughtfully.

"Go? Why should we go? These are our lands, these

are our hills. The glens we have roved these many years. The lands our fathers walked. Where should we go? Why should we leave?"

Wallace had been thinking hard about this, and talking with his family. Fiona, bless her, had a sharp mind, and it was good to talk to her, and learn her ideas. She had started him thinking constructively.

"The English will not leave us in peace," he said thoughtfully. "Where can we go that we will be in peace? My wife has lands in Yorkshire, but not enough for us all to live. And they jeer at me there, and my men. No, that is not the answer," he said to Fiona many a time.

"The Colonies that rebelled and broke away—might we go there?" asked Fiona.

"America? To the United States? We might do this. Yet they might be aye suspicious of us, being Scots and fighting against them those years ago. And many a Highlander fought again in their New Orleans, they remember it well, it was but a couple years back." A shadow came over his face. He had been close to going to America, he had his orders, when word came from Ghent that the peace had been signed.

The word had not been received in New Orleans until after the dreadful battle of New Orleans, where many an Englishman and many a Scotsman had marched forward to his death against the deadly rifles and cannon of the Americans.

"There are the islands of the West Indies," she said, hopefully. "I saw in gazettes some of the advertisements for men to come out there, and run the plantations. Many a wealthy man advertises for managers. Do you know aught of this?"

"Oh, aye," said Wallace gloomily. "I ha' talked to such as came back after a year or two there. Some canna endure the heat there, and the disease, the heavy rains and the storms. And one must direct the work of the blacks that come from Africa. I ha' never worked to order slaves about. Something in me sickens at the thought of the whip and the lash."

Fiona was silent for a time, a strange look on her face. He wondered what she was thinking. Sometimes she seemed hidden from him, like a hill with the mist on it, and he could not see what she was or how she felt. It was strange, they had been married for months, and should be closer than they were. In her was something hidden from him. He realized he knew little of her earlier life. It had probably been passed in innocent pastimes, reading, sewing, riding, dreaming. Yet—a thought came to him from time to time that something more dreadful lay behind her reserve.

His sister Margaret was reserved and quiet, yet he felt he knew her. In passion, she burst out with what she felt, in the poetic words that he understood. She had known suffering, she had endured, she had protected their mother. She was strong, and she was gentle, she was woman for some fortunate man one day. He knew her as his own blood. But Fiona was mystery and mist.

It was as Wallace was walking back in the evening, with the purpling hills spread before him, and his own loch blazing red in the light of the sunset that the idea came to him. "My ain land," he murmured longingly, pausing to gaze hungrily at the scene. "But not my ain lands any longer. They are gone, and my people scattered and hungry. Where can we go? Oh, my good God, whatever shall become of me and mine? How can I protect my people and care for these good folk who depend on me for guidance, as well as on Thee?"

He stood, legs apart, his tartan cloak about his shoulders, gazing steadily to the west. His heart was sick within him, for the croft folks he had seen this day were sick, hungry, and in despair. He thought of the graying woman, not much older than his sister and wife, with four small bairns crying about her, and her man sick on his bed of ferns, and the despair in her blue eyes, and the faltering of her lilting voice.

They would all be sick in another winter, sick and dead in the earth, for the hatreds that lingered still, striking them down into foul death.

138

"We must go," he said aloud to the ringing hills and the sleepy cries of the birds. "We must leave our ain lands, and go forth—and find other place to live. But
They had thought of Yorkshire. They had thought where?"
of the West Indies, but he had rejected that thought. His people would die of the heat and the disease.

The idea came to him, as though some still, small voice said it. "Canada," it said.

"Canada," he said aloud. "Canada!" He said it to the ringing hills, and they answered him, with a soft, whispering echo.

Canada had hills, it had long, beautiful rivers, it had blue glens. It had empty spaces, where a man might build himself a house to shelter his family. It had timber for the house, it had wilderness to roam about, and kill his meat.

He had heard about Canada from men in his regiment. They knew men who had gone there. One had told him, "Some died on the voyage. There was overcrowding and not enough food. The ship ran into foul weather, and many a child died weeping. But the ones who made it to the new land—ah, how they write! They have freedom there, there are not enough English soldiers to stop them, should they go forth into the wilderness to make their own way. Freedom, Frazer!"

He heard the whispering voice of the man, as though it had happened this day, instead of five years ago on the Peninsula. They had gone forth to battle the next day, and the man had died gallantly, another Scots dying in the service of the English. But his words had lingered.

Wallace remained there until past dusk. It was nightfall when he made his way down the mountainside to the loch, and to the boats that waited for him, with three of his Highlanders.

He was silent at the dinner table, turning over the idea in his mind. Fiona, at the foot of the table, directed the footmen as calmly as though she sat in some elegantly furnished dining room, instead of the cruelly cold remains of his old castle.

One day, he would build a fine home for her once more, and she should preside proudly, with her beautiful blue black head erect and her violet eyes shining, in a home suited to her beauty and her upbringing. Their children should grow up in freedom and with laughter in their hearts, instead of grief.

His mind was made up. "We shall all gather in the drawing room, all the family, all the men and women of this household," he said abruptly, into a brief silence, as the tea was brought about.

They looked at him, surprised, hopeful. Had the Frazer made up his mind to their future?

They gathered about him in the drawing room, some spilling out into the Great Hall beyond. Listening, straining, biting lips in excitement, or impassive from long years of hoping and losing.

"It has come to my mind," said Wallace steadily, his gaze searching out his wife's face, "that there is one land like ours, with hills and rivers, with richness as we used to have. There is a land flowing with milk and honey, like the Good Book says. With game for the taking, and no man to say him no, With rich lands for the farming and waters for fishing."

They seemed to hold their breath collectively, listening to the Frazer, the man they would follow anywhere, as they had followed his father and his father's father. Hope flared briefly in some eyes, others were wary.

Fiona was gazing up at him, her violet eyes wide and wondering, her open face eager. He smiled down at her tenderly.

"There is a land," he said slowly, "there is a land of beauty and the wealth of the good earth. That land is Canada."

"Ahhh—Canada—in the Americas! Canada!" He could hear the whispers from one to the other. He let the thought sink in, then he spoke again.

"I have been thinking where we might go, we of the

Clan Frazer, and other good Scots people if they so wish. I have heard from a man—a good man—that Canada is open for settling even to such as us. There is a vast land there, so vast, one said, that one might set several Scotlands in it, and not find them again. In the east there are great lochs, where the canoes paddle and boats sail, and the land is rich with promise. Furs are taken from animals, so many weasels and foxes, so many beaver and bear that one cannot be done finding them. And farther west, the land is vast, untracked, with high mountains and cool hills like our own, and there are fierce Indians there. We will not go there, I am thinking."

"But the ships—I hear that the ships are foul, and many die," one man protested gravely, anxiously.

"We will hire a fine ship," said Wallace, looking at Fiona again rather anxiously. She gave him a tiny nod, firmly. He drew a deep breath. "Yes, we will hire a good ship, with a captain we can trust. I meself shall go to Glasgow to find such a man, and such a ship, and find out the hire price. We best prepare to go in the summer, when the traveling is easier. We will take our own food for our people. Much must be done. If you agree, I shall proceed to Glasgow, and discover all— the hiring of a ship, the price of one, the managing of the land in Canada, how to decide which land is to be ours. It may be that land can be purchased, or tracks of land assigned. I do not know all, but I will find out."

They discussed it all the evening. They were interested, eager as they could be for having had so many disappointments in the past. Wallace went out the next day, with some of his men, and began going about the glen once more. This time he had a message of hope.

Fiona was happy for him, though she dreaded going to a new unknown land. The question of what to do with her Yorkshire lands was not spoken of—too soon for that, she supposed. Wallace was anxious to talk to his people, to see how many would go. Then he would proceed to Glasgow to make more arrangements.

Wallace did speak to Fiona at some length one evening. He had come home weary but with a glow that was different from his discouragement and his hopelessness. There was hope at last, a small glow on the horizon.

"I have not asked you, dear heart. Are you willing for funds to be made available for this purpose? It may cost a vast sum."

"You know that I am," she said sturdily. "I will write to my solicitors. Shall we—sell the Yorkshire house and land?"

"Not yet," he said absently. "Let me discover how many will go, if some should go first to make things ready for the next. I do not know if one hundred will go, or five hundred—we must gather up those in the Glasgow mills, if they wish to depart with us. When I go to Glasgow I will take with me the families from the glen who are willing to go at this time. Some are reluctant to leave the lands of their fathers—God help me, I cannot blame them." And he gave a heavy sigh.

"And you, Wallace, shall you go to Canada with them?" she ventured to ask.

"I know not yet. It means pulling up all—I may not be able to return. Shall I go with the first boatload? Shall I help search out the land? Or am I needed more here, encouraging my people to leave? Or is there some hope that you can get the land back—after all, your father bought it from the Crown. Mayhap the solicitors will be able to get them back. We have only Tilden's word on its status."

She confessed, "I have written to them, asking what they might do. I have also written to the prince regent, telling him of the matter. Whether he is at home, or willing to help—I cannot tell. The matter is so touchy—and the House of Lords has passed the bill against me—"

"Aye, the House of Lords, and with the bill of Lord Morney, I have no doubt!" he said bitterly.

"Probably. He is a vicious man, I think."

"Aye. Well—I must be off again tomorrow—best get some sleep. I think by Monday I shall go to Glasgow, and begin the search for a decent ship and a captain—" He was muttering to himself as he fell asleep on his side of the bed.

She missed his arms about her. He had been so busy and so tired that when he came to bed she had not the comfort of his embrace. Did he blame her for the loss of the lands? If she had not been so hasty in setting up the factory and looms, maybe she would not have brought this on his people. She lay long awake, trying not to stir restlessly, for it might waken Wallace. Yet—she longed to find some place in his plans for her. He had not asked her what she wished to do. She did not even know if she would accompany him, if he went first to Canada with the earliest shipload.

Wallace gathered up some of the outlaws and their families, those who would go with him, and set off for Glasgow. It was a small band of some forty-five persons, many small children, in carriages and farm carts drawn by great dray horses he had hired. Such a stir caused attention from the British soldiers, and Tilden got word of it.

Fiona set out a couple of days later for the small village nearby. Her abigail, Mrs. Owens, went with her, and also Margaret. They wished to speak to the village people, who were sullen and suspicious of the move.

Jamie Frazer rode beside the carriage, his huge frame awkward on the horse. He was so tall, such a giant, that he was uncomfortable on a horse, and preferred to walk. Yet Wallace had left his orders, and Jamie would follow them. When his wife went out, Jamie was to ride beside the carriage always.

In the village, they found the men gathered in the small open pub, drinking. That alone was ominous. Usually they were about, gathering wood for the fires, or cutting peat, the thatchers at work on the roofs, the herdsmen with their few cows. But they were all standing or sitting, talking earnestly, when the carriage drove into the dirt street nearby.

They turned to look at her, and Fiona felt their stares with impact. Wariness—they knew she was English, though the Frazer's wife. Even Margaret was suspect, for she rode with them.

Then from the other side of the village English horsemen rode in. And a carriage with them, with Phineas Tilden. He ordered the carriage stopped near the pub, and hopped out, his dark face red with fury.

"What do you hear?" he cried out to Fiona. "Where is your man? I heard he is taking people from the glen!"

She sat still in the carriage, but her clear voice could be heard in the stillness as women came to the doors of their thatched cottages, and the men stood at the pub and listened.

"I thought that was what you wanted, Mr. Tilden," she said coldly. "You want the Highlanders out of the glen, and sheep put in. Are you not pleased that the Scots people are leaving at last?"

"He'll take away all my workers!" Tilden fumed. "He has no right to encourage anybody to leave! They go only where they are sent!"

"The Scots are free men, Mr. Tilden," said Fiona, in spite of Margaret's urgent pressure on her arm. "They will go where there are jobs and a living to make for their families. And, of course, their families will go with them."

His mean black eyes narrowed suspiciously. "Do they go to Glasgow, then, to work in the mills? Nobody sent for them to work! The city will be overcrowded!"

"Why should they work in Glasgow, Mr. Tilden?" she said calmly. "No, they will go farther, as you shall soon learn."

He picked up the words like a terrier. "Go where? Go where?" he snapped. "Do they go south to make trouble in England? Does he think to lead them into another foolish bootless battle?"

She saw no reason to keep the truth from him, and a little triumph came in her voice. "No, Mr. Tilden. We shall emigrate to the new land, to the Americas. To Canada, where there are lakes and hills, and free men. That is where we will go!"

The women gasped, some muttered words. Mr. Tilden turned purplish red in his fury. He swung his whip, as though he longed to feel Fiona beneath its lash. She had to stiffen herself, to keep from cringing—she remembered the sound and the feel of the lash all too well, that of her father's.

She kept her chin up against his anger.

"They will go to Canada? They will leave without permission? Who will mind the sheep? They have not word to go! We shall see about this!"

She taunted him more openly. "I thought, Mr. Tilden, that you despised the Highlanders. That you would be pleased to see us depart! Then you and the sheep can have the hills to yourself!" And her gaze went deliberately over the red-coated English soldiers.

Someone snickered, then went still as Mr. Tilden stared at her. "Oh—you will say that, will you?" he roared across the space between them. "You speak as a Highlander, do you? You're not one of them! You are an Englishwoman, and the daughter of an Englishman." A curl of triumph came on his mouth. She sensed the words he would say before he said them, and dismay filled her. She had tried him too far. The fuse on his temper was short.

"Do you know who this woman is?" he cried to the crowd.

One man dared to say, "She is the wife of the Frazer of Frazer."

"Oh, yes, she is his wife! Married for her money, for what good it will do him!" cried Mr. Tilden in a shrill high voice. He waved his whip at the crowd. "But her name before marriage was Fiona Cartwright! Yes, yes, Cartwright! And her father before her was Hugo Horace Cartwright, the same that bought the lands of the Clan Frazer when they were confiscate! Yes, he bought the lands, and he drove you from your crofts! It was his orders that caused the burning!"

There was a dead silence as the gazes of the people swung from Mr. Tilden to Fiona. She felt the gathering turned on her. She could say nothing.

"Yes, yes, it was his orders that caused us to burn the crofts! Have to obey orders from the Englishman that bought the Frazer lands!" crowed Mr. Tilden, his mean eyes blazing. "And it was his orders that brought in the sheep! And it is his daughter that sits there in a fine carriage, with silks on her back, and jewels on her hands, bought with the money from the sheep! Aye, look at her, Fiona Cartwright! Daughter of the man I obeyed until the day he died and left all to his stupid daughter!"

The muttering began in the crowd, the women whispering, keening, the men growling. Jamie Frazer rode forward, his red hair flaming in the sunlight.

It was Margaret who spoke, clearly. "And it is her compassion that brought us back to the Highlands. It was her good, kind mind that thought of starting the looms—which Tilden burned! And it is with her money that we shall go to Canada, to begin again where we are not hated and despised! Do not listen to Tilden. Whatever happened to us—"

Her words were drowned out by the growing roar of the crowd. They began to surge forward, toward the carriage holding Fiona, Margaret, and Mrs. Owens. Jamie Frazer grabbed the bit of the lead horse, and forced it forward, and into a run.

"Go, go, go!" he yelled, and the horses raced along the dusty village street, and out into the dense woods beyond. Fiona was gripping the seat with both hands in order not to be thrown out. Jamie was racing after them. But not the English soldiers. Fiona could hear Mr. Tilden's laughter following them.

Jamie escorted them back to the island and saw them safely into the castle. Then he came to Fiona, bonnet in hand. "I will go to the Frazer on his way to Glasgow, and beg him to return," he said somberly. "There will be more trouble, mistress." His blue eyes studied hers, then his gaze dropped.

"Yes, go after him," she said quietly. "Tell him what happened. I will await him here."

His feet shuffled. "I promised him I would stay with

you and protect you while he was gone," he said, troubled. "Yet, I would go after him, for I fear there will be much anger when the word goes about the glen—who you are—"

"Yes, I understand," she said, her heart feeling like cold stone. They would all hate her now. The people should have been told early, and let the hate be done with. There was no time now.

Jamie bowed, and left her, and she wrapped her cloak about her and went out. She sat for a long time on the bench before the ruined castle, staring at the lake as the sunset came and made the waters glow orange and then darkly purple.

Would there be no end to the hate? Did Wallace himself feel hate for her, down beneath the passion he felt for her?

Chapter Thirteen

The days and nights seemed so long. Fiona would
sit outdoors, or when it rained she would sit inside,
staring at the fire. There was no work to do. She heard
the Scots whispering about her, staring at her, distant
from her, grave.

Margaret would come with her sewing or knitting
and sit for a time, not talking, just comforting with her
presence. Mrs. Frazer was ill in bed from a cold and
aching in her bones, and Margaret sometimes attended
on her.

Fiona was restless and tense. What would happen?
She wished Wallace would return soon, but no word
came from him. It was a long distance over the hills
and valleys to Glasgow, and he had much to attend to
there.

One fine morning, she decided on impulse to go out
in the carriage to find some of the hill folk and talk to
them. It was mad, yet she thought she would talk
to them and persuade them that she meant no harm to

them. Must she be condemned for the sins of her father?

She called Mrs. Owens to her and said they would go out for an airing. Mrs. Owens frowned in worry, but bowed in obedience. "As you will, Mrs. Frazer," she said.

She would not take the Scots with her. She called two of her English servants, a coachman and a footman, and had them row her and Mrs. Owens across to the land. There they hooked up the horses, who were in fine fettle.

"I shall come with you, madam?" asked the coachman, worried.

"No, I'll keep to the paths, thank you. We shall return before dusk."

"Aye, madam," he said. He did not like it here, it made him nervous, she knew that. Her English servants were increasingly uneasy in the midst of the Scots people. They heard the gossip, the whispers, about what had been done to the Scots by the English, and the fierce looks confirmed their belief they were not being welcomed here.

Fiona took the reins with more confidence than she felt. She held her blue black head high. She wore her tartan cloak, fastened with the Cairngorm brooch Wallace had given to her.

Mrs. Owens sat beside her in the high seat of the fashionable carriage. She clutched her black cloak about her and looked about uneasily. But she said nothing. Where Fiona went, she would go.

They set out. The coachman and footman watched them go, then settled down to wait their return. They had brought thick slabs of bread and cheese with them, and fishing lines. They would amuse themselves against her return.

It was a beautiful April morning. The birds were singing in the glen, sunlight glinted off the greening trees. The first flowers glowed shyly in the sunshine, golden and reds and pinks. Fiona drew a deep breath of the crisp air that seemed to chill her lungs, and exhilarate her at the same moment. Her cheeks bloomed.

"Ah, this is better, I felt much depressed at the rainstorms we had," she was saying to Mrs. Owens as they drove along.

"Aye, mistress. The storms here are hideous, the winds blustering among the hills and threatening to blow the castle roof from our heads," said Mrs. Owens. She herself liked the more gentle scenes and lands of Yorkshire.

"It is a violent land," said Fiona. The horses were fresh, they had not been exercised for three days. She had trouble holding the reins, they bit into her gloved hands.

They drove along the shadowy grass-grown paths, and up into the hills. She watched carefully for signs of life, and finally in the spring trees she spotted a red tartan. She began to pull up the horses.

She called out gladly, "It is I, the wife of the Frazer! Will you not come down and talk to me? I would speak of the new lands—"

A masculine voice called out hoarsely, "You are not a Frazer! You are Cartwright, and English!"

She felt chilled. They had greeted her warily before, but the children had given her shy smiles, the women had come to know her and talk more freely.

She tried again. "You know me! I have tried to help you; you know what I have tried to do—"

"Your father burned our houses about our heads!" one man cried. She realized suddenly that men were coming down from the hills, ragged, desperate men, with not a woman or child among them. Mrs. Owens clutched her arm.

"Come away, come away, mistress!" she urged. "I do not like their looks!"

Fiona did not either. She thought they had been drinking, their faces were red as their cloaks, they waved their claymores, and some staggered as they walked.

She raised the reins to cluck the horses on. In that

moment, someone let fly with a stone and hit one of the horses. The horses jerked and broke into a run along the uncertain path.

Fiona fought the reins, trying to keep control of the frightened horses. Another stone sang through the air and struck the carriage. Another, and another, then a hail of stone, as they scooped up pebbles and flung them at her wildly.

Mrs. Owens gasped and fell backward into the body of the carriage, her skirts flying up about her legs.

"Mrs. Owens!" cried Fiona, sparing a quick glance at the abigail. The woman's eyes were closed, blood sprang out of her face. Even as Fiona's head turned, a stone came at her, and hit her on the forehead.

It stung, it hurt like fire. Blood began to trickle down into her eyes.

The horses were racing along the path now, driven by fear. She blinked the blood from her eyes and forced herself to think only of keeping the carriage upright as it swayed from side to side.

Now they were out of range of the stones, but the shouts and obscene words and yells followed them for a distance. She found the shore path along the loch and followed it until she could turn about and race along the sandy shore back to the castle.

She felt dazed, incredulous, so shocked that she could not think. In her life, she had known coldness, fury, the beatings of her father. But nothing had prepared her for this mindless, cruel stoning by her husband's people. To have so many turn on her!

She was in a panic, shaking like a leaf; she could scarcely control herself, to say nothing of the horses. They felt it and were in more of a frenzy than before.

She could not look back again at Mrs. Owens. The poor woman's legs were on the seat, she lay on her back in the carriage body, quite limp. Was she dead?

Fiona brushed again at her forehead, her glove came away dark red with blood. There was a constant stream down into one eye. She blinked it away, brushed at it with her cloak. When the castle came in view, she looked at it with dizzy view, it was her refuge.

The coachman and footman sprang up from their fishing, lines forgotten. They ran to catch the heads and bits of the wild horses and dragged them to a stop. The footman held the bits, soothing the horses, while the coachman came to help Fiona down.

"Mistress, mistress, what has happened to you? Did them wild folks hit you?"

"Stoned," she said briefly, wearily. She got down, her hands on his sturdy shoulders, and sagged as she came to the ground. She held onto him for moments, while she got her breath. She could not stop trembling.

When she could stand alone, he lifted Mrs. Owens down. She was unconscious, face white, stained with her own blood. He lifted her into one of the boats and rowed them back to the island. The footman remained to soothe and wipe down the terrified horses.

At the landing, the English footmen and a maid came running. The Scots held back. Fiona looked up, brushing the blood from her eyes, and saw their faces, the faces of those who were her husband's people. She thought she saw a gloomy sort of satisfaction there. And they held back, they did not come to her.

Something crystallized inside her, something grew hard and stony cold. She was not wanted here, they hated her. Even Wallace was gone, and sent no word.

He wanted her money, he was sweet to her for the money, she thought bitterly. Her head high, she walked into the castle.

Margaret sped down the stone stairs, gasped when she saw Fiona. "Ach! What is it, then? What ha' ye done?"

"I went riding, to talk to your people," said Fiona bitterly. "They greeted me—warmly!" She pointed to her head. "Mrs. Owens, there, is still unconscious by their welcome."

Margaret eyed her gravely, worriedly, and drew her to sit down while she bathed her forehead and set a bandage about it. Mrs. Owens was bathed and her wounds examined. She was finally able to speak, and began to weep in fright.

The English servants were muttering among themselves, and drawing back from the Scots. The Scots stood with dark faces, impassive, yet Fiona imagined a sort of triumph in their looks. One Englishwoman hurt—some sort of vengeance!

She knew she was not rational, she knew she should stop and think, but she could not. Her husband was gone, he had no plans for her beyond the use of her money. She could endure no more. They all hated her. Well—she would go. Where she was secure, and welcome, she thought.

She ordered a woman to pack for her. The woman went silently to do so. Margaret tried to protest. Fiona turned to her.

"I will leave with you my tartan cloak, and this brooch," she said. She removed the brooch, of the fine silver chasing and the beautiful smoky quartz stone. "Pray, give it to Wallace. He will know the meaning. Tell him his people hate me, I cannot remain."

"Do but stay, and talk wi' him," Margaret urged gently. "You are afrightened and hurt. Do but stay until he comes again. The Frazer will speak to his people."

"And try to persuade them to accept me? It would be a task beyond him!" Fiona snapped bitterly.

Mrs. Owens was eager to be gone, so was Fiona, and all the English servants. By the next morning, they were packed, the three carriages were loaded, and in the dawn light, Fiona set out. Mrs. Owens was faint, Fiona drew rugs about her, and sat beside her as they set out. Margaret had come ashore to see them off, and stood, in her red tartan cloak, to watch them depart. Sholto, who had remained behind at the castle by Wallace's orders to help guard them, had brought his pipes ashore. He lifted the mouthpiece to his lips as the carriages were started up.

The wild wailing of the pipes rang in Fiona's ears as they drew away from the shore. She thought them a mockery, the triumph of the Scots over the English. She heard the singing and the ringing of the pipes for a long distance, until finally there was no more sound.

The English carried weapons, horse pistols at their fists, swords at their belts, and nervous glances alert as they rode through the dim woods. They knew the way, in general, and they would ride south out of this forsaken land until they had left it. They swore it to each other, whispering out of the sides of their mouths, glancing at their mistress where she sat in the back of the barouche, profile cold and stern.

The white bandage on her head made them furious. The Scots had done this to her. They had dared to stone her! They were well away from this horrible menacing wilderness.

The end of the first day found them at Inverness. The coachman, more resourceful once away from his master, found them comfortable lodging for the night. The next morning, they ate porridge and eggs, drank heavy black tea, and were off early, hoping to make the border by nightfall.

Fiona found her hands full with her ill abigail. The woman vomited several times, apologizing weakly to her mistress, weeping at the shame of it, that madam had to take care of her instead of her caring for her mistress.

"Do not worry, dear Mrs. Owens, I should never have brought you north," said Fiona, bathing her face with cool water from an icy hill stream as they paused.

The illness delayed them. They were still miles from the border when darkness overtook them. Rather than risk going into a small Scottish village, they slept the night on rugs on the damp grass, and both Fiona and Mrs. Owens were ill the next morning, from colds and stiff joints.

One of the footmen had ridden into the nearest village, imitated Scottish talk, and bought some hot oatcakes and sausages grilled on a spit. They ate them, grateful for the hot tea with the food, loaded up the carriages, and went on their way.

They were over the border by late afternoon then, and well on the way to Yorkshire.

It was the next day that they reached home. The gentle rolling green hills, the desolate moors had never looked so fine to Fiona. This was her homeland, this was her refuge. She sighed with relief when the manor door was opened to them. A footman had ridden ahead on horseback to warn them the mistress was coming, and a warm, concerned welcome from the few servants there waited them.

Never had warm beds and home walls seemed so good. No weary traveler returning from a long journey was more glad to be at home, and in his own walls and walking in his own garden. Fiona strolled about the grounds, talking to the housekeeper, issued orders, and packed again for the journey on to London.

There were too many memories here. She would turn the corner of the path and think to find Wallace striding to meet her, weary from a day in the fields, or from hunting. The horses were rested, and ready to ride on.

Mrs. Owens recovered enough to ride on, she bravely reassured Fiona of that. "Yes, indeed, where you wish to go, dear Mrs. Frazer. I shall not be so weak this time."

Also they had cards from Lord Morney. He had heard they had returned, and wished to call upon them. Fiona grimaced in anger. Lord Morney was about the last person she wished to see, recalling his treachery in writing to Phineas Tilden, his bill in the House of Lords taking the Scottish lands from her, and all he had done before.

No. In London, she might be able to approach some important, influential lord, or the prince regent himself, and have her lands restored to her. That was one gift she might give to Wallace. Why did she think of him? she berated herself. He gave little enough thought to her! Yet now that she was more calm, she thought again of Wallace. She wanted to help him—perhaps in

London she could do more good for him than in Scotland, where his people hated her.

She put her hand to her forehead. The scar had not yet healed, and sometimes her head pained her. The welcome of her husband's people, once they had learned her true identity! She would never be one of them.

They would never accept her. They hated her, with a wild passion related to all the past centuries; she could not defeat and overcome that hate.

She could not look into the future, and she was too weary even to consider the present.

She would go to London, and so she went, leaving no note for anyone, even the kindly squire who had called once. Squire Reid had been blusteringly angry when he saw Fiona's forehead.

"Why dast do that to you, Mrs. Frazer? I'll take a sword to them myself!" he had raged.

"Let be, let be," she had said wearily. "Do take my regards to your good wife and children." And she had offered him tea and cut the conversation short, pleading weariness.

She and Mrs. Owens set off for London within three days of arriving at Yorkshire. She would go to her godmother's town house, to be cosseted and comforted. There she might gather up the threads of her life and decide what to do next.

She could not seem to think clearly. She felt deserted, cut off from her husband and his people. All she had was her godmother, and the thought of the spritely white-haired woman, her gentle face, and soothing spirit drew Fiona.

She would go to Mrs. Trent and rest with her for a time.

The horses were put to the barouche and the other carriages, and they set out in stately manner for London once more.

Chapter Fourteen

Jamie Frazer came to Wallace in Glasgow as Wallace was trying to hire a ship and finding little help from the suspicious English captains. They wanted money in down payment for the voyage, especially since he wished to hire all the places on the ship for his people.

He had been thinking, desperately, that money had to pay for all. If one did not have money, he had nothing, no respect, no consideration, no honor. He in his shabby tartans was an object of suspicion on the waterfront. Several first mates even tried to press him onto their crews.

"Let be, let be," he told them haughtily. "I am here to hire a ship, not to sail one!"

Yet they watched him off the dock, striding into the office, their hands on their hips, watching, eyes narrowed.

Jamie came to him at his lodgings near the waterfront. Frazers crowded several houses nearby. They waited for word of sailing, eager, yet not counting on anything. Women washed the clothes and cooked the food, the children played on the wharf, wary eyes out for any press gangs, for they would even take young boys to work the ships.

"Ye best come hame to the castle," Jamie told him briefly when Wallace had returned to the lodging that night. He stood, so tall and red head high, waiting for his chief. "That odious Tilden—he told the clan that the Frazer's wife is a Cartwright. There be murmurs in the glen, talk against her. They be that bitter."

Wallace stared at him, then gave a groan and an obscene word or two. He ruffled his red hair. More problems. "I must go back to her, but nothing has been settled. I hoped to send word to her so that money might be sent from London to pay for hire of a ship."

His thoughts went to Fiona. She would be terrified, he thought. She was gently bred—English bred! He felt a curious chill even yet when he thought of her father and herself. He loved her with passion, yet when he was away from her, his mind recalled the many horrors that father had visited on him and his people.

The crofts burned about their heads. The castle wantonly burned, the paintings ruined, the tapestries torn down and burned. The Highlanders ran off the land, the sheep moved in in their stead. "Highlanders turn no profit, sheep do," as the crude saying went.

And he had served ably, though unwillingly, when forced into their regiments! He thought of the years in the army, the years in the Peninsular wars, the final horror of the Battle of Waterloo, when so many brave tartan-clad men had been mowed down by cannon and rifle.

Yet—he could not help his people without money, and Fiona had the money. She must not be scared away. His mouth turned rueful and grim as he thought of his own plans. Yes, he desired, loved, wanted her. But he needed her money!

"I must go back," he said, and they went the next day, just him and Jamie Frazer, riding through the small towns and villages, along the Great Glen, and off to the Highlands.

They arrived on a rainy, stormy night, when great gusts of wind blew through the pines and oaks and made the sturdiest trees sway. The little animals had gone to hiding, their horses shivered, heads down, against the blinding pelting of the rain. Wallace Frazer and Jamie had their cloaks wrapped about them, yet were soaked through to the bone by the time they reached the shore opposite their own island.

Jamie lit a torch, waved it, and soon a boat came over for them. The Scotsmen cheered softly to see their chief returning.

"It is a good night for your returning," one said as the salt spray beat into his tanned face.

Wallace grinned, and took their hands in turn before springing into the boat. "How goes all? Is it well?" he asked eagerly.

They were silent, bending to the oars. He repeated his question. "Is all well with ye and with my house?"

Sholto finally muttered, "The lady Margaret, she will tell ye of the happenings."

His heart seemed to turn cold and stop for a moment. "And my own lady Fiona? My lady Frazer?" he asked. "How is she?" Could she be dead, and all were frightened? They would not have dared—

"The lady Margaret, she will tell ye," said Sholto again. "I did pipe her away, when she left," he hastened to add, with a sigh. "She didna turn her head to listen, nor to lift her hand."

"Left?" burst out Wallace incredulously. "She has left me?"

They were silent, rowing more sturdily, to get him there the faster, before his rare anger burst on their heads.

At the castle, Wallace swept in; his rain-drenched cloak, dripping, was cast into the hallway, and he went into the drawing room where the fire burned. Margaret stood to wait upon him. She greeted him, with a kiss of his cheek.

"You are wet—do go and get on dry clothes, my dear Frazer," she said gently.

"Nay. Tell me first."

"It is a long story, and ye will wish to hear the all of it," she insisted.

"Is Fiona gone?"

"Aye," she said. "She has returned home—to England."

His red head drooped, he went without a word up to his bedroom. He dried himself, and put on fresh clothing, rubbed his wet red head with a towel, all unnoticing of the warmth and comfort after the cold, long ride.

He then went to his mother's bedroom, greeted her, noted with deep concern how frail and ill she looked, and refrained from questioning her.

"My dear son—home," she quavered, and smiled at him.

"Aye, mother. All will be well," he said gently, not believing it ever. All had gone ill for them for years, why should it change and be good now? He thought it bitterly and went draggingly down the stone stairs to the drawing room. Margaret had set a small table, with hot soup for him, and bread and cheese, and a good dram of Scotch. When he came in, she took the hot poker, and thrust it into the mug of liquor, so that it sizzled and steamed. He drank it off, and felt the burning warmth go through him.

He sat down to the meal. Margaret sat opposite him, filling his mug again, and supplying the bread as he wished. There were no words between them until he had finished. She was aye an understanding woman, he thought.

But Fiona!

He pushed himself back from the table and fixed his gaze on her. "Now, the tale of it," he said.

She nodded soberly, her blue eyes so like his, steady and firm of look. "Aye. Jamie will ha' told ye of the day when we rode into the village, and Tilden—God blast him—burst out with his spiteful tale of how your lady is the daughter of the Cartwright. Aye?"

"Aye. And what then?"

"Your good lady brooded over it many a day and night, she slept little, I am thinking." Margaret went on to tell him of how she had gone out in the carriage, how she had returned. Wallace listened with head erect, his gaze on his sister's face as she told the story.

Margaret has sympathy for Fiona, she likes her, he thought. She told the story well, with her poetic words.

"Aye, she was bitter wi' it," she concluded. "I couldna blame her, though I begged her to remain and speak wi' ye about the matter. But fire burned in her heart, and shone in her eye, and she couldna separate ye from your clan, and blamin' ye for being gone this time. She is not secure in her love, I'm thinking, if ye will forgive me for being so personal, Wallace."

He touched her worn hand gently on the table and nodded. "Ye are right, we are not secure in each other, being strangers at times. But we love, and it shall come right," he added firmly and saw the relief lighting her eyes.

She told how the stones had injured Fiona and her abigail, and his brow darkened. His fists clenched on the table. "I'll beat them with my claymore, daring to attack my wife!" he raged.

"They are but ignorant folk, and red and wild with drink, and worn with the running and the hiding," Margaret said gently. "Yet, how my heart did keen when I saw the blood running down her dear pretty face, and the daze in her bonny violet eyes, like the spring flowers."

He hit his fist against the table, and the dishes clattered. "I'll go out tomorrow and speak to them, aye, and more than speak! They shall be punished for daring to stone my wife—my wife!"

He slept little that night, for all his weariness. He rose early. The clan would know he had returned, they had their watchers. He dressed with dignity, in full clan dress, with black velvet suit and white ruffled shirt, and his red tartan dried and cleaned. He fastened the Cairngorm brooch to his shoulder. He had the smaller brooch Fiona had left to him, and he fastened that also below his own. That she should have left it to him, and her tartan cloak! It made his heart ache, both his pride as a husband, and his grief that she should have felt so desperately unwanted.

Jamie, Ossian, and Sholto came with him that day. They rode about the glen, and he talked to the clan wherever he found them. He raved at them in tone like thunder, he told them about his dear wife, and how gentle and good she was.

"But she is daughter of the man who burned us out!" one man dared to reply.

"Aye," said a woman, "and her all dressed in London fashion, and smart bonnets, riding among us!"

Wallace glared at her. "And with my tartan plaid about her body, and my Cairngorm brooch protecting her heart! And you dared to stone her—the Frazer's wife!" He lashed them with his tongue, and they bent their heads meekly.

"What will ye do with us?" asked one woman. "Will ye leave us, then, to return to your English wife?" The words were bitter. The others were listening, wary with him.

He quieted. "I had planned to take all of you would go with me—to the new world, to Canada, to start again. Now—I do not know. I ha' not the money to do it, without the money of my wife," he said, brutally frank. "Whether she will pay for this, I know not. All I know is, she is my wife, body of my body, heart of my heart, and I will go after her. I will discover if she will forgive you, my people, or if we must be strangers to each other!"

They stared after him as he rode off. They did not call after him, but they looked thoughtful. And they were sober today.

"Would ye do it?" asked Ossian gravely.

"What?"

"Leave us entirely? Frazer of Frazer? Will ye refrain

from leading us again? We shall be as lost sheep," he said sadly, his red head uncovered, his hair blowing in the wind.

Wallace sighed. "I storm and rage, but I canna put off my people. I will return again, but when, I do not know," he said.

He remained at home only two days and set off with only Jamie to accompany him, south to England, to Yorkshire. They rode nights and rested days, half-hidden in the bracken against the English soldiers, who were all too willing to set up a fight against any Scots with fine horses and weapons.

He reached Fiona's Yorkshire home in three days, but she was not there. The housekeeper made him welcome, though, she and the others liked this grave-eyed Scotsman with the hard, bitter lines about his mouth, and the soft speech with them. He had gone through much, they said to each other.

"She was gone to London, to her godmother," said the housekeeper.

Wallace Frazer went to the squire, who made him welcome. They talked a bit, and the squire told of his fury. "Aye, how it made me furious to see the wound on the fair forehead of Mrs. Frazer," he said frankly. "I would have cursed your people, yet I know of the deep bitterness there. Will it never end?"

"I do not know. But I must go after my wife. Said she aught to you—of her plans, of where she went?"

"She said nothing to me."

"I am grateful to you," said Wallace after a pause. "I hear you have looked after the lands and helped Mr. Proudfoot to manage the cattle sales. It is good of you."

"The lands are vast, they need much care," said the squire carefully, puffing at his long pipe. "Will you not come back to Yorkshire and care for them? Mr. Proudfoot can do much, but he has not the authority to do all that should be done."

Another burden. Wallace's shoulders felt heavy with them. "I will think on it, I thank ye," he said, and departed after a fine tea and a pleasant talk with Mrs. Reid.

It was unfortunate that as Wallace was leaving the squire's, Lord Morney should ride up with Captain Ainsworth. No doubt, he thought later, they had seen Jamie at guard before the house, unmistakable with his height and flaming head.

"Ah, you have come chasing after your runaway wife," smiled Lord Morney, tapping his whip on the saddlehorn before him.

Wallace stiffened and eyed him with that deliberately blank expression he had used so often during the wars under this officer. "Good afternoon, sir, I must be off."

"Not so fast!" he drawled, and waved his hand at the village. "Why do you not have a cup with me? We'll adjourn to that pub, it is quite decent, though small."

"I canna stay today, I regret, my lord."

"I am telling you, I wish to speak with you!"

"Not today, my lord."

"Oh, very well, I'll say it in public, then! It's a poor man who cannot hold his wife! But I could have told you before you married that the marriage would not last! A poor Scotsman and a rich Englishwoman! And a frigid woman at that!" Lord Morney grinned down at him tauntingly from his high perch on the fine black horse. Captain Ainsworth did not look amused, he gasped, and his horse moved with his restlessness.

Wallace stiffened with rage. His head went back. He was no sergeant under this major now! "You'll keep your tongue off my wife!" he blazed. "Look to your own household, my lord! I'll mind mine!"

Lord Morney laughed, pleased to have drawn a response. The whip went snap, snap against the saddle, and his horse shifted in alarm at the sound over his head.

"No one expected the marriage to last," he went on, with his lazy drawl. "There is passion in you, though you hide it well—yes, I schooled you well, Frazer! You had good training in my hands! But the passion in you wasn't matched by the ice maiden you married! I could have told you she was cold!"

Involuntarily, in spite of his anger, Wallace thought of the passionate nights, with Fiona in his arms, under his hands, moaning with desire, wild with her rising ecstasy. He half smiled, and Lord Morney watched him sharply.

"It is not your concern, my lord," he said. "Now I bid you good day."

"Not so fast!" Lord Morney was bored, this was the first exciting encounter he had had in a week. He was about ready to go to London to stir up more trouble, he was so bored. He moved his horse to cut off Wallace's approach to his horse. Jamie moved forward, protectively, his hand to his sword. "I'll have more speech with you! What about the lands in Scotland? Has the factor taken them over under my direction?"

Wallace came to a halt, his angry temper ready to boil over. So Lord Morney was going to take over those lands, was he? Then he remembered—he and his people were leaving, God and Fiona willing! He would leave the empty glen, the silent hills, the implacable mountains and cold storms to Lord Morney—and let him do his worst! There would be no people there to taunt and bully!

He put his hands on his hips, looking up at Lord Morney dispassionately. The blond hair was lanky and limp, the green eyes bleary with too many late nights and too much drink. He was developing a pot belly also, the long years of campaigning were over, and with them his strong, muscular form was dissolving into fat. Wallace ran his gaze down over the form insultingly. Morney flushed, and raised the whip. Wallace stared at him.

"Aye? So ye will have the Frazer lands, my lord?" asked Wallace calmly. "I wish ye joy of them. Oh, and look to your factor, keep a close eye on him. He has been known to keep back monies, and to cheat his master before this!" He smiled, knowing the barb was going home.

He pushed at the horse's head and went past to his own mount. Morney shouted at him. "Stay here! Do not disobey me! Stand fast! I would hear more of this!"

Wallace swung into his saddle easily. He thought of the beautiful stallion he had lost to Morney and Jenks. "I have no reason to *obey* you, my lord," he mocked. "I am not in your service now. But only that of my lady, whom I love—with passion! I bid you good day, I am anxious to ride on to follow her!" And he smiled, and swung his horse away.

People in the street were staring curiously at them, pausing in elaborately casual little groups, muttering to each other, obviously listening.

Morney shouted after him. "If you catch up with your cold lady, I wish you pleasure in her! She is all ice! And she will not hand out money freely to your poor ragged Scots people! Her father earned it too dearly. She will not fling it away! I am sorry that your marriage has turned out so poorly!" And he flung back his head and laughed aloud.

People gasped, stared at Wallace in surprise and with pity. His mouth tightened, but he did not try to answer. He swung his horse away to face Captain Ainsworth who had said little up to now.

The captain looked troubled, his brown eyes worried. "I say, my sympathy, Frazer. I did not know all this—I wish you well in the marriage—you have my best wishes—"

"Keep them," said Frazer savagely. "And to the devil with ye both!"

And off he rode, with Jamie racing after him on the tall horse that was the only one that could carry him. Lord Morney's mocking laughter rolled after them as they thundered up the dusty street of the village, with all staring after them.

Chapter Fifteen

April turned to May as Wallace traveled down from Yorkshire to London with Jamie at his heels. People in the villages they passed stared at the two red-haired Scots, but the men did not stop in any town.

They ate cold bread and cheese and slept nights in the fields, wrapped in their plaids, as they had for many a year, in and out of campaigns.

Wallace was trying to think ahead, to figure out what might happen. He felt helpless. He loved his wife, though he felt so chilled about her birth. Yet he loved his people, obstinate and difficult though they were. His clan was his responsibility, he owed them his life work, his heart, his mind. He was Frazer of Frazer.

Many a clan chief had given up and flung away his duties. Many a former chief closed his eyes to the plight of his people, said, "I can do no more for them, it is against the laws of England," and gave himself to thinking of his own close family alone. Many a clan had dissolved, their members scattered like lost sheep.

A few clan heads had even taken back their lands and put in sheep, as the English had.

However, from the time Wallace Frazer was a wee small lad, he had had his own servant, his own piper. His father had instilled in him by words and by example what it meant to be responsible for hundreds of people. His duties in wartime had increased his sense of what it meant to be chief over men, how he might direct them, how he might keep them safe even in times of battle. He must be clever in maneuvers, close-mouthed before the English, noble in battle, always at the front of his troops, spying out the land before them, always thinking ahead—

The burden never left him, it was part of his head and shoulders, it lay heavy on him waking and sleeping. And he had added a wife to his burdens, and that duty puzzled the man. Where did his duties and chivalry to her end, and that to his people take hold? Were they one and the same? How could he manage to reconcile the two which seemed so opposite?

When they arrived in London in late afternoon, instead of going to Mrs. Trent's town house, Wallace and Jamie proceeded to the boardinghouse where they had lived before. The woman made them welcome, though her house was full. She put out two quarrelsome men with much aplomb and put Wallace and Jamie in their room as soon as she had had a manservant to clean it thoroughly.

"No trouble, they are pigs in a sty," she said cheerfully and sat them down to hot meat and drinks as they waited.

She had a maid to wash their clothing, and a man to clean their boots. By morning, they were fresh and alert once more, ready to start out.

They proceeded to Mrs. Trent's home. Jamie took up his stance outside the door, bonneted head high, beside the elderly white-wigged footman. They exchanged a few wary but kindly words—they knew each other—and Jamie settled down to wait.

Fiona was not at home. Mrs. Trent told him at once,

taking one of his big tanned hands in both her own little ones. "My dearest Frazer!" she exclaimed. "If I had but known you were coming—and why do you not stay with us?"

"I must speak with my wife first. Where is she?" He glanced about, saw reassuring signs of her presence in the house, a blue shawl tossed over a chair, one of her bonnets on a table, cards in a bowl on the hall table bearing her name.

"Out early and late," sighed Mrs. Trent. "She does her best in your cause, my dear man, do not fret for that. Today she went the morning to the solicitors, they are pursuing the matter of the Frazer lands in the glen. She thinks to get them back for you, yet the signs are not hopeful for that. Someone else has requested them, and paid."

"Aye. Lord Morney," said Wallace grimly, settling down gratefully into a large chair near the fireplace. The house, though small, was homely and cheery, with flowered chairs, light draperies at the windows, a warmth to it.

"That dreadful man!" exclaimed Mrs. Trent, toasting her small feet at the fender, and looking as fierce as her daintiness would manage. She seemed a delicate porcelain doll, more so today, with a tiny white lace bonnet on her white hair, a violet flower sprigged dress setting off her blue eyes. "Ugh, I detest him, he makes me feel—unclean!"

Wallace managed a smile, for all his desperate feelings. "Aye, that is a good word for it. As though swamps were about, and little pesky whining bugs flitting through the air and biting their little stings."

"Precisely. Dear me, whatever shall you do?" She gazed at him in anxious sympathy.

He leaned back his red head, feeling at home and at rest for the first time in a month. "First, I must talk to Fiona. Has she recovered—from the head injury?" he asked anxiously.

"To her head, yes, but not to her heart. She droops too much for my liking," said Mrs. Trent frankly.

"Now you are here, she shall recover quickly, I am sure."

"I could hope so," he said, rubbing his red head with a fretful hand. "I ha' scolded my people, pointed out their errors, told them I will ha' no more of such foul deeds. And against my ain wife!" He looked quite fierce.

"It sticks in their craw that she is English, so Fiona tells me," she said gently, and it drew him out.

"Oh, aye, and in mine, I am afraid," he said, meeting her bluntness with his own. "I love her, she is beautiful to my heart. Yet—when I think who her father was, and how she lived a life of ease and luxury while my people starved—"

They were silent for a little time. He stirred restlessly, she was studying him gravely.

He said, "When does she return?"

"Not until evening, I fear. She lunches with a baron who might do your cause some good. His wife is kind, and sympathetic to the Scots, having a cousin who married into a Scots family. She wears herself to the bone, flitting from one person to another, from one office to another, trying to find someone who will help her get the lands back, and restoring some employment to the Highlands."

"I fear it will do no good. Lord Morney holds to whatever he manages to steal," said Frazer bitterly. "I think Canada is our best chance to start afresh, away from our beloved lands, and the bitterness that follows us still."

"And your own bitterness, Mr. Frazer?" Mrs. Trent asked gently. "I think you hold Fiona's parentage and wealth against her, knowing little of what she herself endured."

He lifted his head from brooding contemplation of the fire and gazed at the little Dresden doll beside him. "You have hinted before of her suffering. She tells me nothing about it. Will you not speak to me of something of this life?" he asked anxiously. "It stands between us that I know nothing of what she was as a

170

child, as a girl. And I fear I have been so busy with my people, I have not questioned her as I should, to make more understanding between us."

"She will not willingly speak of it, yet you should know," sighed Mrs. Trent. "I knew, because of my closeness to her mother, my dearest Glynis. How she suffered! How she must have suffered, looking down from heaven, where she surely went, to see her daughter so abused by that Cartwright!" And her blue eyes flashed with unusual temper.

"Abused?" asked Wallace slowly, and his big fists clenched on the arms of the chair. "Tell me of it."

"It is time you should know. Fiona has shut it from herself and does not mention it. Perhaps she thinks I know little. However—" She settled herself in the chair and proceeded. "My dearest Glynis was a friend of my childhood and girlhood. She was married off to Hugo Horace Cartwright when she was but seventeen, her family was poor, he was becoming wealthy, and seemed entranced with lovely young Glynis. Indeed, at their wedding, I felt hopeful of the match, for he was gentle and enamored of her."

Wallace listened quietly as she went on, after a thoughtful pause. Her small feet on the fender tapped a little in her agitation, then her discipline of years held her still.

"I went to their home in Yorkshire when Fiona was born. She was christened Fiona Elizabeth, after me, and I held the small babe in my arms in the church, and how good she was, small and wee and sweet." She smiled in reminiscence. "I think the first few years were good. But he was a hard man, Cartwright. He drove himself and others. He had acquired the Frazer lands, as I discovered later, and went up there to oversee their disposition. Then, he became harder, for no son came, and Glynis was often ill. She had two still-births, I don't know how many other—accidents," she said delicately.

Wallace nodded, watching her face alertly, anxiously. "Yes, and so?"

"Dear little Glynis died when Fiona was seven, in another stillbirth. It would have been a son," said Mrs. Trent, with regret. "That might have pleased Hugo Cartwright. The loss enraged him and turned him hard and angry. I was no longer welcome there. I insisted on going, and stayed with the rector there sometimes, just to see my Fiona. At twelve—" She stopped, and put her hand on her face. "Dear me, I still get so distressed," she said, in a choked little voice.

"Tell me," Wallace insisted gently, iron behind his tone. He felt he was coming to the heart of the mystery behind his wife's reserve.

"Yes, yes. It seemed that Hugo had no wish to marry again. He—indulged himself—with village maids. There was a girl in the household, quite a nice little girl, of whom Fiona was fond. She played with Fiona, they rode together, a nice girl of fourteen. Cartwright conceived a momentary passion for her and tried to lock her into his bedroom against—the night. Fiona rescued her and helped her get away to her uncle's, a place on a farm far from Cartwright's reach. I was arriving, quite innocent of all these developments. He refused me entrance, I got in the back way by connivance of a devoted housekeeper—he since turned her off. I found Fiona—in her room. She lay face down on her bed, stoical, not weeping. Her back was in ribbons," and Mrs. Trent's voice faltered. "He had whipped her mercilessly. And it was not the first time. He seemed—he had the habit of whipping her."

"My—God—" whispered Wallace, shocked and stunned. "He—whipped her—a small wee girl—"

"Yes, I found marks of old beatings on her back. I tried to take her away with me, he refused to let her go. She was, after all, his heir, and he meant to beat her into shape, he told me, enjoying my displeasure and grief. He seemed to turn on all those days, on all." She stopped and sat quietly, her hands on her heart until she felt more calm.

Wallace bit his lips, he wanted to cry out in rage against such treatment. He knew men beat their sons sometimes—but a girl? A delicate, beautiful girl like Fiona— "And he did—continue with this?" he asked, in a strangled voice.

"Yes. I tried to help her, my efforts enraged him, and I had to desist. It would but reflect on Fiona and make her sufferings worse. I told her to stay away from him when he drank, not to defy him, to meet his fury with meekness, to keep her own temper calm. She learned to show a cool face to him, to avoid him, to keep herself icy calm. It was not easy for her, a spirited girl, but she managed to do so. And she made herself useful, in the household, helping the housekeeper, instructing the maids, even learning to prepare his favorite dishes, to deflect his growing senseless furies. And—two years ago—a little more now—he went to some horse fair, bargained for an animal, and lost, lost his temper, and fell down raving. It killed him, he died before he reached home."

Wallace drew a deep breath, schooling the fury inside him. The man was dead, and thank God for it. But now he knew the secret of those marks on his wife's back, the chill calm of her manner, the unusual discipline of her control of herself. Such a girlhood, deprived of a mother's love, and her godmother's must be at a distance. Enduring the mad beatings of a man going insane, keeping herself within herself—

"I have often thought, since your marriage," Mrs. Trent finally continued, after a long silence. "I have often considered what irony God visits on us his people. Cartwright caused much suffering among your Scots people and yourself. He and his factor were cruel and brutal. And Cartwright treated Fiona in such a way also, with brutal savagery. And now the money he reluctantly left to her, his only heir, must go to help relieve their sufferings. I said as much to dear Fiona the other evening. Fate makes a pattern, we follow it, and sometimes it leads us along surprising paths, don't you agree?"

"Aye. Surprising paths," he said, liking that. He

thought of Lord Morney, the way he had interfered in his own life, the challenge he had issued, which had resulted in Wallace's marriage to Fiona. "I can but hope it comes to some good ending," he sighed. "My people have suffered much—so has my wife."

Mrs. Trent smiled and patted his big hand timidly, like a small bird pecking anxiously for a crumb. He turned his hand and clasped hers. "You will treat her—more gently?" she asked. "Her happiness is more dear to me than my own."

"Oh, aye, I shall," he said solemnly. He felt as though his heart had softened utterly to Fiona, now knowing what she had suffered. He wanted to make up that misery to her. They sat and talked for a long time that morning, and over luncheon, in the pretty, sunny sitting room. She told him stories of Fiona, opening to him all the little incidents which revealed the girl's character to her husband.

Fiona's carriage returned about four o'clock. Wallace had been watching anxiously for her, and walked out the door as soon as he saw it driving up. He saw Fiona's bent head, in the blue straw bonnet, with a fine, brave blue ribbon on it. But her face when she lifted it at his greeting was strained and pale.

She stared, not believing her eyes.

"My dear," he said, and helped her from the carriage. He helped Mrs. Owens down, then turned back to Fiona, tucked her hand in his arm and escorted her into the house. They walked into the sitting room, which Mrs. Trent had tactfully left to them. Mrs. Owens went upstairs to rejoice with Fiona's godmother that Mr. Frazer had returned.

Fiona's hands were cold. Wallace stripped off her gloves and chafed the hands in his. Her gaze had not left his during the time, and her violet eyes were solemn.

"You came," she said softly.

"Aye. Once I had heard. Jamie came for me. Oh, my dear one, how sick at heart I was when I heard. I

174

pray your forgiveness for my misguided people. I gave them a tongue-lashing, and longed to put a stick at their stiff backs for the stoning of—of my dearest wife." He swallowed. She had put off her bonnet, and he saw the red scar still visible on her white forehead. He touched it gently.

"You came," she said again. "Oh—Wallace—"

"Aye." He drew her to sit down with him on the comfortable sofa. Her head went naturally to his shoulder, and he held her in his arm, and stroked back her dark hair. She shuddered in relief and seemed to wilt against him. "And I find my wife, running about London, trying to do good for those who harmed her."

"I have tried and tried, Wallace," she said, her voice dragging. "My solicitors had worked on the problem, they are eager to help, and most angry at the action taken against us. Yet we keep running against a stone wall. No one in power will listen to us."

"Not for the Scots, I warrant." He said it dispassionately, not liking to upset her tonight, or ever again. The poor wee bairn, he thought of the picture her godmother had painted of her lying on her stomach, stoically enduring the lashes on her back, the blood running down— "I think it best for us to remove to Canada. Ha' ye a mind to that removal?"

"Whatever you decide, Wallace," she said. "However, there are the Yorkshire lands. What shall we do with them?"

"Tomorrow, or another time, we shall decide it," he said. He kept stroking her head soothingly, his fingers running through the thick, dark hair. "How I missed ye," he whispered. "My heart aches sore for ye."

She turned up her face. "And mine—for you." He pressed a kiss on her cheek, moved his lips slowly to hers, where they clung for a long moment. Then he put his cheek against hers, and they sat there for a time, gazing into the heart of the fire, soaking in the goodness of being together once more.

After a tactful interval, Mrs. Trent returned to have

tea with them. It was night before Wallace could talk to Fiona alone again. He wanted to question why she had run away, why she had not trusted him to take care of matters. But not tonight, while both were so weary.

He sent Jamie to pay the kind landlady, and they moved into Mrs. Trent's house again. He slept in the small room next to Fiona's, while her abigail removed herself to a servant's room.

He had thought he would not ask Fiona to sleep with him until they had talked things out and come to some agreement. He would know her heart, and tell her his.

During the next days, they talked together, tentatively at first, then more openly. She was distressed that Mrs. Trent had told him of the early years. "I wished to forget them, Wallace," she said.

"I wanted to hear, to know more about my wife." he told her gently. "There had been some mystery about, and I was puzzled. Now I feel I know you better, that is good."

They talked about his people, he sensed she was sore of heart still about the stoning, and he did not blame her. His own anger flared up inside him when he thought of it.

He went out with Fiona, saw the solicitors, and had their pessimistic verdict about the chances of recovering the Frazer lands. "They have been sold to a Lord Morney, Mr. Frazer. He claims possession of them, and the Crown supports his claim. He has the ear of the prince regent, who finds his cynical wit amusing," sighed one man, shaking his white head. "Sad, that, when the law of England is flouted to make way for a rogue. But on the subject of Scotland and the lands of the Scots, many in England close their minds, and live on prejudice."

Mr. Proudfoot wrote, asking questions about what to do with some horses, and the fields that had been sowed with wheat. Fiona and Wallace consulted about it, worrying about whether to return to Yorkshire so soon, or try to remain in London in the hope of doing some good here.

They grew closer in their common problems. And one night he allowed his pride to be stilled that she had left him, and he went to her bed.

He looked down at her in the light of the single bed candle beside her and marveled at her loveliness, her blue black hair in a cloud about her face, her slim form in the violet silk nightdress trimmed in the fine white lace she liked.

He blew out the candle and lay down beside her and felt her move shyly yet eagerly into his arms. His big hand stroked down over her rounded softness, and he felt the same desire rise in him, more tender and devoted than before, yet hot and passionate, wildly beating at his control.

He kissed her from her forehead, lingering over the little scar, down to her straight nose, around to her cheeks, and to the sensitive lobe of her ear. Her hand moved over his bare arm, fingering the hard, muscled upper arm, to his shoulder.

"Ah, it has been—such a time," she whispered.

"Such a long time—too long—"

His mouth found the soft curve of her throat, around to the pulse that beat at its base, down to the shadowy valley between her breasts. He laid his head on her breast and kissed the perfumed sweetness there, his hand under her body, stroking slowly up and down her back. He remembered those scars, and hot anger at her father overcame him for a moment, so that he stiffened.

"What is it?"

"The past," he said. "Will it always hurt us so? Do ye hate thinking of the past?"

"The past no longer matters to me, now I have you," she said, so low, he scarcely could hear the words. "Happiness—wipes out the pain—I never thought to be happy—"

His heart was humbled again at her humility, at the trust she put in him against the odds.

"I would make the rest of your life so happy, my love," he whispered, "that you would never feel a moment of pain again."

She put her hand gently on his lips. "All life has its pain. How else would we know that we have pleasure? It is the contrast, the pain and the pleasure, the joy and the grief. I do not begrudge pain its moments, so long as you stay with me, and give me the joy of loving me."

It was so generous that tears flicked in his eyes, and he had to blink them away. "Ah, me love, my joy, my heart," he said against her shoulder.

He drew over on her, and they came together, so sweetly that it made them both catch breath. It was more close than they had ever been, for body matched body, and also mind to mind, so they were one body and one mind and heart, together in that bed that night. Never so close before, never so desirous of being a part of the other.

She was wild in his arms, at the last, moving under him, clutching at him, moaning her pleasure in little gasps of delight. He groaned, also, with the deep release of the emotion and built-up passion. When he finally lay back, they were out of breath, unable to speak, clinging with wet hands and arms and legs.

Incongruously, as he lay back, spent, he thought of Lord Morney wishing him joy of the Snow Maiden! He gave a little chuckle, and Fiona at once asked, "What is it, why do you laugh?" She sounded puzzled.

He could not say his thoughts, he did not welcome the thought of Lord Morney so near his bed anyway! He said, "Ye are so delightsome, my ain wife. I am so happy. No matter what happens, no problem is too big that we cannot solve it together."

She cuddled close to him and rubbed her cheek on his arm. "Aye, we can do anything—together," she agreed sleepily.

And he lay there, grinning like a fool, he thought, at

the joy she had brought him, and the thought of Lord Morney's haughty, disdainful face, his amazement should he be able to peep into that bedroom! No Snow Maiden was his Fiona!

Chapter Sixteen

Fiona and Wallace finally came to the reluctant conclusion that they could do the Frazer cause little good in London, not at that time, in that climate of opinion.

One of the elderly solicitors told them gravely, "Our one hope, I fear, is that the said Lord Morney, owner now of the lands, is without heir. One day, when he is dead, if his wife does not remarry, and is without issue, the lands might revert to the English Crown. In that case, you might then apply for restoration of them."

"All that seems rather distant and remote," sighed Fiona.

"Yes, I fear that it is. However, we will put in claim for financial remuncration for the taking of the lands. The law courts move slowly, yet one day there might be some money received from them. We will continue to work on the case for you."

And in the meantime, the Yorkshire lands demanded their care. Fiona knew that Wallace was reluctant to return there, he hated the thought of being so close to Lord Morney and his home. Yet they must go. Mr. Proudfoot could not carry on alone forever.

So they packed up, bade farewell to Mrs. Trent, who wished to remain out the London season for the sake of the concerts and plays. Fiona had no heart for merry-making, and was glad to quit smoky and smelly London for the June countryside she loved.

Wallace rode in the great barouche with her, while Mrs. Owens, the maids and footmen took care of the other carriages and the luggage. Part of the time, Fiona rode with Wallace's arm about her, to ease the jolts along the rough roads, and her heart sang for his tenderness and concern.

He had become different to her. He was no longer seized with fits of melancholy and remoteness. He opened his mind to her, and they spoke freely on many matters. He consulted with her anxiously to make sure they were in agreement on what to do. In short, he was a devoted husband, as loving in daylight as in nighttime in their bed.

She felt the difference in him joyously. If only she had confided in him earlier! But something in her still cringed at thought of the early days of her young life. She hated thinking and speaking of those horrible times, when she had merely endured from one day to the next, trying to keep out of her father's path, anxious to shield the maids from him, keep the grooms from his tempers, making all go smoothly so he had little cause for his ungovernable tempers.

All that was past, she thought, leaning her head on Wallace's shoulder as they gazed at the English countryside. The hedges seemed to glow with primroses and pink hedge roses. The lilacs were almost finished, but other flowers and peonies bloomed in gardens, the wheat was green, the paddocks rich with grass.

They arrived home in good time, and Mr. and Mrs. Proudfoot greeted them happily. "Oh, it is good that you came, you will enjoy the English spring," they said. "And the summer promises fair. Squire and Mrs. Reid inquired of you at church, and we were able to tell them you would return home shortly. They will be calling upon you."

Fiona smiled and thanked her but later turned to Wallace. "I do not feel social," she said slowly. "It would be the same again, Lord Morney and his hatefulness. Could we not plead some reluctance? Could we not refuse invitations?"

"I have no wish to see that lot again," said Wallace, a hard line about his mouth. "Let us hope they will be away for the summer."

They learned Lord Morney had been in the Highlands, discharging his factor, one Phineas Tilden, for cheating him. That did amuse and please them. "Fate grinds slowly, but exceeding well," murmured Fiona.

Then Lord Morney had gone off to London for the season. They hoped to see little of him. They set to work, and Wallace was out daily, from morning to dusk, with Mr. Proudfoot, inspecting the lands, ordering some damming of a stream where it overflowed. There were the sheep to count, the horses to be considered. Should some be sold? Did they need so many to fill that enormous stable?

Fiona worked happily about the home, though always with the thought in the back of her mind that they might leave and emigrate to Canada. Would she miss this house? Perhaps, a little. But she had known heavy sorrows and pain here, as well as her new delights. No, she liked the house itself, but she would not be sorry to leave it.

She had not spoken again to Wallace about emigration. She was timid about inquiring, and thought he would speak of it when he was ready. When he spoke of the clan, he would frown, and she knew he was still angry with those who had stoned her.

They had not been home above two weeks, when a great procession startled them. Half a dozen Highlanders in full regalia riding down the road, with three full carriages of ladies, trunks, hatboxes, and Margaret Frazer leaning out a window and a rare smile on her lips as she waved frantically to them.

Wallace's mother and sister had come. Anxious about Fiona, concerned about the marriage, his mother had risen from her sickbed, said, "It is spring, I can travel and I shall," and ordered the carriages set up.

They had had to travel slowly, but they had made the journey, and Fiona hugged her mother-in-law tenderly, then put her right to bed in a warm, comfortable room. "How could you risk the journey?" she scolded. "But I am so glad to see you!"

The fragile little Mrs. Frazer smiled up wearily from her white pillows, no whiter than her delicate face, and said, "But we had to come. Dearest Fiona, how sick I was to hear of that cruel stoning. Have ye forgiven us for such a dreadful thing?"

Fiona bent and kissed the thin cheek. "I never held it against you," she said simply. "Now, rest and sleep, and tomorrow we shall converse as much as you like!"

Margaret sat up with them for a time, chatting of events in the glen. Morney's men had come, with their master a-ranting and a-raving, as Margaret said, gleams of humor in her blue eyes. He had pounced on the books of the factor, one said who had been there. The accounts had sent him into a driveling fury, and out went Tilden into the stormy night, according to Margaret.

"No one was sorry to see him go. But the man in his place is aye so cruel again. The clan hides, the men are in grumbling anger, and the women keening. I think no one wishes to remain in sight of the new factor, nor will any take work wi' him. Aye, many went off to Glasgow, and await the coming of the Frazer of Frazer," and she looked to Wallace.

He was rubbing his chin and frowning in thought. "I dinna ken what to do as yet," he said. "I ha' been sa busy with the farms here."

"Aye, there be time," she said, comfortable as could be.

Mrs. Frazer and Margaret settled into the routine of the house. Margaret insisted gently on helping with the duties, and her deft hand with the maids, her presence in the kitchen freed Fiona to ride out with her husband to inspect the lands.

Squire and Mrs. Reid came to call, they received them, liking them. But they were not at home to the county, Fiona had no wish to open doors for Lord Morney to walk in. They accepted no invitations to dine out, making the work their excuse. They had been gone all the winter, said Wallace to any he might meet in his rare visits to the village on errands of supply: "Maybe in the winter there may be time."

Fiona did not approach the village at all. She confided in Margaret she had no wish to take up acquaintance that might be broken as quickly. "I do not know what Wallace will decide, but I am thinking it will be Canada. He is not happy here, he will not be happy in the Highlands with Lord Morney's men about."

"I have heard that Canada is no sich bad a place," said Margaret. "I talked wi' a lady who came back to visit her old mither, and persuaded her to come back with her. A land of rich earth and blue skies, much like ours, with hills and bonny rivers flowing, and a thousand sheep on the hills, and no man to call another servant."

"It sounds good," said Fiona thoughtfully, and they talked some together about the prospects of life in a new land. Yet—could Fiona go with the Clan Frazer? Would they still hate and resent her for what her father brought on them?

Mrs. Rose Frazer came to Fiona one day as Fiona worked on accounts in her sunny little sitting room at the back of the house. Fiona looked up to see the fragile gray-haired lady hesitating in the doorway. She jumped to her feet.

"Come in, come, sit down, please! Should you be walking up and down stairs?" she reproached.

"I had to see you and talk wi' ye alone," said Wallace's mother. "There was something on me mind."

Fiona saw her seated comfortably on a sofa, with cushions at her back, and an embroidered footstool under her small feet. Then she sat down opposite her. "Now, are you quite happy?" she smiled.

The little lady did not smile, she surveyed Fiona's face with troubled look. "My dearest daughter," she said gently. "I am so sore of heart about the things my people did to ye. I had to question ye about them. I do hear but a bit here and a bit there, and nobody to tell me the truth of it. Did the Frazer men really stone ye? Could they be so gone in drink they would strike the wife of the Frazer?"

Fiona's face shadowed. She hesitated, then told her the truth of it. She concluded, "I think it was my fault for going out when they were—upset and not knowing where to turn. They saw me only as English, and daughter of an enemy."

Mrs. Frazer sighed, her hand on her heart. Fiona wondered anxiously if this was all too much for her.

"I pray ye will not hold it against them. When men are desperate, their wives sa thin and worn, and their bonny children pale and weak with hunger—they be wild men," she said simply. "Do ye hold it against us all?"

Fiona bent to her and took the frail hand in hers and put it to her cheek. "No, not any more," she said honestly. "Wallace's love is much to me, and the love of Margaret and you. His men cleave to him and are honorable to me. No, it was the work of a few wild, desperate men, as you say. I will not hold it against them."

They talked a little longer, and Mrs. Frazer was comforted. She came and sat with them more evenings and seemed better of health and spirits, to Fiona's relief.

One afternoon, they heard that Lord Morney had returned. He dared to come riding up to the house, and try to enter. The English butler refused him entrance, standing stiff and formal. "I regret, my lord, they are not receiving this summer. They have that much work to do."

Lord Morney was furious, and about to take a whip

to him, but Jamie came out and glared at him, and he and Captain Jenks and Captain Ainsworth rode off. Kate Grenville, Lady Morney, then tried to call and leave her card. The butler took her card but told the same tale that the Frazers were not receiving that summer, to his regret. She was smiling and gracious, sending sharp curious looks at the house, as though hopeful of seeing some glimpse of them.

It was Margaret Frazer, to their surprise, who involuntarily received one of them. She was in the gardens, dreamily leaning on the sundial, with a basket of roses in her hand, enjoying the cool morning.

Captain Benedict Ainsworth rode up and swung from his horse just outside the gate to the garden. He strode in eagerly, ignoring the house, the servants, just going into the garden, as though the sight of the red-haired girl with the roses drew him like a star.

"Miss Margaret! I had hoped to see you one day! This is my lucky hour!" He came up to her. She stood upright, startled, a wary look to her. He took her free hand, caught it up to her lips before she could wrench it away. His lips lingered on the hand.

"Sir!" she said haughtily.

"How beautiful you are, like the morning!" he breathed. She stared up at him, the tall slim form, the brown hair, the eager brown eyes. Away from his mentor, Lord Morney, he seemed to lose the dissipated look, the mocking smile he copied.

"We are not receiving, sir," she said, drawing back.

"I know, I know, I shall not be formal," he said impatiently. "I heard you had come, I longed to see you. When shall you be at home to the county?" He took one of the yellow roses from the basket and put it to his lips, not taking his gaze from her fresh pink-cheeked face.

"We shall not be at home—this summer, sir," she said. She looked about uneasily, but on that side of the house, with no one at the windows, no rescue was in sight.

She drew herself up.

"I must go inside, and arrange the flowers," she said.

He stood in her path, not boldly, but definitely, smiling. "Do not go in yet, the day is so lovely," he said, his eyes giving the compliment to her face and form. "May I call upon you one day, perhaps on Sunday afternoon?"

"Sir, I am not at home to anyone."

His face grew more serious. "I heard about the Frazer lands. I say, I am sorry about that. I told Lord Morney I thought he had gone too far with the matter. To take lands from Mrs. Frazer! And Frazer was a good chap in the service, a fine soldier."

He sounded sincere, she could not fault him for that. As she hesitated, he coaxed, "Will you not invite me to remain for tea? I would speak further with you on the matter. I told Lord Morney I thought he should give back the lands. He was furious with me and almost threw me from his house."

"It was good of you to take our part," she said evenly, not quite knowing whether to believe him. "I canna invite ye to tea, sir, no one is at home."

"On Sunday afternoon, then, may I come?"

She hesitated again, then said, with sweet disarming frankness, "We do not mean to be at home to Lord Morney, nor Lady Morney, nor Captain Jenks. My sister canna like them, nor do I, and so I think—"

"I shall not tell them!" he said impetuously. "Pray, let me come! I would speak with Wallace Frazer about the Frazer lands. What I know of the matter. Will he not let me tell him of that?"

She bit her lips. He pressed the matter.

"I pray you, I shall be good and not cause a quarrel between us," and he smiled with a likable manner, warm, brown eyes shining. "I would be friends with your brother, I like him immensely. He saved my life twice, you know."

"He did?"

"Yes, once in the Peninsula, when I was surrounded by Frenchies. Another time, at Waterloo, when I thought I was gone. He dragged me free from my fallen horse, took me up behind him, and got me off the field until I could get another horse and go back."

She studied him gravely. He was the kind of man she could have liked—but that he was English. Fine, brave, not bragging. He had gone back into battle—that counted for her. She knew of men who had run away and had not been found until after, paralyzed by fear.

Impulsively, she said, "Come, then, about three on Sunday. But I warn ye—if Lord Morney accompanies ye—the door shall be tight shut!"

He caught her hand, kissed it, and let it go, so quickly she had no time to protest. "You are too good and kind, Miss Frazer! I will wait anxiously for Sunday. The days will be long and gray until then!"

He would have stayed on, talking, teasing, flirting with her, making court with his eyes, but she dismissed him finally, shaking her red head at him severely, and going into the house with her basket of roses. He had kept the one yellow rose, however, and had it in his hand as he mounted his horse at the gate.

Wallace received him reluctantly on that Sunday. Mrs. Frazer came to study him with shrewd eyes. Fiona sat back and let them talk, for Captain Ainsworth kept his word and told Wallace what he knew of the matter of the Frazer lands. He confirmed much of what they had heard by rumor. Morney did not really want the Highland lands, he had done it to spite Wallace Frazer, and now found himself with a burden on his shoulders. And his wife Kate was furiously angry with him for spending money on stupid lands, as she called them, when she might have had more for jewels and fine dresses.

"Perhaps you might buy them back from him," said the captain hopefully, looking sideways at Margaret.

Wallace shook his head, Fiona said nothing. Margaret knew their thoughts. The lands had been taken from them once, confiscate to the Crown, and could be taken again. It would be throwing money away.

The duty done, he turned to his courtship of Margaret. The girl found it rather delightful, suspicious though she was of him, to hear teasing compliments, to find him springing up when she stood, to see him put a cushion to her mother's back, gallantly. He was a gay charmer, when away from Lord Morney. They could not forget his close association with the man, however.

Fiona drew him on shrewdly to tell of his brother and his family. "Ah," he shrugged. "That brother of mine—he wants nothing to do with me. When he had no sons, he suspected I was after the property, it is entailed, you know. But now he has four sons, and three daughters, there is no worry, is there? Yet I am not welcome at Fairlands. We have had no correspondence for these two years. To him, I am a burden, for he is ten years older, and had my schooling to pay for when I was a lad. He still throws it up to me." He laughed, but Margaret sensed the hurt behind it.

He was groping to find a home and family of his own, she thought. The poor younger brother, what a curse it could be, for the laws of inheritance fell harshly on the younger ones. If the elder did not care, then the younger went poor.

When he reluctantly took his leave after two hours, he turned to Margaret. "You will see me to the gate?" he asked.

Wallace lifted his head sharply, glared at Margaret, but she stood and shook out her ruffled green skirts. "I will see ye to the gate," she said, and went out with him through the open French windows, avoiding the hallway and the stiff butler.

They strolled through the garden. Benedict Ainsworth kept staring down at her, scarcely noticing how he went, over grass or path. She finally took his sleeve and guided him to the path.

"We shall not thank ye to trample all the wee grass," she said severely.

"Oh, I am sorry! Forgive me!" He looked down at his great brown boots sheepishly.

"Nay, nay, it is no matter."

"May I come again tomorrow morning?" he asked eagerly.

She caught her breath. His face was open, transparent. He wished to court her. They could not even be friends, she thought sadly. She shook her head.

"Why not? Tuesday, then? I am free all the day."

"It would be best if ye do not come again, Captain," she said, not wanting to hurt him. "My brother canna like any man who consorts with Lord Morney."

"He has been good to me these years," said Ainsworth. "I know he can be cruel and hard, and the lands matter is no light one. Yet—he was good to me and keeps me in his circle. I have few friends without him. May I not come to see you anyway?"

She stood her ground and turned to face him, looking up at him with clear blue eyes. She saw few signs of dissipation about him—yet he rode with Lord Morney.

And he was English.

"Sir, ye are English, I am Scots, and my people have suffered much. I canna see ye, nor take ye seriously. I am sorry, sir."

His face darkened, she thought he would be furious. He stood biting his lips and gazing down at her, then he put out his hand. She kept still, and he put his fingers gently on her cheek.

"You are very lovely, Margaret. I would see you again."

"It is best not, sir."

"Let me come one morning, and just talk with you."

"It is to no purpose."

"Roses are to no purpose," he said quietly. "A lark singing in a blue sky and piercing the heart is to no purpose. Yet it gives comfort to a sore heart—"

She shook her head, in silence, the red curls flying about her white neck. She saw him look at the neck and the curls as though he wished to touch them, and she grew afraid—not of him, but of herself, and her too-soft heart.

"I bid you good day, sir."

"Because I am English—and friend of Lord Morney?"

"Aye, it is so."

He bent his head and went slowly down the winding path to his horse. She watched him ride away and felt a little pang in her. There went a lonely man.

Chapter Seventeen

The Frazers tried to keep to themselves that June and into the warm days of July. They were busy with the house and farms, it was not difficult to refuse invitations. Yet Squire and Mrs. Reid were eager to meet with them, they had them to dinner twice.

"We must do something," sighed Fiona to Margaret one day. "It is difficult to remain strangers in the county, when we know everyone. I could wish we would sell up and go. Yet—if Wallace wishes to keep these lands—I do not know."

"Aye, it is difficult," said Margaret, a droop to her young mouth. Fiona wondered if she thought of Captain Ainsworth, a personable young man, though in bad company.

Kate Grenville, Lady Morney, called again when Fiona was alone. Fiona hesitated, her mouth compressed. She was about to instruct the butler to turn the lady away, when Lady Morney swept in past him.

"I will come in," she said gaily, smiling. "Dear Mrs.

Frazer, do let me talk to you! I have apologies to make to you! Dear Morney has acted so abominably, I did not speak to him for a week!"

Fiona stood up stiffly, nodded to the butler, and he departed. She did not send for Margaret, and Wallace was off on the lands.

"Pray, be seated, Lady Morney," she said coolly. "How cool and lovely you do look today."

"You are too kind to say so," smiled Kate Grenville, settling her pale green ruffled skirts. Her tall blond form moved so gracefully, her hands waved so languidly she would catch the eye anywhere. Today in her green and cream bonnet, her face looked unusually lovely, with the smile on her red lips instead of the usual discontent.

"We had not meant to receive this summer, I beg you will excuse us. There is so much to do, and we are not socially inclined." Fiona meant to make that clear.

"I know. And you are furious with Lord Morney! So am I!" Lady Morney, confessing, with her head on one side, and a twinkle in her green eyes, was difficult to resist. "When I heard that he had forced you from your Scottish lands and bought them, I was livid with him! Not just for your sake, dear Mrs. Frazer. But for my own! What did he want with those horrid wild lands? I asked him. Just for spite, and he could not deny that! Indeed, I believe he is already sorry that he did so."

She chatted on in that manner for a half an hour, drank some tea which Fiona requested for them. When she stood up to leave, she put her hand briefly on Fiona's arm.

"Dear Mrs. Frazer, do not let us be strangers to each other," she said seriously. "There are few enough in the county of our rank, and most of them are such—bores!" She wrinkled up her nose. "I miss London frightfully, yet Derek must return to Yorkshire, and so must I, to take care of our property. If it were not for kind Mrs. Reid, I should go mad! And now if you will befriend me, I shall be happy!"

Fiona smiled in a strained manner and bade her farewell. She told Wallace that evening of the encounter in a troubled manner. "I felt sorry for her, my dear," she said. "I cannot really like her, yet she made a real effort today to be friendly and kind. And she told me of the Scottish lands, that Lord Morney finds them a burden to him, and regrets having purchased them."

"Hummm," said Wallace, frowning. "I would mistrust the lady. Yet, mayhap she is lonely here. She has few friends of her standing. Her reputation, however, is not the best."

"I shall not receive her again, if you do not wish."

"It is as *you* wish, my dear," he said. "If she amused you, let it be. But I do not wish to exchange visits with Lord Morney! It will be difficult to receive one, and not the other."

When Kate Grenville came again several days later, Fiona was of two minds as to whether to receive her. Yet—she had been most gracious in her apologies for her husband's conduct. She finally asked the butler to show her in.

This time, Mrs. Grenville was in fine form. She had brought some London gazettes with her and gossiped happily about mutual acquaintances, and was so amusing that she had Fiona laughing with her. She told the latest on-dits of the prince regent, her green eyes sparkled as she talked of one matter and another, and she left reluctantly after an hour.

"It has quite made my week to talk with you, dear Fiona!" she exclaimed as she rose to leave. "You will allow me to call you by your name, will you not? And you must call me Kate! Derek scowls at me for coming to visit, but I shall not mind him. He has his own cronies, and I have mine!" Though she laughed, her eyes were sad, and she bit her lips.

"Of course—Kate. And do come again when you have the time."

"You are too good!" the lady exclaimed as she left, with a wave of her white-gloved hand.

She came again in another week and had the new London gazettes which she left with Fiona, "to amuse you," she said. She had also some dress patterns on which she wished Fiona's opinion. Was the neckline too daring? Would the county endure the latest in fashion? And what did Fiona think of the bonnet line here? It was flattering to be asked her opinion as though it mattered.

They were beginning to feel isolated here. Kate Grenville's visits were rather welcome to Fiona. She even brought her news of Mrs. Trent, a friend had called on Mrs. Trent, and written to Kate that she had attended a concert with her. Fiona was glad of the news and resolved to write her again soon.

Yet—they missed the social events of the county. Fiona had accepted no invitations to the county events, the summer cotillion, the squire's garden party, the children's end-of-school pageant. They were quite left out, on Wallace's wishes.

Fiona began to wonder if it was right. They were, after all, one of the chief families of the district. Lord and Lady Morney dutifully attended all of the events, bored though they might be. They were, many of them, his tenants, he had the livings of the five churches in his care, he gave generous gifts to the churches and schools.

She thought, We also have duties here. My father attended to them, much as he hated all the running around. She could remember his presence on the platform of political events, his reading of the Scripture at church, his solemn face at weddings and funerals, at christenings and openings of civic buildings.

She could not bring herself to speak to Wallace. He seemed to prefer a solitary life. He worried about his clansmen and the glen, he seemed to feel no duties toward the English.

Fiona began to wonder if he was right, or if he should be urged gently toward consideration of new duties here. Margaret was absorbed in her care of her mother, the household chores, and the gardening which she enjoyed so much. Fiona set down her pen and brooded over the household accounts.

Was this all there was to life? She thought of Kate Grenville's witty account of the town hall opening, and the funny events and serious speeches that had occurred. The Frazers should have been there.

Margaret said, that evening, something about missing the life in the glen. "We used to have singings," she said wistfully. "And the dancing—remember the dancing, Wallace? We should teach Fiona the ways of the Highland dances," she added.

Wallace smiled. "All in good time," he said. "Do ye miss the London dances, my dear?" he asked Fiona.

She grimaced at herself and nodded. "I confess I do. It was at a dance that we met first, Wallace, remember?"

He smiled across at her. "Could I ever forget?" he asked gently. "How beautiful and untouched you looked."

"Perhaps—this autumn—if we remain—we should receive again," said Fiona timidly, watching his face warily. "The Frazers have a position in the county, you know. I am sure Squire Reid would wish us to come to his annual summer cotillion, also. It is always in August."

Wallace turned aside to knock out his pipe against the mantel. His face was hidden from her. "That is the future, and I do not know it, my dear," he said, and his voice dragged.

Margaret stared down at her embroidery, and her hands did not move for a time. Finally she picked it up again and began putting in the tiny beautiful stitches in the butterfly and floral design of the pillow cover. Did she miss any gaiety? Fiona thought she did. She was young, lovely, had had a difficult, enclosed life. From her mention of the Highland singing and dancing, Fiona decided that Margaret also missed social events.

By the end of the summer, she must gently convert Wallace to her way of thinking, she decided. They could not remain enclosed forever in a cocoon of

196

selfishness. They owed duties to the county, and they owed each other a social debt to be neighborly and welcoming. They had not even visited any tenants of their own, leaving it to Mr. Proudfoot to convey requests for repairs or problems.

Fiona was thinking along those lines as she was out riding with her groom one afternoon. Wallace had turned off to inspect some fences, and she was turning toward home, when a carriage drew up behind them.

She and the groom rode aside to the verge to let the carriage pass. Instead it was pulled to a halt. Kate Grenville leaned out. She seemed quite excited, and hailed Fiona.

"My dear Fiona! Just the lady I wanted to see!"

Fiona smiled and rode up beside the carriage. She had misjudged Lady Morney, she thought. The woman could be quite pleasant and charming.

"How are you, Kate? What brings you out today?"

"Oh, poor dear Mrs. Reid!" exclaimed Kate. "I have just now heard—a broken leg and all those children! The household is quite distracted! I am riding over to offer my aid, if it is any good to them," she added with a grimace. "I am not that good with children—having none of my own—" And a wistful tinge came to the green eyes.

"Oh, dear me! How dreadful! I had not heard."

"It must have happened just this morning. I am riding over at once to see if I can be of assistance. Would you like to come with me? I am sure you are better with children than I! You have such a nice pretty voice, and children always like that."

Fiona was not immune to such flattery, and besides she liked Mrs. Reid immensely. She gave her reins to the groom and accepted his offer of a help down. She got up into the carriage with Kate.

"Oh, this is very good of you," said Kate, after Fiona had told the groom to tell her household she would not be back until she had seen to Mrs. Reid's comfort. Lady Morney nodded to her own coachman, and she settled back in the carriage beside Fiona. "I am afraid I am hopeless with children. I suppose the best thing will be to assist in hiring someone in the village to help. Do you know of anyone who is free to do so?"

They discussed that matter for a little time. Fiona was so absorbed, she really did not notice where they were traveling. She sat up with a start when they reached a deserted tavern in the midst of the country, at a crossroads where two country roads met.

"But this is not the village! Kate—whatever is the matter? Your coachman is not driving—" Out of the tavern two men came, grinning.

Lord Morney and Captain Sidney Jenks.

Even then Fiona did not understand. She turned impatiently to Kate. "I have no time for visiting! We must be on to Mrs. Reid's—"

"Smart work, Kate," said Lord Morney, in his hateful drawl. He reached up and dragged Fiona from the carriage by her arm, and she felt it wrenched as he pulled her. She opened her mouth to scream. He clapped the other hand over her mouth.

Sidney Jenks helped him, lifting her easily in his rough hold. Kate sat laughing, then reached over as they struggled with the furious Fiona. She tapped her cheek with her whip, not lightly.

"Stupid woman! I said it would be easy, Derek! Enjoy yourself with her, my dear! I shall be amused by your account of it all!" And she laughed her shrill, cruel laugh and leaned back in the carriage.

Fiona's heart was beating so hard it hurt her. The two men were dragging her to the bleak, dirty tavern. There were no handymen in the stable yard, no one seemed about.

When they loosed her in the struggle, she screamed, and Lord Morney slapped her across the mouth. "Shut up," he said. "Be easy, and you'll enjoy it as much as we do. Eh, Jenks?" and he laughed coarsely.

She fought them angrily, fury giving her renewed strength. They tore her bodice in the pulling and pushing to get her into the tavern. The black hacking jacket was ripped from her back. Her hat went tumbling into the dusty yard. Her whip followed, when she tried to use it on one of them, hitting out wildly.

"I'll use my whip on you if you don't stop scratching," yelled Captain Jenks.

Lord Morney laughed. "I like a woman who fights. Makes it more enjoyable—after."

They dragged her to the stairs inside. The stairway was narrow, they panted and struggled as they fought her to get her up the stairs. She held herself rigid, caught her foot on the railing, and held until they wrenched it loose. Fear was fluttering in her throat, terror gripped her.

Those monsters! And Kate Grenville—fooling her into such a trap! She should have known better! Margaret was right—the English could not be trusted! These—her own people—could not be trusted! Lord Morney meant the worst by her, she knew that.

And Wallace—he would be so angry—would he cast her off? Spoiled goods! She could see it in his eyes—he was so honest, so good. Oh, God, what could she do?—

She fought and struggled, panting, in spite of the hard arms clamped about her.

"A sweet one," crowed Captain Jenks, in his hoarse voice, and she smelled the rum drink on his breath. He fondled her and Derek Grenville cursed him.

"Not now, you fool! Get her into the bedroom, safely locked in! Old Pete will be back betimes—come on!" They dragged and pushed and yanked her until her arms and legs felt as though they would come off, and got her into the bedroom. She clung to the lintel, resisting stubbornly. Her hat off, her hair flying about her face and shoulders—fire in her eyes—her cheeks flushed—

"By glory, she is a beauty!" cried Captain Jenks, pausing to admire her greedily.

"Frazer will kill you," she said coldly, her violet eyes flashing blue fire at them. "He will not stand for this, let me warn you! Let me go! He will be furious enough if I come to no harm—but if you—" She stammered to a halt before their sniggering faces. The contempt in their look, the greedy way they eyed her up and down—she felt dirty with their gazes, as well as their fondling hands.

"I say!" said another voice. Captain Benedict Ainsworth was coming up the stairs. "I found a lady's jacket in the yard. Have you got a woman up here—I say—it's Mrs. Frazer!" The voice changed to surprise and shock.

"Come in and shut up," said Lord Morney.

"But—Mrs. Frazer! Is she willing?—" began Benedict, staring at them in amazement.

"They tricked me here!" cried Fiona. "Frazer will kill you all! Let me go—you villains!"

"I say, she ain't willing," said the captain. "The lady ain't willing! Let her go." He tried to put a hand on Morney's arm. Morney turned on him with a snarl.

"You can join us or get out!" he said viciously.

Ainsworth stared at them all, last of all to Fiona, with her torn garments, her blue black head held high, the shame in her flushed face. "Mrs. Frazer, I'll take you home," he said, and offered his arm. "They are drunken, and do not know what they are doing."

She began to step forward, suspicious, but willing to risk his company. But Jenks knocked his arm down and shoved him from the room. "Get away!" cried Jenks. "You won't spoil our fun! And keep your trap shut!"

They fought with Fiona as she cried out. Jenks slammed the lock on the door, slammed the bolt home at the small, dirty door. And Fiona felt that the last friend she had in the world had departed as she heard Ainsworth's boots clattering down the stairs.

Chapter Eighteen

Wallace was riding slowly about the rim of the field, eyeing it critically. He could not get over how lush and green it was. How wheat flourished here, unlike the Highlands. All the lands seemed to give forth exuberantly, in the rich soil.

He heard a shrill yell, and looked up. Jamie was on the far side of the field, near the road, and now the man gave a wild Highland yell for danger.

Wallace lifted the reins and kicked the horse into a run. He raced around to the road to find Captain Ainsworth there, waving his arms distractedly, his face red and flushed.

"What is it?" asked Frazer sharply as soon as he was within hailing distance.

"Mrs. Frazer! At the crossroads tavern! Lord Morney has her! Come—at once—no time to lose!" And the captain turned his wet, trembling horse and started back along the road.

Wallace felt his heart drop out of him. He felt cold

and shaken. He could not believe it. Was this a trick? No, the anguish on young Ainsworth's face was real.

"Jamie, get the others," he said sharply and raced after Captain Ainsworth, down the dusty road toward the empty countryside.

Incredulous rage was twisting and turning in him, making him numb to the beauty of the wheatfields, the hedges of July roses, the flame lilies. He caught up with Ainsworth, the other's horse was tiring, yet he whipped it on as though mad.

"What happened?" he asked sharply as he came alongside.

"Don't know," gasped the young man. His face was red with exertion in the July sun. "Saw a woman's black jacket in the stable yard—went in—old Pete said—room upstairs—went up—Mrs. Frazer fighting them—"

"Them?" snapped Frazer.

"Lord Morney—Captain Jenks. Had her—her bodice ripped off—hair down—she was scratching and fighting—they shoved me out—locked and bolted the door—oh, God—"

Fury ripped through Wallace. He was so angry, so full of fear—for Fiona! His own beloved! In their hands! Those filthy, ravaging hands! His own fault! He should have ridden home with her, instead of leaving her with the groom— Always too absorbed in his work, neglecting her—oh, God, Fiona, he was groaning to himself as he whipped the horse.

Behind him, hoofs pounded. He turned slightly in the saddle. Jamie followed, and behind him raced Ossian, Rory, Sholto, their bonnets whipped from their heads, their red hair flaming in the sun, their claymores at the ready, as though for battle.

"How far?" he snapped at young Ainsworth.

"Another mile," gasped the young man. "I would have—got the stablehands to break in—could find nobody but old Pete—and him well paid to stay out of sight—"

"Planned, then?"

"God, I am afraid so—I did see Mrs. Grenville—Lady Morney—driving away in her carriage—she was laughing—"

Wallace's lips compressed. He stared ahead of him, blinking against the dust of the road. Rage was boiling in him, a red rage that clouded his sight.

"I say—" gasped Ainsworth.

"Yes?"

"Door locked and bolted—too much time to break it down."

"Any windows?"

"Two small ones—near the front of the tavern—"

It was like old days, against the French in the Peninsula. Planning a campaign, a battle plan against the riding. The hot blood was up, Ainsworth was gleaming-eyed, in a rage, like himself. Could he trust the man against his own friends? Yes, thought Wallace. He had ridden to the rescue—unless it was yet another plot!

He was close friends with Lord Morney—yet a decent enough chap. He must take the chance with Benedict Ainsworth—

Fiona. Wallace was groaning in his heart. His own beloved, who had undergone such torment and misery—to have another such torture—those two greedy bastards—those two—loose with women, evil—

The four Highlanders were not far behind them as Wallace and Benedict Ainsworth raced into the dusty stable yard before the small, grimy tavern. Wallace stared up at the windows grimly.

"Which ones?" he asked.

Ainsworth pointed. "The front room there on the right."

They were large enough. Jamie pounded up, the other three behind him. "Ladders," snapped Wallace. Jamie ran to the stable yard and came back with two.

The men were up the ladders, and Wallace raced into the building to the sound of their pounding at the windows. They had their claymores out, and as the two ran up the stairs, the sound of window glass smashing could be heard.

By the time they reached the locked and bolted door, Jamie and the others were inside the room. They could hear the cries, the yells, the sounds of swords slashing, steel on steel. Then Jamie was at the door, unlocking it, and opening it to his master.

Wallace went in, sword in hand, his face grim. His gaze went first to Fiona, rising from the bed, ashy white. She had a cup clutched in her hand, liquor had spilled over her torn bodice. Her eyes, wild at first, met him steadily.

"Ah, Frazer!" cried Lord Morney. "I have enjoyed your wife immensely!"

"That is a lie," said Fiona steadily. "I fainted, they gave me liquor when I roused, to—to warm me up— he said. Thank God you are in time!"

Wallace let out a grateful sigh. She met his look without flinching, and her petticoat beneath the torn skirt was intact. He believed her.

Captain Jenks was backing uneasily into a corner, his sword out, but eyeing the two Highlanders who loomed over him with wary black eyes.

Jamie had his sword to Morney's throat. "Should I finish him, Frazer?" he asked, as easily as though he would finish a stoat.

"Now, now, this is between gentlemen, I do not fight with rabble," said Lord Morney.

But Morney should not get off. He turned to him, sword upraised. "I'll take him, Jamie," Wallace said quietly.

"Not up here!" cried Morney. "The room is too small. Come now, as gentlemen! Let us set a time and place— Tomorrow, with seconds—"

And he would arrange all to his advantage, thought Wallace. As Morney had so often in the past. He would not wait for the clever bastard to set up one of his schemes. He well remembered that hill in Portugal, the young man with the sun in his eyes—

"We will go outside to the yard to discuss this," he

said. "Ossian, you will look to my lady." And he bowed to her, before he stood back for Jenks and Morney to follow Jamie from the room.

Ainsworth stood uneasily, out of breath, red of face, yet his brown eyes troubled. He followed them down the narrow stairs. Morney gave him a hard look.

"I didn't think you would be the babbling kind," he said. He gave him a sharp-toothed grin. "We learn as we live. You ran to the Frazer, did you? What favor do you think to get from him?"

"His respect," said Ainsworth simply.

Morney laughed, his shrill voice echoing through the tavern as they walked through. Once outside, he glanced about. The stablehands had miraculously reappeared, old Pete stood hunched near the horses, watching the gentlemen uneasily.

"Well, tomorrow, then, at dawn. I'll send you my seconds," said Morney easily. "And a doctor, yes, we must have a doctor—if you live to need one," and he laughed again and began to turn away.

"Nay," said Wallace. "We fight here. Now. Just the two of us."

Morney turned out sharply. His usually neat silk suit was disarranged—from fighting with Fiona Frazer. Wallace thought of that, and rage boiled up in him again. But he would not let anger blind him. He would fight the man, and kill him.

Morney saw that in his face, and stood back involuntarily. He recovered himself, laughed again. "Ah, no! I fear I am not ready."

"What man is ready for death to come for him?" asked Wallace somberly. From the corner of his eye, he saw Fiona in the doorway, Ossian at her hand. She had put on the torn skirt, arranged her hair swiftly into a sort of braid. On her back was Ossian's jacket, covering her bareness. She said not a word.

"Would you run to death before your lady's eyes?" jeered Morney. "Nay, tomorrow is time enough. It will give you the chance to write your will and sign it—"

"Now," said Wallace, and the stablehands shrank

back before the steel in his voice. "Ainsworth, I thank you for what ye did. Jenks, if ye interfere, it will be my sword in ye. Now—Morney—for all the nastiness ye have done to me and mine—I shall finish ye."

He set himself on guard, and Morney must do the same, after one last helpless look about. The man had courage, you must say that for him. But he liked not the odds. He always wanted them in his own favor.

The four Highlanders stood about, in casual but purposeful arrangements, one in each of four corners of the yard. Ossian kept to my lady's hand, ready to protect her with his drawn steel.

The stablehands gasped. Rarely did gentlemen put on such a show. They would have much to gossip about this night! Old Pete was not so sure. It would give his tavern a bad name. He should have thought before he accepted the coins to let the gentlemen have the tavern to themselves for an hour.

But too late for any such regrets. The steel blade slid on steel, and the two gentlemen were at it.

Wallace had tossed off his jacket, and Jamie held it reverently. Bonnet off, also, and Fiona held it tight clenched in her bloody fingers. She tasted whiskey on her lips, where Morney had forced her to drink—to warm her up, he had said, laughing hatefully. She had come to, with a jolt, on that husk-mattressed bed, with Jenks, holding her feet, and Morney with his arm about her shoulders, and thought herself despoiled. She had fainted with her exertions, and a blow to her face which now showed a dark bruise.

But they had not done it—Wallace had been in time. Oh, thank God. Her hands clenched tighter on the gay tartan and blue bonnet of her beloved. She followed the action with anxious eyes, but stiffly, proudly, for he fought for her.

They were well matched, she could see it. The two lithe forms, Wallace the thinner and more muscular. Lord Morney had gone to too much drink, his face was flabby, his belly showed a paunch. His wind was short also, his face showed it. His mouth was open, he gasped for breath, even as they circled each other warily.

Wallace stood almost still, moving only his feet in a slow, easy movement. He let Morney do the running about him, and turned only to face him. The sun was high in the sky, there was no advantage to the sun in one's face.

Silence in the stable yard. Only the chink, chink of the steel as one blade struck and then slip off. The narrowed, alert eyes. Wallace kept watching Morney's face. Not the sword blade, just the face.

A strike, and the sleeve of Wallace's shirt was torn from his arm. Jenks let out a squeal of shrill delight. "Oh, you have him, you have him!" he cried.

Jamie drew a deep breath, blew it out slowly between pursed lips, his concentration unfaltering. Ossian stood just behind Fiona, she felt his tension, the sword tip rested just on the dirt of the ground. He was ready, should any get into the action beside Wallace and Morney. She felt him turned toward Jenks.

Circling, circling again, Morney looked for another opening. Wallace stood quietly, letting him come to his body, then his sword blade flashed, and a red glaze of blood followed on the back of Morney's right hand. Morney winced, and backed up.

Circling, circling, Morney attacked again, more wildly. He slashed forward, the steel glinting in the moonlight. Fiona watched until her eyes ached with it, but both men were cautious again. Morney smiled with his lips, his green eyes were narrowed to little slits.

Wallace was impassive. His face showed nothing, not the turmoil and the hate inside him. He was all attention to the battle, nothing else mattered.

It went on, on. Fiona shifted from one foot to the other, and felt herself cold inside.

Then Morney dashed forward and slashed at Wallace. The sudden move made Ossian gasp and half lift his sword. But Wallace was not there. With a lithe move of his hips, he was out of the path, and his sword slashed and clashed on the other's steel.

Morney was off-balance. Wallace's sword came up and struck at the left arm. He drew blood again. Morney's feet danced back.

His eyes began to swerve anxiously. "We should stop the fight," cried Jenks. But no one paid any attention to him. "Blood drawn! Get the doctor!" he cried again. No one moved.

Now Wallace pressed forward. He followed Morney in a deadly circle, pacing himself. Morney was backing up, moving in a desperate backward dance, his left arm hung limp. His right arm held the sword up, though, its deadly tip trying to find the way to Wallace's heart.

Then, so rapidly the movements were a blur before Fiona's eyes, Morney plunged forward, in a last desperate bid. He had his sword tip at Wallace's chest, and Jenks yelled, "Get him, get him!"

In that moment, while Morney was vulnerable, Wallace leaned forward also. Ignoring the sword tip which touched his chest, he lifted his sword and plunged it straight into Morney's throat and down.

The man clutched at himself, his sword dropped from nerveless hands. Eyes glazed, he sank to his knees, choking, blood streaming from his throat and mouth.

He toppled over in the dust, a huddled heap.

Wallace stared down at him. Jenks ran forward, sword in hand. "You devil! You killed him!"

Ossian's sword spun from his hand, and Wallace caught it in midair, caught the hilt, and turned on Jenks. Fiona had not even gasped before he had faced the man, with fresh sword in grip.

Over the dead man's body, they fought, Jenks with a maniacal fury. Wallace cool again. Impassive, cold. As they moved away from the body of Morney, Rory dared to move up and yanked at the man's boots so he could pull him out of their path.

The swords flashed again in the sun, Fiona felt it was a deadly dance that would go on forever. But Jenks was hampered by his fury and his fear. Wallace stalked him, and Jenks began to back up, backing in a circle, just as Wallace forced him to do.

The deadly sword flared out, again so swiftly that Fiona could scarce catch the move. Jenks' right arm was slashed, and the sword dropped from him.

He cried out, in fear, as Wallace stood ready with bloody sword. "I yield! I yield! My God, my arms!" He huddled on his knees, moaning over his arm, which ran blood.

Wallace hesitated, then stood back. Rory bent to the man and looked at the arm, first removing the sword further from him with a kick of his boot.

"He canna use the arm, Frazer," he said respectfully and stood back.

Wallace nodded. Jamie came forward, solemnly removed the swaying sword from Morney's throat, and drew it in the dust to clean it. Then he finished the cleaning, with a brisk polish on his tartan.

Then Jamie went on one knee before Frazer and presented the blade across his arm. "Frazer of Frazer," he said solemnly, and the other Highlanders sent out a wild, cheering yell.

Wallace stood stiffly, bent his head, his heels clicked together proudly, and he took the sword, then thrust it again into his belt.

Fiona gave a great sigh. Wallace turned to her. "Shall we go home, my lady?" he asked, and gave her his arm, as the stablehands gasped.

Sholto came forward, the reins of the horses over his arm. He gave Wallace Frazer his horse first, and Wallace lifted Fiona into the saddle, then mounted behind her.

He turned the great black horse and they left the stable yard.

Old Pete regained his wits and ran after them as the three other red-tartaned men followed their chief.

"But what shall I do with them?" he cried.

Wallace did not give him a glance. They rode away, with the old man shrilling after them. "How shall I tell the county? What shall I do with them?"

Fiona leaned back against Wallace. She could find no words. The events of the day had moved so swiftly. It had been but three hours since she had ridden out with Wallace on a beautiful July day. And now one man lay dead in the dust, and another moaned over his injuries.

But her own man was alive, and well. And she herself—she had been saved from those beasts.

She felt as though the sun was cleansing them as they rode slowly homeward.

Chapter Nineteen

The entire county and beyond shrilled with the excitement. The story grew with the telling. Fiona and the other Frazers kept to themselves, but the world would not leave them alone.

Kate Grenville, Lady Morney, brought charges against Wallace Frazer for the murder of her husband, and he was brought to trial. The county wished the story out anyway, and the officials were anxious to have all clear.

Captain Jenks was there, one arm useless forever, hanging at his side, his black eyes watery with much drink. They had some chance against the Frazer. He was Scots, and they were English.

The prosecution lawyers, hired by Lady Morney, tried to make out that Frazer was a troublemaker, had a grudge against Lord Morney, that Fiona had come to him willingly.

Wallace had trouble keeping his face impassive, his arms folded tight, as the trial went on day after hot.

August day. Fiona had hired lawyers, her solicitors had sent them from London. They had the whole story and presented an impressive case.

The village doctor testified. Both the dead man and Captain Jenks had the marks of a woman's fingernails all over their faces, and the blood marks were fresh. Some woman had fought them bitterly.

The stablehands testified. It had been a fair fight, man against man, in the yard, and one man gave a very graphic description of it that had them all gasping. He was so pleased with himself that he repeated the story of the fight every Saturday night for many years.

Fiona testified, and it had great weight. In a steady voice, she related the story of her father, his purchase of the Frazer lands, how he had installed a factor, and treated the Frazers cruelly. She had been trying to make amends and give the Scots work to do, as she told them, when Lord Morney had interfered. By his work, he had taken the lands from her, and purchased them himself.

That had the Crown officials whispering on the bench gravely, wigged heads together. The prince regent had sent them on the case; his old friend and witty companion, Lord Morney, had been murdered, and he was in a fine rage about it. This put a different complexion on the matter, and they would report to him of the wrongs done to the Frazers. To take lands from an Englishwoman, without giving her a chance to defend the matter! It was all more grave than they had thought.

At Kate Grenville's urging, the prosecution lawyers attacked Fiona's character, and her behavior with the man who had become her husband. That brought the blood to her face, and fire to her eye. She defended him passionately, and well.

"He is a splendid man!" she said. "You do not know him! He has worked hard all his days for his clan! He is Frazer of Frazer! All who truly know him honor him! I am privileged to be his wife, his partner in his life's work!"

"But did he not send his own men to attack you in the glens of Scotland?" asked one lawyer shrewdly. "Were you not stoned, and injured gravely, so that you left Scotland?"

"The Scots people were so upset by Lord Morney's actions that they were grieving," she said bravely. "When the factor burned the looms and told them I was the daughter of Hugo Cartwright, they lost their wits, a few of them. Yes, some men did attack me. It was a time when my husband was away—"

"He left you often?" smiled the lawyer. "That does not sound like devotion!"

"He was in Glasgow to see some of his people there," she said quietly. "One of his men, one Jamie Frazer, his cousin, went for him, and he left his people, to follow me to England. He has loved me always," she added proudly, her blue black head high, and her violet eyes shining.

"One can see that she is prejudiced," said the lawyer smoothly. "He has cunningly convinced her he had nothing to do with violence shown to her. Or she hides the truth, for her lover, Lord Morney, has died at the hands of her husband—"

The defense lawyers were rising to their feet to protest when Fiona flashed out swiftly, "That weasel! He was never my lover! I despised him, and Captain Jenks as well! Unable to gain even a look from me, they called me the Snow Maiden! They resorted to trickery to get me to that tavern, as you have heard!"

The prosecution then called Captain Benedict Ainsworth. "As a friend of Lord Morney," said the lawyer ponderously, "you will tell us the truth of it."

The young man was pale. He had been living with Squire and Mrs. Reid this past month since the events at the country tavern. He had moved out, bag and baggage, at once.

He spoke honestly, and directly, without fancy

213

words. "Lord Morney was a friend of mine, yes. He befriended me when others did not, as a poor younger brother. I followed him blindly, I admired him in battle. However, in his personal life, I was coming to see him as he was—"

He was cut off, points of law shot back and forth for a time before he was permitted to continue.

He told the story of the events. He had come to admire Mrs. Frazer, for her devotion to her husband and the Scots people, for her honesty and courage and her honor in all matters. "She is a splendid woman, one whom I admired from afar," he said quietly. "When I saw her in that tavern room, fighting Lord Morney and Captain Jenks—"

The lawyer brought him back sharply as to how he had happened to be at the spot. He told how he had seen Lady Morney driving away in her carriage, laughing. How he had seen the woman's jacket in the stable yard, and the stable yard deserted. How he had gone up the stairs and found Mrs. Frazer in the room with Captain Jenks and Lord Morney.

"You say she was fighting them?" asked the lawyer silkily. "Were they rather not fighting each other for her favors, and she encouraging them?"

"Never," he said. "She scratched their faces wildly with her nails, she was kicking and struggling. It fair made me ill. They shoved me from the room when I offered to escort her from the place. They locked the door and barred it. I was off at once to fetch Mr. Frazer, praying we would be in time." He wiped the sweat from his forehead, his face was ghastly, remembering the horror. "I whipped my horse as I never had," he added.

They took him through the story again and again, and he did not change it. Lady Morney eyed him grimly, furious. She would see to it that he was never again received by her crowd! Not only had he betrayed their friendship, he had cost her a wealthy husband. Now a distant relative was going to claim Morney, for

214

the lord had left no children. She was going to live in practical poverty, as she had wept privately.

The trial went on for days, but the testimony of Fiona Frazer and that of Captain Ainsworth finally turned the day. Wallace Frazer was acquitted of the charge of murder. The prince regent did send a stern warning about dueling, however. He had forbidden it in England.

The Frazers gathered in their living room, the evening after the verdict had been returned. Fiona felt drained, and Margaret brought the coffee cup to her.

Wallace was sitting, frowning over his cup. He had been gloomy and very silent for the weeks of the trial. Now it was early September, and how sick they were of Yorkshire, and of England itself, thought Fiona bitterly.

She roused and turned to the elderly solicitor who had stuck by them, though his gray head waggled with weariness, and his aged brown-spotted hands quivered.

"I think it would be best if we should leave England, do you not, sir?" she asked quietly. Wallace looked up, his eyes lighting.

"Where would you go, dear lady?" asked the elderly man. "Scotland is in turmoil still, and the Scots hated."

"To Canada," said Fiona, looking at her husband. He nodded.

"Aye—to Canada—to begin again. Is it possible to start over once more?" The Frazer was sighing as he spoke.

"Will your people go with us?" asked Fiona timidly. "Or do they—hate me?"

"Nay, they do not hate ye," said Wallace gently. "Some will go, some willing to give up what little they have left in the land of their birth. I will persuade all I can."

"How many will go?" asked Margaret practically. "Some three hundred? Will we need more than one ship?"

Captain Benedict Ainsworth was with them, at the

rather quiet celebration of the end of the trial. They treated him cautiously as a friend, and he sat to one side.

Now he looked at Margaret. Fiona saw the look and was sorry for him. He adored the bright-haired girl. And he had few other friends, his rough crowd had fallen away from him.

They talked of the matter for a time. The solicitor advised them to sell the Yorkshire lands and have money invested for them for use later in Canada.

"Yes, we might be able to buy a large tract of land and set out a small village of our own," mused Frazer. His face was lighting up. "We can remain together, then, rather than hiring out to others. We can till the land, cut timber in the forests, catch the fish in the lochs—"

"Yes, and begin the looms once again!" said Fiona eagerly. "I know it could be done! We could grow sheep once more, and use the wool for fine blankets and plaids! Oh, Frazer, we could be self-sufficient," and she looked eagerly about the circle.

They talked it over in the next few days, but their minds were already inclined to a new start in Canada. They would put behind them the gossip and the whispers, the torments and the anguish which had been their lives in Scotland and in England.

To begin again! "How few ha' the chance to begin again," mused Margaret one day over tea. "It is heaven-sent. And the land be fine, so they do say, with blue skies, and blue lochs, and the green trees between, like Scotland was centuries ago, so the wise ones said."

Captain Ainsworth said, in a low tone to Frazer, and Fiona overheard, "I would ask a favor of you, Frazer."

"Ask away. We are in your debt."

"No, not for that reason," said Benedict blushing furiously. "Think not of debts. I did but my duty and told the truth of it. What I did in court—"

"I was thinking of what you did that black day when the villains had my wife," said Wallace bluntly. "You did not stay to think on't. You came for me, half killing yourself and horse. And you backed me on the stairs. I'll not forget it ever."

"I have your respect, then? I am glad of it. I would like—if it does not displease you—" Ainsworth hesitated again, looking toward Margaret, who was now listening to their talk, turning from her mother.

"Say it," said Wallace, his mouth gentling. He too had noted the looks between the young man and woman.

"I would go with you to the new lands," said Benedict. "I would sail with you, and share your new life, be it hard or soft, good or bad. I am fair sick of my life here."

"Hummm," said Wallace, sucking on his pipe, then knocking it out against the fender. "What say you, Fiona?"

"It is as he wishes," said Fiona. "He is our friend forever."

"And you, Margaret?" asked Wallace, deliberately looking at his sister, who was now blushing with a fiery red.

In her delicate green muslin, and the red tartan shawl about her shoulders, the blue-eyed girl looked wildly about her for aid. All eyes were on her, some curious, some smiling.

"Why, it is to you, you are the Frazer of Frazer," she tried to send it back to her brother.

Humor lightened his face. "Nay, it is for you to say; he is, I am thinking, looking to your approval, my sister."

Fiona half opened her mouth to scold her husband. Margaret was covered with blushes. Then she realized his intent. The girl was so loyal a Scots she might resist forever. She must declare herself before them.

"He has aye been friend to us," said Margaret finally, demurely. "I would say he would come, and welcome."

Ainsworth sprang to his feet and made his way to

her. He bent, and lifted her white hand and kissed it fervently. "Thank you—Miss Frazer," he murmured. "I will never betray my loyalty—to you."

A little later, when the evening grew dusky, the pair wandered alone into the garden, with Wallace only looking after them thoughtfully. When they returned, it was hand in hand, and Ainsworth looked as though someone had given him a crown and scepter.

Wallace talked at length to Fiona about the Yorkshire lands. It was her suggestion to offer them to Squire Reid. The squire came to call, and they talked for a long time. They settled on a price, and the squire was generous about the amount.

He was jubilant as well. "Now I shall have more land and influence than the new Lord Morney, however he may be. I shall hope it is a good man, but knowing the blood, I shall not count on it. This way I shall have more say in the governing of the county and lands hereabouts. I thank you both!"

"I know you will have a good care of the people," said Wallace, that burden lifting from his shoulders. "Mr. Proudfoot will be happy to serve under you, you both understand each other."

"That we do, and I shall be happy to have him and Mrs. Proudfoot working in my employ."

Fiona made a hasty visit to London to say a tender and lasting farewell to Mrs. Elizabeth Trent. They both wept a bit, for they did not think to see each other again in this world.

"But you have a good man and husband," said Mrs. Trent, bravely wiping away the signs of sorrow. "I shall write to you, and you shall write to me, as we always did. Blessings on you, my dearest blest goddaughter. May you always be so happy."

While in London, Fiona and Mrs. Owens purchased blankets, stocks of foodstuffs, which they sent to Glasgow to the ship wharf there, coats and shoes and warm boots. They had heard it was not easy to find such things in the new land. And the ship supplies came but once or twice a year.

Finally they were all packed, and a grand procession of carriages conveyed them to Scotland. Fiona bade farewell to her English coachman, her footmen and maids, they would return to seek other employment, some with Squire Reid, others in London. She thanked them all for their loyal service and paid them in gold coins against their future.

Then she was alone, but for Mrs. Owens, among all the Scots. No, one more English! For Captain Ainsworth had kept to his word and was one of their company now. He was tireless, helping to order supplies, striding about the warehouses seeing to the packing of the goods in stout wooden cases, inspecting the meats and other foods with the keen eye of a soldier.

Fiona had one more great fear. Remembering vividly their stoning of her, she dreaded meeting Wallace's Scots people again. Especially those wild fellows from the glen. He had told them they had all come, the glen was practically empty of Frazers now.

"All have come, but a few stubborn folk," he said proudly. "There shall be five hundred and sixty of us on the two ships we have hired."

The moment she had feared came all too soon. As she was on the wharf, wrapped warmly in her red tartan of the Frazers, one blustery-faced man came up to her, urged on by a small black-haired woman behind him.

"I ha' come to apologize to ye, Mrs. Frazer," he said solemnly. "I was one of thim what stoned ye, and I wish to say here and now——" He blushed wildly and stopped dead, gazing helplessly into her violet eyes.

His wife gave him a poke in the ribs. "I was mistook in my feelings," she hissed.

"I was mistook in my feelings, and sore drunk with rage and too much good Scotch," he went on obediently. "We all do ask ye to forgive what was a stupid matter, and forgive and forget."

He came to the end of his speech with a sigh of relief. Fiona suppressed a smile and forgot her own fears.

"I thank you for your apology on behalf of yourself and your fellows," she said formally. "I suggest we do as you suggest, forgive and forget. And here's my hand on it," she added impulsively. Her slim white hand was swallowed up in the great hairy paw.

His wife came up next to say her piece more quickly. "And we do wish to say we know now how hard ye tried to aid us and help us. Ye was good to us, and we are mighty grateful to ye and to our chief and to the good kind Lord, who is leading us into the land of Canaan," she said.

"I hope Canada will prove to be our promised land," said Fiona, more relaxed now, and she gravely shook the small, spritely woman's hand.

"They will hope for it," murmured Margaret, overhearing them. "Let us not hope too much. There is hard work and sorrow ahead of us, but perhaps more joy than we have known before."

Captain Ainsworth had her by the elbow and drew her close to him. "But we will have each other," he whispered.

She blushed and gazed up at him. She had promised to marry him just before they departed, her marriage would take place on Scottish soil.

And so it was done, the marriage took place on the wharf, with the Frazers all about them, and Jamie piping. Wallace gave his sister away, and Fiona attended her, all their dresses and cloaks and kilts whipped wildly by the wind off the sea.

Then they got on the ships, and the captains gave out instructions. Fiona leaned on the rail, waved to the people ashore who had come, curious and wondering, to see them off. The other ship went out first, and they waited, then when the wind was right again, their ship followed, slipping into the dark sea waves. Soon they would be into the Atlantic, on their way across the wild ocean, to Canada.

Wallace's arm slipped about Fiona's waist, and his cloak came about her to warm her against the wild, whipping wind. He looked up at the billowing white sails as they burst from their ropes as the sailors released them.

"On our way, at last. To new lands, and new beginnings."

"Yes, Wallace." Her hand went to his, as he pressed it to her waist. She knew how he felt, half-sorrow, half-joy, to be leaving his own land, his own hills and glen. But they had known so much grief there—surely the new would be better?

She said as much. "The new will be good, Wallace."

"Aye, I hope so. We shall work hard to make it so. We have our good arms and our strong backs, and our will. And our love to keep us warm of nights," he added, with the little teasing smile she had not seen for a time.

She leaned to his shoulder and pressed his hand more closely to her. "And more," she said softly. "Our child was conceived in the old land, but he will be born in the new."

He stiffened. "What did ye say?" he asked incredulously.

Fiona smiled up at him adoringly. "A new Frazer of Frazer," she whispered. "God willing. Though he will be Canadian born, and a fine boy in the new world we will be making for him. Does it please you?"

"It joys me," he said soberly. "But the sea voyage—Fiona, will it not be too much for ye? We would ha' waited for the spring."

She shook her head. "Nay, I want my child born in the new world," she said serenely. "He is but a few weeks along, I am thinking. Mrs. Owens knows of such matters, and she will care for me well. Do not be worried for me, Wallace."

He pressed his cheek to her hair, his arms about her. A last flutter of handkerchief waved from the wharf, a last shout reached them across the growing length of water between them. Fiona looked her last on Scotland, which had given her grief, and much more of love.

She would never forget the land of her birth, England, and the land of her love, Scotland. But she looked forward eagerly to the land of her future, Canada. There they might at last work, in peace, and laughter, and warmth of love.

GREAT ROMANTIC NOVELS

STERS AND STRANGERS   PB 04445 $2.50

y Helen Van Slyke

Three women—three sisters each grown into an inde-
endent lifestyle—now are three strangers who reunite to
nd that their intimate feelings and perilous fates are
twined.

HE SUMMER OF THE SPANISH WOMAN

                     CB 23809 $2.50

y Catherine Gaskin

A young, fervent Irish beauty is alone. The only man
e ever loved is lost as is the ancient family estate. She
es to Spain. There she unexpectedly discovers the sim-
ering secrets of her wretched past . . . meets the Spanish
oman . . . and plots revenge.

HE CURSE OF THE KINGS   CB 23284 $1.95

y Victoria Holt

This is Victoria Holt's most exotic novel! It is a story
romance when Judith marries Tybalt, the young arche-
logist, and they set out to explore the Pharaohs' tombs on
eir honeymoon. But the tombs are cursed . . . two arche-
logists have already died mysteriously.

8000

MASTER NOVELISTS

CHESAPEAKE   CB 24163 $3.9
by James A. Michener

An enthralling historical saga. It gives the account
different generations and races of American families wh
struggled, invented, endured and triumphed on Maryland
Chesapeake Bay. It is the first work of fiction in ten yea
to be first on *The New York Times Best Seller List*.

THE BEST PLACE TO BE   PB 04024 $2.5
by Helen Van Slyke

Sheila Callaghan's husband suddenly died, her childre
are grown, independent and troubled, the men she mee
expect an easy kind of woman. Is there a place of con
fort? a place for strength against an aching void? A nov
for every woman who has ever loved.

ONE FEARFUL YELLOW EYE   GB 14146 $1.9
by John D. MacDonald

Dr. Fortner Geis relinquishes $600,000 to someone th
no one knows. Who knows his reasons? There is a histor
of threats which Travis McGee exposes. But why does th
full explanation live behind the eerie yellow eye of a mut
lated corpse?

800